CHARITY GIRL

Charity Girl

GEORGETTE
HEYER

NEW YORK
E. P. DUTTON & CO., INC.

CHARITY GIRL

CHAPTER I

As far as it was possible for an elderly gentleman suffering from dyspepsia and a particularly violent attack of gout to take pleasure in anything but the alleviation of his various pains the Earl of Wroxton was enjoying himself. He was engaged on the agreeable task of delivering himself of a diatribe on the shortcomings of his heir. To the uninitiated his strictures must have seemed unjust, for Viscount Desford bore the appearance of a son of whom any father must have been proud. In addition to a goodlooking countenance, and a lithe, athletic figure, he had the easy manners which sprang as much from an innate amiability as from his breeding. He had also a considerable store of patience, and a sense of humour which showed itself in the smile which lurked in his eyes, and which was thought by a great many persons to be irresistible. His father was not of their number: when a victim of gout, he thought it exasperating.

The month was July, but the weather was so far from sultry that the Earl had caused a fire to be kindled in his library. On either side of the hearth he and his heir were seated, the Earl with one heavily bandaged foot on a stool, and his heir (having discreetly edged his chair away from the warmth of the smouldering logs) at his graceful ease opposite him. The Viscount was wearing the coat, the buckskin breeches, and the topboots which were the correct morning-attire for any gentleman sojourning in the country, but a certain elegance, deriving from the cut of his coat, and the arrangement of his neckcloth, gave his father an excuse for apostrophizing him as a damned dandy. To which he responded, in mild protest: "No, no, sir! The dandy-set would be shocked to hear you say so!"

"I collect," said his father, glaring at him, "that you call yourself a Corinthian!"

"To own the truth, sir," said the Viscount apologetically, "I don't call myself anything!" He waited for a moment, watching

7

with as much sympathy as amusement the champing of his parent's jaws, and then said coaxingly: "Now, come, Papa! What have I done to earn such a trimming from you?"

"What have you done to earn praise from me?" instantly countered the Earl. "Nothing! You're a skitterbrain, sir! A slibberslabber here-and-thereian, with no more thought for what you owe your name than some rubbishing commoner! A damned scattergood—and you've no need to remind me that you're not dependent on *me* for the money you waste on your horses, and your betting, and your bits of muslin, for I'm well aware of it, and what I said at the time, and say now, and always shall say is that it was just like your great-aunt to leave her fortune to you, and exactly what might have been expected of such a shuttlehead as she was! As well have handed you a carte blanche to commit every sort of—of extravagant folly! But on that head," said his lordship inaccurately, but with perfect sincerity, "I shall say nothing! She was your mother's aunt and *that* circumstance seals my lips."

He paused, throwing a challenging glance at his heir, but the Viscount merely said, with becoming meekness: "Just so, Papa!"

"Had she stipulated that her fortune was to be used for the support of your wife and family I should have thought it a very proper bequest," announced his lordship, adding, however: "Not that I was not at that time, and at this present, able and willing to increase your allowance to enable you to meet the added expenses consequent on your entry into the married state."

He paused again, and the Viscount, feeling that some comment was expected, said politely that he was much obliged to him.

"Oh, no, you're not!" said his lordship grimly. "And, what's more, you won't be until you provide me with a grandson, no matter how fast your great-aunt's fortune burns in your pockets! Upon my word, a pretty set of children I have!" he said, suddenly enlarging his scope. "Not one of you cares a straw for the Family! At my age I might have expected to have had a score of grandchildren to gladden my last years! But have I? No! Not one!"

"In fact you have three," replied the Viscount disconcertingly. "Not that it has ever seemed to me that they gladdened you precisely, but I do feel it to be only just to Griselda that her offspring should be mentioned!"

"Girls!" snapped the Earl, sweeping them aside with a contemptuous gesture. "I take no account of them! Besides, they're Broxbourne brats! What I want is sons, Ashley! *Carringtons,* to succeed to our Name, and our Honours, and our Tradition!"

"But scarcely a score of them!" protested the Viscount. "One must be reasonable, sir, and even if I had obliged you by marrying when I was twenty, and my unfortunate wife had presented me with twins every year, you must still have been at least two short of your expectation—setting aside the probability that there would have been several girls amongst such a bevy of grandchildren."

This attempt to win his parent out of his ill-humour might have succeeded (for the Earl was fond of the ridiculous) had not a sudden twinge in his afflicted foot caused him to wince, and to utter in a menacing voice: "Don't be impertinent, sir! I would remind you that you—I thank God!—are not my only son!"

"No," agreed the Viscount, with unruffled cordiality. "And while I can't but feel that Simon is too young to be setting up his nursery I have great hopes that Horace may oblige you—when the Occupation ends, as, from all accounts, it will do in the not too far distant future—and he returns to us."

"Horace!" uttered his lordship. "I may think myself fortunate if he doesn't come home with some French hussy on his arm!"

"Oh, I don't think that very likely!" said the Viscount. "He is not at all partial to foreigners, sir, and quite as mindful of what is due to the Family as you are."

"I shan't be alive to see it," said the Earl, seeking refuge in decrepitude, but slightly damaging his effect by adding an acrimonious rider: "Much any of you will care!"

The Viscount laughed, but with a good deal of affection. "No,

9

no, Papa!" he said. "Don't try to pitch the fork to me! I haven't been on the town for nine years—and intimately acquainted with you for *twenty*-nine years!—without learning when a man is trying to come crab over me! Good God, sir, you're all skin and whipcord—saving only a tendency to gout, which you may easily overcome by *not* drinking the best part of two bottles of port at a sitting—and you'll hold for a long trig! Long enough, I've little doubt, to rake down a son of mine as you're raking me down today!"

The Earl could not help being gratified to know that his heir considered him to be in very good condition, but he thought it proper to say austerely that he neither understood nor approved of the cant expressions so deplorably in use amongst the young men of the day. He toyed for a moment with the impulse to inform the Viscount, in forthright terms, that when he desired his opinion of his drinking habits he would ask him for it, but discarded this notion, because he knew that no dependence could be placed on Ashley's receiving a snub in filial silence, and he had no wish to embark on an argument in which he stood on very unreliable ground. Instead, he said: "A son of yours? I want no base-born brats, I thank you, Desford—though I daresay you have a score—any number of them!" he amended hastily.

"Not to my knowledge, sir," said the Viscount.

"I'm glad to hear it! But if you had agreed to the marriage I planned for you a son of yours might have been sitting on my knee at this moment!"

"I hesitate to contradict you, sir, but I find myself quite unable to believe that any grandchild attempting—at this moment—to sit on your knee would have met with anything but a severe rebuff."

The Earl acknowledged this hit by giving a bark of laughter, but said: "Oh, well, there's no need for you to take me up so literally! The thing is that you behaved very badly when you refused to make Henrietta Silverdale an offer! Never did I think to meet with such ingratitude, Desford! Anyone would have supposed that I had chosen a bride for you whom you disliked, or with whom you were unacquainted—which, I may tell you, was not an uncommon thing to happen in *my* day! Instead of that, I chose for you a girl with whom you had been closely acquainted all your life, and to whom I believed you to be sincerely attached. I might have looked much higher, but all I desired was your happiness! And what has been my reward? Tell me that!"

"Oh, for God's sake, sir——!" exclaimed the Viscount, for the first time showing impatience. "Must you hark back to what happened nine years ago? Can't you believe that Hetta had no more wish to marry me than I had to marry her?"

"No—and if you mean to tell me you were not attached to her you may as well spare your breath!"

"Of course I was attached to her—as though she had been my sister! I still am: we are the best of good friends, but a man don't wish to marry his sister, however fond he may be of her! The truth of the matter is, Papa, that you and Sir John hatched the scheme between you—though how the pair of you could be such gudgeons as to suppose that to rear us almost as though we *had* been brother and sister would further this precious scheme is something that has me in a puzzle to this day! No, no, don't rattle me off for calling you a gudgeon! Recollect that I did say it has me in a puzzle!"

"Ay, you've a soft tongue, and think to turn me up sweet with it!" growled his father.

"Alas, I know well I can't!" said the Viscount ruefully. "But I wish you will tell me, sir, why you, who didn't become riveted until you were past thirty, were so determined to see me leg-shackled before I had even attained my majority?"

"To keep you out of mischief!" replied the Earl, with more promptitude than wisdom.

"Oho!" said the Viscount, quizzing him wickedly. "So that was it, was it? Well, I've long suspected that you were not—in your day—such a pattern of rectitude as you would have us believe!"

"Pattern of rectitude! Of course I was no such thing!" said the Earl, repulsing the suggestion with loathing.

"Of course you weren't!" said the Viscount, laughing at him.

11

"No! I sowed my wild oats just as any youngster must, but I never consorted with rake-shames!"

This announcement put a quick end to the Viscount's laughter. He directed a searching look at his father from under suddenly frowning brows, and demanded: "What's this? If it is to my address, you'll permit me to tell you that you've been misinformed, sir!"

"No, no!" replied his lordship testily. "I'm talking of Simon, muttonhead!"

"Simon! Why, what the devil has he been doing to provoke you?"

"Don't tell me you aren't very well aware that he's for ever on the spree with a set of rascally scrubs, knocking up disgraceful larks, committing every sort of extravagant folly, creating riot and rumpus——"

"Well, I do tell you so, sir!" said the Viscount, interrupting this wholesale indictment without ceremony. "I don't see much of him, but you may depend upon it that I should hear of it fast enough if he'd got into the sort of company you're describing! Good God, anyone to hear you would suppose Simon had joined the Beggars' Club, or ended up each night either in the Finish, or in a Round-house! I daresay you wouldn't care for the set he runs with—I don't care for them myself, but that's because I'm nine-and-twenty, not three-and-twenty, and have outgrown the restiness of my salad days. But they're not *rascally,* and they're certainly not *scrubs!* Coming it much too strong, Father, believe me!"

"It's a pity you *don't* see much of him!" countered the Earl. "I should have known better than to think you might make it your business to do so!"

"Well, yes, I think you should!" replied the Viscount frankly.

"I take it," said the Earl, visibly controlling his temper, "that I should be wasting my breath if I asked you to take the young wastrel in hand!"

"You would indeed, Papa! Lord, what heed do you think he would pay to me?"

"Oh, well," replied his lordship grudgingly, "for all your

faults you're good ton, you're a member of the Four-horse Club, and—thanks to my training!—a pretty accomplished fencer. They tell me that the younger men are inclined to follow your lead, so there's no saying but what you might have more influence over him than I have."

"If you had had any brothers, Papa," said the Viscount, smiling, "you would know that the junior members of the fraternity are very much more likely to run directly counter to what their eldest brother advises than to follow his lead, even if he were a far more notable sportsman than I am! I am sorry to disoblige you, but I must firmly decline to meddle in Simon's career. I don't think there's the least need for anyone to do so, but if you do think so it's for you to curb his activities, not me!"

"How the devil can I curb them?" demanded his father explosively. "He's a curst care-for-nobody, and although you may consider me a gudgeon I promise you I'm not such a gudgeon as to stop his allowance! A pretty thing it would be if he got himself rolled-up and I were forced to rescue him from some sponging-house! Not but what it would do him good to be locked up!"

"You know, sir, you are taking much too gloomy a view of young Simon's prospects! I wish you won't tease yourself over him—even if he *has* put you all on end!"

"I might have known *you* wouldn't tease yourself!" said the Earl, assailed by another stab of pain. "You're all alike! Why I've been saddled with a pack of selfish, worthless, ungrateful brats I shall never know! Your mother spoilt you to death, of course, and I was fool enough to let her do it! As for you, damme if you're not the worst of the bunch! I wash my hands of you, and the sooner you take yourself off the better pleased I shall be! I don't know what brought you down here, but if it was to see me you might have spared yourself the pains! I don't want to see your face again!"

The Viscount got up, saying with perfect affability: "Well, in that case I'll remove it from your sight, sir! I won't ask you for your blessing, for your sense of propriety would compel you to bestow it on me, and I'm sure it would choke you to utter the

13

words! I won't even offer to shake hands with you—but that's to save myself a wounding snub!"

"Jackanapes!" said his parent, thrusting out his hand.

The Viscount took it in his, dropped a respectful kiss on it, and said: "Take care of yourself, Papa! Goodbye!"

The Earl watched him cross the room to the door, and, as he opened it, said, in the voice of a man goaded beyond endurance: "I suppose you came home because you wanted something!"

"I did!" replied the Viscount, throwing him a look brimful of mockery over his shoulder. "I wanted to see Mama!"

He then withdrew in good order, firmly closing the door on the explosion of wrath which greeted this parting shot.

When he reached the hall of the house he found that the butler was there, and encountered such a glance of mournful sympathy from this aged and privileged retainer that he broke into a chuckle, saying: "You're looking your last at me, Pedmore! My father has cast me out! He says I'm a worthless skitterbrain, and a jackanapes, besides a number of other things which I can't at the moment remember. Would you have believed he could be so unfeeling?"

The butler clicked his tongue disapprovingly, and shook his head. Sighing deeply, he replied: "It's the gout, my lord. It always makes him mifty!"

"Mifty!" said the Viscount. "What you mean is that it sets him at dagger-drawing with anyone unwise enough to cross his path, you old humbugger!"

"It would not become me to agree with your lordship, so I shall hold my peace," said Pedmore severely. "And, if I may venture to proffer a word of advice—being as I have known your honoured parent for many years longer than you have, my lord —I would respectfully beg you not to set any store by anything he may say when he's in the gout, for he doesn't mean it—not if it's you! And if you was to take snuff he'd be regularly blue-devilled—he would indeed, my lord, whatever he may have said to you!"

"Bless you, Pedmore, do you think I don't know it?" said the

Viscount, smiling affectionately at him. "You must think I'm a lunkhead! Where shall I find my mother?"

"In her drawing-room, my lord."

The Viscount nodded, and ran lightly up the broad stairway. His mother greeted his entrance to her sanctum with a warm smile, and a hand held out to him. "Come in, dearest!" she said. "Have you been having a *dreadful* peal rung over you?"

He kissed her hand. "Lord, yes!" he said cheerfully. "He rattled me off in famous style! In fact, he has informed me that he doesn't wish to see my face again."

"Oh, dear! But he doesn't mean it, you know. Yes, of course you do: you always understand things without having to have them explained to you, don't you?"

"Do I? It seems very unlikely! And I don't think it can be true, for both you and old Pedmore seem to believe that I must need reassurance! I don't, but I claim no extraordinary powers of understanding for that! No one who was not a confirmed sap-skull could suppose—being intimately acquainted with Papa!—that his violent attacks spring from anything but colic and gout! I feared the worst when I saw him partake so lavishly of the curried crab at dinner last night; and my fears were confirmed when he embarked on the second bottle of port. Pray don't think me captious, Mama, but ought he to regale himself quite so unwisely?"

"No," replied Lady Wroxton. "It is very bad for him, but it is quite useless to remonstrate with him, for it only puts him out of temper to be offered the wholesome dishes Dr Chettle pre-scribes, when he has expressed a desire for something *most* indigestible, and you know what he is, Ashley, when he is thwarted! And when he flies into one of his odd rages!"

"I know!" said the Viscount, smiling.

"It is even worse for him when he does that, because he becomes exhausted, and then falls into a fit of dejection, and says that he is burnt to the socket, and has nothing to do but to wind up his accounts. And it is quite as bad for the household, for even Pedmore, who is so *very* devoted to us, doesn't like to have

15

things thrown at him—particularly when it chances to be mutton-broth."

"As bad as that?" said the Viscount, considerably startled.

"Oh, not always!" his mother assured him, in a comfortable voice. "And he is in general very sorry afterwards, and tries to make amends for having behaved with so little moderation. I daresay he will be a trifle twitty tonight, but I have the greatest hope that tomorrow he will be content to eat a panada, or a boiled chicken. So you have no need to look so concerned, dearest: very likely it will be several weeks before he indulges himself again with his favourite dishes."

"I am concerned for you, Mama, far more than I am for him! I don't know how you are able to bear your life! *I* could not!"

"No, I don't suppose you could," she responded, looking at him in tolerant amusement. "You weren't acquainted with him when he was young, and naturally you were never in love with him. But I was, and I remember how gay, and handsome, and dashing he used to be, and how very happy we were. And we still love one another, Ashley."

He was frowning a little, and asked abruptly: "Does he subject you to that sort of Turkish treatment, Mama?"

"Oh, no, never! To be sure, he does sometimes scold me, but he has *never* thrown anything at me—not even when I ventured to suggest that he should add some rhubarb and water to his port, which is an excellent remedy for a deranged stomach, you know, but he would have none of it. In fact, it put him into a regular flame."

"I'm not surprised!" said the Viscount, laughing at her. "You almost deserved to have it thrown at you, I think!"

"Yes, that's what he said, but he didn't throw it at me. He burst out laughing, just as you did. What made him suddenly so vexed, dearest? Did you say something to make him pucker up? I know you haven't *done* anything to displease him, for he was delighted to see you. Indeed, that is why we had the dressed crab, and he made Pedmore bring up the best port."

"Good God, in my honour, was it? Of course, I dared not tell him so, but I'm not at all fond of port, and I had to drink the

16

deuce of a lot of it. As for what vexed him, it was certainly nothing I said, for not an unwise word passed my lips! I can only suppose that the crab and the port were responsible." He paused, thinking of what had passed in the library, the frown returning to his brow. He turned his eyes towards his mother, and said slowly: "And yet—Mama, what made him hark back, after all this time, to the match he tried to make between Hetta and me, when I was twenty?"

"Oh, did he do so? How unfortunate!"

"But why did he, Mama? He hasn't spoken of it for years!"

"No, and that is what one particularly likes about him. He has a shockingly quick temper, but he never sinks into the mops, or rubs up old sores. The thing is, I fear, that it has all been brought back to his mind because he has been told that at last dear Henrietta seems likely to contract a very eligible alliance."

"Good God!" exclaimed the Viscount. "You don't mean it! Who's the suitor?"

"I shouldn't think you know him, for he has only lately come into Hertfordshire, and I fancy he very rarely goes to London. He is old Mr Bourne's cousin, and inherited Marley House from him. According to Lady Draycott, he is an excellent person, of the first respectability, a thousand agreeable talents, and most distinguished manners. I haven't met him myself, but I do hope something may come of it, for I have the greatest regard for Henrietta, and have always wished to see her comfortably established. And, if Lady Draycott is to be believed, this Mr—Mr Nethersole—no, not Nethersole, but some name like that—seems to be just the man for her."

"He sounds to me like a dashed dull dog!" said the Viscount.

"Yes, but persons of uniform virtues always do sound dull, Ashley. It seems to me such an odd circumstance! However, we must remember that Lady Draycott is not wholly to be relied on, and I daresay she has exaggerated. She thinks everyone she likes a pattern-saint, and everyone she doesn't like a rascal." Her eyes twinkled. "Well, she says *you* are a man of character, and *very* well conducted!"

17

"Much obliged to her!" said the Viscount. "To think she should judge me so well!"

She laughed. "Yes, indeed! It is a striking example of the advantage of having engaging manners. What a sad reflection it is that to have powers of captivation should be of much more practical use than worthiness!" She leaned forward to pinch his chin, her eyes full of loving mockery. "You can't bamboozle me, you rogue! You *are* a here-and-thereian, you know, exactly as I am persuaded Papa told you! I wish you might form a tendre for some very nice girl, and settle down with her! Never mind! I don't mean to tease you!"

She withdrew her hand, but he caught it, and held it, saying, with a searching look: "Do you, Mama? Did you, perhaps, wish me to offer for Hetta, nine years ago? Would you have liked her to have been your daughter-in-law?"

"What a very odd notion you have of me, my love! I hope I am not such a pea-goose as to have wished you to marry any girl for whom you had formed no lasting passion! To be sure, I have a great regard for Hetta, but I daresay you would not have suited. In any event, that has been past history for years, and nothing is such a sad bore as to be recalling it! I promise you, I shall welcome the bride you do choose at last with as much pleasure as I shall attend Hetta's wedding to the man of *her* choice."

"What, to the pattern-card whose name you can't remember? Are the Silverdales at Inglehurst? I haven't seen Hetta in town for weeks, but from what she told me when we met at the Castlereaghs' ball I had supposed that she must by now have been fixed at Worthing, poor girl!"

"Lady Silverdale," said his mother, in an expressionless voice, "finding that the only lodging she could tolerate in Worthing was not available this summer, has recollected that the sea-air always makes her bilious, and has chosen to retire to Inglehurst rather than to seek a lodging at some other resort."

"What an abominable woman she is!" said the Viscount cheerfully. "Oh, well! I daresay Hetta will be better off with her pattern-card! I'll drop in at Inglehurst tomorrow, on my way

18

back to London, and try to discover what this fellow, Nether-what's-it, is really like!"

Slightly taken aback, Lady Wroxton said, in mild expostulation: "My dear boy, you cannot, surely, question Hetta about him?"

"Lord, yes! of course I can!" said the Viscount. "There are no secrets between Hetta and me, Mama, any more than there are between Griselda and me—in fact," he added, subjecting this confident assertion to consideration, "far fewer!"

CHAPTER II

VISCOUNT DESFORD left his ancestral home on the following morning without seeking another interview with his father. Since the Earl rarely left his bedchamber before noon, this was not difficult. The Viscount partook of an excellent breakfast in solitary state; ran upstairs to bid his mother a fond farewell, issued a few final directions to his valet, who was to follow him into Hampshire with his baggage, and mounted into his curricle as the stable clock began to strike eleven. By the time the echoes of its last stroke had died he was out of sight of the house, bowling down the long avenue that led to the main gates.

The pace at which he drove his mettlesome horses might have alarmed persons of less iron nerve than the middle-aged groom who sat beside him; but Stebbing, who had served him ever since his boyhood, had a disposition which matched his square, severe countenance, and sat with his arms folded across his chest, and an expression on his face of complete unconcern. As little as he betrayed alarm did he betray his pride in the out-and-outer whom he had taught to ride his first pony, and who had become, as well as an accomplished fencer, a first-rate dragsman. Only in the company of his intimates did he say, over a heavy wet, that, taking him in harness and out, no man could do more with his horses than my Lord Desford could.

The curricle which Desford was driving was not precisely a racing curricle, but it had been built to his own design by Hatchett, of Longacre, so lightly that it was very easy on his horses, and capable (if drawn by the sort of blood cattle his lordship kept in his stables) of covering long distances in an incredibly short space of time. In general, Desford drove with a pair only under the pole, but if he set out on a long journey he had a team harnessed to the carriage, demonstrating (so said his ribald cronies) that he was bang up to the knocker. He was driving a team of splendid grays on this occasion, and if they were not the sixteen-mile an hour tits so frequently advertised for sale in the columns of the Morning Post they reached the Viscount's immediate destination considerably before noon, and without having once been allowed to break out of a fast trot.

Inglehurst Place was a very respectable estate owned, until his death some years previously, by a lifelong friend of Lord Wroxton's. Its present owner, Sir Charles Silverdale, had inherited it from his father when still at Harrow, and he had not yet come into his majority, or (according to those who shook sad heads over his rackety ways) shown the least desire to assume the responsibilities attached to his inheritance. His fortune was controlled by his trustees, but since neither of these two gentlemen whose lives had been devoted to the Law had any but a superficial understanding of country matters the management of the estate was shared by Sir Charles's bailiff, and his sister, Miss Henrietta Silverdale.

The butler, a very stately personage, accorded the Viscount a bow, and said that he regretted to be obliged to inform him that her ladyship, having passed an indifferent night, had not yet come downstairs, and so could not receive him.

"Come down from your high ropes, Grimshaw!" said the Viscount. "You know dashed well I haven't come to visit her ladyship! Is Miss Silverdale at home?"

Grimshaw unbent sufficiently to say that he thought Miss would be found in the garden, but his expression, as he watched Desford stride off round the corner of the house, was one of gloomy disapproval.

The Viscount found Miss Silverdale in the rose-garden, attended by two gentlemen, one of whom was known to him, and the other a stranger. She greeted him with unaffected pleasure, exclaiming: "Des!" and stretching out her hands to him. "I had supposed you to be in Brighton! What brings you into Hertfordshire?"

The Viscount took her hands, but kissed her cheek, and said: "Filial piety, Hetta! How do you do my dear? Not that I need ask! I can see you're in high force!" He nodded and smiled at the younger of the two gentlemen present, and looked enquiringly at the other.

"I don't think you are acquainted with Mr Nethercott, are you, Des?" said Henrietta. "Mr Nethercott, you must let me make you known to Lord Desford, who is almost my foster-brother!"

The two men shook hands, each swiftly weighing the other up. Cary Nethercott was rather older than Desford, but lacked the Viscount's air of easy assurance. His manners, though perfectly well-bred, held a good deal of shy reserve. He was taller and more thick-set than Desford; and while he was dressed with propriety there was no suggestion about him of the man of fashion: his coat was made of Bath cloth, but only a clodpole could have supposed it to have come from the hands of Weston, or Nugee. He had a well-formed person, regular features, and if his habitual expression was grave it was also kindly, and his rare smile held a good deal of sweetness.

"No, I fancy we've never met," said Desford. "You have only lately come into the district, haven't you? My mother was speaking of you yesterday: said you were old Mr Bourne's heir."

"Yes, I am," replied Cary. "It seems very strange that I should be, because I scarcely knew him!"

"All the better for you!" said Desford. "The most crotchety old rumstick I ever met in my life! Lord, Hetta, will you ever forget the dust he kicked up when he found us trespassing on his land?"

"No, indeed!" she said, laughing. "And we weren't doing the least harm! I do hope, Mr Nethercott, that *you* won't fly into a rage if I should stray on to the sacred ground of Marley House!"

"You may be very sure I won't!" he said, smiling warmly at her.

At this point, young Mr Beckenham's evil genius prompted him to embark on a tangled speech. He said throatily: "For my part, I can promise Miss Silverdale that if ever she should stray on to *my* land I should think it hallowed ground thereafter! At least, what I mean is I should if it *were* my land, but that's of no consequence, because it will be, when my father dies—not that

23

I wish him to die!—and, in any event, he would be as happy as I should be to welcome you to Foxshot, if there were the least chance of your *straying* on to our land! I only wish Foxshot had been situated within walking distance of Inglehurst!"

He then perceived that Cary Nethercott was looking very much amused, and subsided into blushful silence.

"Well said!" approved the Viscount, patting him on the shoulder. "If you're not very much obliged to him, Hetta, you should be!"

"Of course I am!" said Henrietta, smiling kindly upon her youthful admirer. "And if Foxshot were not fifteen miles distant I expect I *should* stray on to it!"

"In the meantime," quietly interposed Cary Nethercott, "I believe it is time we both took our leave, and allowed Miss Silverdale to enjoy a comfortable cose with his lordship."

Mr Beckenham could not gainsay it; and although Henrietta said merrily that she and his lordship were more likely to come to cuffs than to indulge in a comfortable cose she made no attempt to deter the departure. Mr Beckenham reverently kissed her hand, but his older and less demonstrative rival merely shook it, begging her to convey his compliments to her mama. He then bade the Viscount goodbye, expressing a conventional hope that he might have the pleasure of meeting him again, and took himself off.

"Well," said the Viscount, critically watching his withdrawal, "he's better than I looked for! But I don't think it will do, Hetta: he ain't the man for you!"

Miss Silverdale had very fine eyes. They were, indeed, her only claim to beauty, for her mouth was held to be too large, her high-bridged nose too aquiline, and her hair of an undistinguished brown; but her eyes dominated her face, and were responsible for the generally accepted dictum that she had a great deal of countenance. Their colour was unremarkable, being of that indeterminate colour which passes for gray, but they were subject to changes seldom to be seen in the more admired blue, or brown eyes. If she was bored, they looked to be almost lightless, but as soon as her interest was roused they darkened, and glowed; they could sparkle in anger; or, more frequently, in amusement; and they were at all times reflective of her moods. As she turned them now upon the Viscount, they held surprise, a hint of anger, and a good deal of laughter. She said: "Do you think so indeed? Well, if you're right what a fortunate circumstance it is that he hasn't made me an offer! Who knows but what, at my age, I might have accepted it?"

"Don't hide your teeth with me, Hetta! It's as plain as a pikestaff that he *will* make you an offer! I daresay he's a very worthy man, and I can see he has good, easy manners, but he wouldn't do for you! Take my word for it!"

"What a dog in the manger you are, Ashley!" she exclaimed, between indignation and amusement. "You don't want me yourself, but you can't endure the thought that I might marry another man!"

"Nothing of the sort!" said the Viscount. "I may not wish to marry you—and don't try to hoax me into believing that you've been wearing the willow for me these nine years, because there's nothing amiss with my memory, and I remember as clearly as if it was yesterday how you begged me *not* to offer for you, when that abominable plot was hatched between your father and mine! —but I'm devilish fond of you, and I'd be happy to see you married to a man who was up to your weight. The thing is that Nethercott ain't! You'd be bored with him before the end of your honeymoon, Hetta!"

"You can't think how much obliged to you I am, Des, for having my interests so much at heart!" she said, with immense, if spurious, earnestness. "But it is possible, you know—just faintly possible!—that I am a better judge of what will suit me than you are! Since your memory is so good there can be no need to remind you that I am not a silly schoolgirl, but in my twenty-sixth year——"

"No need at all," he interrupted, with one of his disarming smiles. "You will be twenty-six on the 15th of January next, and I know already what I mean to give you on that occasion. How could you think I would forget your birthday, best of my friends?"

"You are quite atrocious, you know," she informed him, in a resigned voice. "However I should miss you very much if we ceased to be the best of friends, for there's no denying that it is a great comfort to be able to turn to you for advice whenever I find myself in a hobble—which, to do you justice, you've never failed to give me. So do, pray, let us leave this nonsensical argument about poor Mr Nethercott before we find ourselves at outs! You said it was filial piety which brought you home: I do hope this doesn't mean that Lord Wroxton is ill?"

"Not unless rage has caused him to fall into an apoplectic fit," he responded. "We parted on the worst of bad terms last night—in fact, he said he never wanted to see my face again—but Mama and Pedmore have assured me that he didn't mean it, and I believe them. Provided I don't make the mistake of intruding my phiz upon him too soon, I daresay he will be quite pleased to see it again. Of course, it was quite cockleheaded of me to have let him see it twice in less than two months!"

She laughed. "From which I collect that he is in the gout again! Poor Lord Wroxton! But what made him rip up at you? Has some tattle-box been carrying tales about you to him?"

"Certainly not!" he replied austerely. "There are no tales to carry!"

"What, have you cast off the dasher I saw you with at Vauxhall a month ago?" enquired Miss Silverdale, artlessly surprised.

"No, she cast me off!" he retorted. "A lovely little barque of frailty, wasn't she? But much too expensive, unfortunately!"

"Oh, that's too bad!" she said sympathetically. "And haven't you found another to take her place? But you will, Des, you will!"

"One of these days you will be found strangled—very likely by me!" the Viscount warned her. "Pray, what business has a delicately nurtured female to know anything about such things?"

"Ah, that's one of the advantages of having outgrown one's girlhood!" she said. "One need no longer pretend to be an innocent!"

The Viscount had been lounging beside her on a rustic seat, but this utterance startled him into straightening himself with a

26

jerk, and exclaiming: "For God's sake, Hetta——! Is that how you talk to people?"

Her eyes twinkled mischievously; she said, on a choke of laughter: "No, no, only to you, Des! That's another of the ways in which you are a comfort to me! Of course, I do talk pretty freely to Charlie, but he's only my younger brother, not my elder brother! Does Griselda never talk frankly to you?"

"I can't remember that she ever did, but I had only just come down from Oxford when she got herself hitched to Broxbourne, and I don't see much of her nowadays." He gave a sudden chuckle. "Would you believe it, Hetta? My father suddenly ripped up an old grievance which I had thought dead and buried years ago, and raked me down in thundering style for not having coaxed you to marry me!"

"Oh, good God!" she cried. *"Still?* Why didn't you tell him that we didn't *wish* to marry one another?"

"I did, but he didn't believe me. To be sure, I didn't tell him that we knew all about the plot he and your father had so inexpertly hatched, and had decided what we must do about it. Believe me, my dear, that would never do!"

"No," she agreed. "And it wouldn't do for Mama either! I did tell Papa, and he perfectly understood our feelings, and never once reproached me. But Mama never ceases to do so! I do wish you would do something to give her a disgust of you, instead of making yourself agreeable to her! Every time she meets you she complains of my ingratitude until I could scream, and begs me not to blame her when I find myself at my last prayers. According to her, you are everything that is most desirable, and I must be all about in my head! What she might say of you if you were not heir to an Earldom I haven't asked her!" Her little spurt of temper subsided; she gave a rueful laugh, and said: "Oh, dear, how very improper of me to talk like that about her! Let me assure you that I do *not* do so to anyone but you! And how shocking it is that I should be glad she is feeling not quite the thing today, and doesn't mean to leave her room! I do hope Grimshaw can be trusted not to tell her you have been here!"

27

"Well, it may be shocking, but I don't scruple to tell you that I was even more glad to learn that she wasn't receiving visitors!" said the Viscount candidly. "She makes me feel I'm some sort of a heartless loose-screw, for she's got a way of sighing, and smiling sadly and reproachfully at me when I accord her the common decencies of civility." He drew out his watch, and said: "I must be off, Hetta. I'm on my way to Hazelfield, and my aunt won't like it if I arrive at midnight."

Henrietta rose from the seat, and accompanied him towards the house. "Oh, are you going to visit your aunt Emborough? Pray give her my kind regards!"

"I will," he promised. "And do you—if Grimshaw should have disclosed my presence here!—say all that is proper to your mama! My compliments, and my—er—regret that I should have paid her a morning visit when she was indisposed!" He bestowed a fraternal hug upon her, kissed her cheek, and said: "Goodbye, my dear! Don't do anything gooseish, will you?"

"No, and don't you do anything gooseish either!" she retorted.

"What, under my Aunt Sophronia's eye? I shouldn't dare!" he tossed at her over his shoulder, as he strode off towards the stableyard.

CHAPTER III

LADY EMBOROUGH was Lord Wroxton's sole surviving sister. In appearance they were much alike, but although persons of nervous disposition thought that the resemblance was very much more than skin-deep they were misled by her loud voice and downright manners. She was certainly inclined to manage the affairs of anyone weak-minded enough to submit to her autocracy, but she was inspired quite as much by a conviction that such persons were incapable of managing their own affairs as by her belief in her own infallibility, and she never bore anyone the least malice for withstanding her. She was thought by some to be odiously overbearing, but not by those who had sought her help in a moment of need. Under her rough manners she had a warm heart, and an inexhaustible store of kindness. Her husband was a quiet man of few words who for the most part allowed her to rule the household as she chose, a circumstance which frequently led the uninitiated to think that he was henpecked. But those more intimately acquainted with her knew that her lord could check her with no more than a look, and an almost imperceptible shake of his head. She took these silent reproofs in perfectly good part, often saying, with a good natured laugh: "Oh, there is Emborough frowning me down, so not another word will I utter on the subject!"

She greeted her nephew characteristically, saying: "So here you are at last, Desford! You're late—and don't tell me one of your horses lost a shoe, or you broke a trace, because I shan't believe any of your farradiddles!"

"Now, don't bullock poor Des, Mama!" her eldest son, a stalwart young man who bore all the appearance of a country squire, admonished her.

"Much he cares!" she said, laughing heartily.

"Of course I don't!" Desford said, kissing her hand. "Do you take me for a rabbit-sucker, ma'am? None of my horses lost a

29

shoe, and I did not break a trace, or suffer any accident whatsoever, and if you mean to tell me I've kept you waiting for dinner I shan't, of course, be so disrespectful as to accuse *you* of telling farradiddles, but I shall think it! The thing was I called at Inglehurst on my way, and stayed chatting to Hetta for rather longer than I had intended. She told me to give you her kind regards, by the way."

"Inglehurst! Why, have you come from Wolversham?" she exclaimed. "I had supposed you to have been in London still! How's your father?"

"In the gout!"

She gave a snort. "I daresay! And no one but himself to blame! It would do him good to have me living at Wolversham: your mother's too easy with him!"

The violent altercations which had taken place between Lord Wroxton and his sister when last she had descended upon Wolversham still lived vividly in the Viscount's memory, and he barely repressed a shudder. Fortunately, he was not obliged to answer his aunt, for she switched abruptly to another subject, and demanded to be told what he meant by instructing his postilions to lodge at the Blue Boar. "I'll have you know, Desford, I'm not one of these modern hostesses who tell their guests they won't house any other of their servants than their valets! Such nipcheese ways won't do for me: shabby-genteel *I* call 'em! Your groom and your postboys will be lodged with our own, and I want no argument about it."

"Very well, ma'am," said the Viscount obediently, "you shall have none!"

"Now, that's what I like in you!" said his aunt, regarding him with warm approval. "You never disgust me with flowery commonplaces! By the by, if you were expecting to find the house full of smarts you'll be disappointed: we have only the Montsales staying here, and young Ross, and his sister. However, I daresay you won't care for that if you get good sport on the river, which Ned assures me you will. Then there's racing at Winchester, and——"

She was interrupted by Lord Emborough, who had entered

30

the room in the middle of this speech, and who said humourously: "Don't overwhelm him with the treats you have in store, my love! How do you do, Desford? If you can be dragged away from the trout, you must come and look at my young stock tomorrow and tell me how you like the best yearling I've bred yet! He's out of my mare, Creeping Polly, by Whiffler, and I shall own myself surprised if I haven't got a winner in him."

This pronouncement instantly drew the five gentlemen present into an exclusively male conversation, during the course of which Mr Edward Emborough loudly seconded his father's opinion; Mr Gilbert Emborough, his junior by a year, said that although the colt had great bone and substance he couldn't rid himself of the conviction that the animal was just a *leetle* straight-shouldered; Mr Mortimer Redgrave, who had entered the room in Lord Emborough's wake, and was the elder of that gentleman's two sons-in-law, said that for his part he never wanted to see a more promising young 'un; and Mr Christian Emborough, in his first year at Oxford, who had been reverently observing the exquisite cut of his cousin's coat, said that he would be interested to hear what he thought of the colt, "because Des is much more knowing about horses than Ned and Gil are—even if he doesn't boast about it!" Having delivered himself of this snub to his seniors, he relapsed into blushful silence. The Viscount, not having seen the colt, volunteered no opinion, but engaged instead in general stable-talk with his host. Lady Emborough allowed the gentlemen to enjoy themselves in their own way for quite a quarter of an hour before intervening, with a reminder to her sons and nephew that if they didn't rig themselves out for dinner at once they would get nothing but scraps to eat, since she did not mean to wait for them. Upon which the male company dispersed, young Mr Christian Emborough confiding to his cousin, as he went up the broad stairway beside him, that he happened to know that a couple of ducklings and a plump leveret were to form the main dishes for the second course. The Viscount agreed that it would be a shocking thing if these succulent dishes should be spoilt; and young Mr Emborough, taking his courage in his hands, ventured to ask him if

31

he had tied his neckcloth in the style known as the Oriental. To which the Viscount responded gravely: "No, it's called the Mathematical Tie. Would you like me to teach you how to achieve it?"

"Oh, by Jupiter, wouldn't I just?" exclaimed Christian, the ready colour flooding his cheeks in gratification.

"Well, I will, then," promised Desford. "But not just at this moment, if those ducks are not to be over-roasted!"

"Oh, no, no! Whenever it is perfectly convenient to you!" Christian stammered.

He then went off to his own bedchamber, more than ever convinced that Des was a bang-up fellow, not by half as top-lofty as his own brothers; and filled with an agreeable vision of stunning these censorious seniors by appearing before them in a neckcloth which they must instantly recognize as being slap up to the mark.

When the Viscount went back to the drawing-room, he found that the party was rather larger than his aunt had led him to expect, for besides the persons she had mentioned, it included Miss Montsale; both the married daughters of the house, with their spouses; a rather nebulous female of uncertain age, in whom he vaguely recognized one of Lady Emborough's indigent cousins; and the Honourable Rachel Emborough, who was the eldest of the family, and seemed to be destined to fill the rôles of universal confidant, companion of her parents, wise and reliable sister of her brothers and sisters, and beloved aunt of their offspring. She had no pretensions to beauty, but her unaffected manners, her cheerfulness, and the kindness that sprang from a warm heart made her a general favourite. And finally, because Lady Emborough had discovered almost at the last moment that her numbers were uneven, the Honourable Clara Emborough had also been included. This damsel, who had not yet attained her seventeenth birthday, was not considered to have emerged from the schoolroom but, as her mama told the Viscount: "It don't do girls any harm to attend a few parties before one brings 'em out in the regular way. Teaches 'em how to go on in Society, and accustoms 'em to talking to strangers! Of course I wouldn't

32

let her appear at formal parties until I've presented her! And I can depend on Rachel to keep an eye on her!"

The Viscount, who had been watching Rachel check, in the gentlest way, Miss Clara's mounting exuberance, intervene to give her brothers' thoughts a fresh direction when an argument which sprang up between them threatened to become acrimonious, and attend unobtrusively to the comfort of the guests, said impulsively: "What a good girl Rachel is, ma'am!"

"Yes, she's as good as wheat," agreed Lady Emborough, in a somewhat gloomy voice. "But she ain't a girl, Desford: she's older than you are! And no one has ever offered for her! Heaven knows I shouldn't know what to do without her, but I *can't* be glad to see her dwindling into an old maid! It ain't that the men don't like her: they do, but they don't fall in love with her. She's like Hetta Silverdale—except that Hetta's a very well-looking girl, and my poor Rachel—well, there can be no denying that she's something of a Homely Joan! But each of them would make any man an excellent wife—a much better wife than my Theresa there, who is so full of whims and crotchets that I never expected her to go off at all, far less to attach such a good bargain as John Thimbleby!"

Aware that Mr Thimbleby was seated well within earshot, the Viscount shot an involuntary glance at him. He was relieved to see a most appreciative twinkle in this gentleman's eye, and to receive from him something suspiciously like a wink. He was thus able to reply to his aunt with perfect equanimity: "Very true, ma'am! But there is no accounting for tastes, you know! However, you're out when you say that Hetta has no suitors! I could name you at least four very eligible *partis* whom she might have had for the lifting of a finger. Indeed, when I saw her this morning I found her entertaining two more of them! Perhaps neither she nor my cousin Rachel wishes to become a mere wife!"

"Gammon!" said her ladyship crudely. "Show me the female who doesn't hope for marriage, and I'll show you a lunatic past praying for! Yes, and if you wish to know what *I* think—not

33

that I suppose you do!—you're a shuttlehead not to have married Hetta when I daresay she was yours for the asking!"

The Viscount was annoyed, and betrayed it by a slight contraction of his brows, and the careful civility with which he said: "You are mistaken, my dear aunt: Hetta was never mine for the asking. Neither of us has ever wished for a closer relationship than that of the friendship we have always enjoyed—and, I trust, may always enjoy!"

As little as Lady Emborough resented the quiet checks her husband imposed upon her exuberance did she resent a deserved snub. She replied, laughing: "That's the hammer! Quite right to give me a set-down, for what you do is no business of mine! Emborough is for ever scolding me for being too wide in the mouth! But, wit-cracking apart, Desford, isn't it time you were thinking of matrimony? I don't mean Hetta, for if you don't fancy each other there's nothing to be said about *that,* but with Horace still in France, and Simon, from all I hear, sowing even more wild oats than your father did, in his day, I can't but feel that you do owe it to your father to give him a grandson or two —legitimate ones, I mean!"

This made the Viscount burst out laughing, and effectually banished his vexation. "Aunt Sophronia," he said, "you are quite abominable! Did anyone ever tell you so? But you are right, for all that, as I've lately been brought to realize. It is clearly time that I brought my delightfully untrammelled life to an end. The only difficulty is that I have yet to meet any female who will both meet with Papa's approval, and inspire me with the smallest desire to become riveted to her for life!"

"You are a great deal too nice in your requirements," she told him severely; but added, after a moment's reflection: "Not but what I don't wish any of my children to marry anyone for whom they don't feel a decided preference. When I was a girl, you know, most of us married to oblige our parents. Why, even my bosom-bow in those days did so, though she positively disliked the man to whom her parents betrothed her! And a vilely unhappy marriage it was! But your grandfather, my dear Ashley, having himself been forced to contract an alliance which was *far* from happy, was resolute in his determination that none of *his* children should find themselves in a similar situation. And nothing, you will agree, could have been more felicitous than the result of his liberality of mind! To be sure, there were only three of us, and your Aunt Jane died before you were born, but when I married Emborough, and Everard married your dear mama, no one could have been more delighted than your grandfather!"

"I am sorry he died before I was out of short coats," Desford remarked. "I have no memory of him, but from all I have heard about him from you, and from Mama, I wish that I had had the privilege of knowing him."

"Yes, you'd have liked him," she nodded. "What's more, he'd have liked you! And if your father hadn't waited until he was more than thirty before he got married to your mama you *would* have known him! And why Wroxton should glump at you for doing exactly what he did himself is something I don't understand, or wish to understand! There, you be off to play billiards with your cousins, and the Montsale girl, before I get to be as cross as crabs, which they say I always do when I talk about your father!"

He was very ready to obey her, and she did not again revert to the subject. He stayed for a week in Hampshire, and passed his time very pleasurably. After the exigencies of the Season, with its ceaseless breakfasts, balls, routs, race-parties at Ascot, opera-parties, convivial gatherings at Cribb's Parlour, evenings spent at Watier's, not to mention the numerous picnics, and al fresco entertainments ranging from quite ordinary parties to some, given by ambitious hostesses, so daringly original that they were talked of for at least three days, the lazy, unexacting life at Hazelfield exactly suited his humour. If one visited the Emboroughs there was no need to fear that every moment of every day would have been planned, or that you would be dragged to explore some ruin or local beauty spot when all you wished to do was to go for a strolling walk with some other like-minded members of the party. Lady Emborough never made elaborate plans for the entertainment of her guests. She merely fed them very well, and saw to it that whatever facilities were necessary to

enable them to engage in such sports or exercises as they favoured were always at hand; and if any amusement, such as a
race-meeting, happened to be taking place she informed them
that carriages were ready to take them to it, but if anyone felt
disinclined to go racing he had only to say so, and need not
fear that she would be offended.

She adhered strictly to this admirable course when she disclosed to Desford that she had promised to attend a party on the
last night of his visit, taking with her her two elder sons, as
many of her daughters as she thought proper, and any of the
guests she would no doubt have staying with her at Hazelfield
and who did not despise quite a small, country ball. "I shall be
obliged to go," she said, in the resigned voice of one who did
not expect to derive any pleasure from the offered festivity.
"And Emma and Mortimer mean to go too. Theresa has cried
off, but that won't surprise Lady Bugle, for she knows very well
that Theresa is increasing. The Montsales don't wish to go
either, and there's no reason why they should when I *must* go,
and can chaperon Mary for them. Ned and Gil mean to go, but
Christian don't: he hasn't started to dangle after pretty girls
yet. And if you don't fancy it, Desford, there's no reason why
you shouldn't remain here, and play whist with the Montsales
and John Thimbleby! In fact, I strongly advise you to do so,
because it's my belief you'll think the Bugles' party a dead bore."

"Think it a dead bore when that glorious creature will be
present?" ejaculated Mr Gilbert Emborough, who had entered
the room in time to hear the last part of this speech. "Nothing
could be a bore when *she* is there!"

"Come, this is most promising!" said Desford. "Who is this
glorious *she*? Am I acquainted with her?"

"No, you ain't *acquainted* with her," replied Gilbert, "but you
have seen her! What's more, you were much struck—well, anyone would be!—and you asked Ned who she was."

"What, the ravishing girl I saw at the races?" exclaimed
Desford. "My dear aunt, of course I will go with you to this ball!
The most exquisite piece of nature I've seen in a twelve-

month! I hoped Ned might present me to her, and very unhandsome I thought it of him that he didn't do so."

Gilbert gave a crack of laughter. "Afraid you'd cut him out! See if I don't roast him for it!"

"But who is she?" demanded the Viscount. "I didn't properly hear what Ned said, when I asked him that question, for at that moment we were joined by some friends of his, and by the time we had parted from them the next race was about to start, and I thought no more about the Beauty."

"Shame!" said his cousin, grinning at him.

"Her name is Lucasta," said Lady Emborough. "She's the eldest daughter of Sir Thomas Bugle: he has five of 'em, and four sons. Certainly a very handsome girl, and I daresay she may make a good marriage, for she has all the men in raptures. But if her portion is above five thousand pounds I shall own myself astonished. Sir Thomas's fortune is no more than genteel, and he hasn't the least notion of trying to sconce the reckoning."

"Poor Lucasta!" said the Viscount lightly.

"You may well say so! Her mama brought her out in the spring, and there was never anything so unfortunate! Would you believe it?—within three days of her being presented at Court Sir Thomas received an express letter from Dr Cromer, informing him that *old* Lady Bugle had been suddenly taken ill! So, of course, they were obliged to post home in a great hurry, because she *was* very old, and even though one knew she was as tough as whitleather there is always the chance that such persons will be perfectly stout one day, and dead the next. Not that she did die the next day: she lasted for more than two months, which naturally made it impossible for her mama to take Lucasta to balls and assemblies until they are out of black gloves. This dance Lady Bugle has got up is to be quite a small affair. She gives it in honour of Stonor Bugle's engagement to the elder Miss Windle. A good enough girl in her way, but it's not an alliance I should welcome for one of *my* sons!"

"I should think not indeed!" said Gilbert. "Why, she's downright knocker-faced!"

Lady Emborough called him sharply to order for so rudely exaggerating Miss Windle's appearance; but when, on the following evening, the Viscount was presented to the lady he could not feel that Gilbert had been unjust. But he felt also that her homeliness would not have struck him so forcibly had not Lady Bugle caused her to stand side by side with Lucasta Bugle, to receive the guests.

Lucasta was certainly something quite out of the ordinary way, for besides a countenance of classic beauty her figure was good, and her teeth, when she smiled, were seen to be very even, and as white as whalebone. She had luxuriant hair, which only jealous rivals stigmatized as gingery: it was, in fact, the colour of ripening corn; and her proud mama had frequently been known, when accepting compliments on her burnished curls, to whisper confidentially that they had never to be papered. She seemed to have acquired habits of easy intercourse, in spite of the abrupt curtailment of her first season, for she betrayed none of the signs of shyness which so often made it difficult for their partners at a ball to talk to girls who had only just emerged from the schoolroom. Her manners were assured; she had a fund of social chit-chat at her tongue's end; she was all delight and cordiality towards her mama's guests; she was animated, and laughed a great deal; and seemed to be an expert in the art of light-hearted flirtation.

The Viscount had the honour of standing up with her for the dance that was forming when the Emborough party arrived, and since he was more expert in this art than she was he gratified her by responding in the most obliging way to the encouragement he received to pay her just the sort of compliments he judged likely to be the most acceptable. His cousin Edward, indignantly observing the progress he was making into the Beauty's good graces, and the arch, laughing looks which she threw at him, was torn between envy of his address, and cynical reflections on the advantages attached to being the heir to an Earldom. For these he took himself severely to task, telling himself, with dogged loyalty, that the divine Lucasta was merely trying to put a stranger at his ease. But when Gilbert, who had never con-

38

trived to grow higher in the Beauty's esteem than had his elder
brother, encountered him for a fleeting moment, and said, with a
malicious wink: "Des is devilish taken with her, ain't he?" he
was unable to disagree. All he could think of to say was that he
was sure it was no wonder. But when he saw his divinity waltzing, a little later in the evening, with Desford, he would, had he
not been a very goodnatured young man, have taken his cousin
in violent dislike. The waltz was still considered by old-
fashioned persons to be an improper dance, and was seldom
played at country assemblies. One or two dashing hostesses had
caused it to be played, but Ned, having painstakingly mastered
the steps, had found that he had wasted his time: Lucasta never
waltzed.

He had not expected that it would figure amongst the country
dances and the boulangers offered to the company in the Bugles'
establishment, but Lady Bugle, hopeful that Lady Emborough
would bring to her little party her tonnish nephew, had warned
the musicians to be prepared to strike up for one, and had told
Lucasta that if the Viscount did happen to ask her to dance it
with him she might do so.

"For there can be no objection to your doing so *here,* my
love, amongst our particular friends. In London, of course, the
case would be different—until, as I need scarcely remind you,
you have been approved by the Patronesses of Almacks; but I
should be excessively mortified if any of our guests thought it a
dowdy party, and if dear Lady Emborough does bring Lord
Desford to it you may depend upon it that he will expect to hear
waltzes played, for he is quite one of the Pinks of the Ton, you
know!"

Lord Desford did ask her, saying, as he led her off the floor at
the end of the country dance, that he hoped she would stand up
with him again, and adding, with his attractive smile: "Dare I
ask you to waltz with me? Or do you frown on the waltz in
Hampshire? I wonder if my aunt does? How stupid it was of me
not to have asked her! Now, don't, I do beg of you, Miss Bugle,
tell me that I've committed a social solecism!"

She laughed, and said: "No, indeed you have not! I *do* waltz,

39

but whether Mama will permit me to do so in public is another matter!"

"Then I shall instantly ask Mama's permission to waltz with you!" he said.

This having been granted, he was presently seen twirling round the room with an arm lightly encircling Lucasta's trim waist: a spectacle which Lady Bugle regarded with complacency, but which was watched by the Viscount's two cousins, and by several other young gentlemen equally enamoured of the Beauty, with no pleasure at all.

After this, the Viscount did his duty by Miss Windle, and Miss Montsale, and then asked his cousin Emma to stand up with him.

"For heaven's sake, Ashley, don't ask me to dance, but take me out of this insufferably hot room!" replied Mrs Redgrave, who had inherited much of her mother's forthrightness.

"With the greatest pleasure on earth, cousin!" he replied, offering his arm. "I've been uneasily aware for the past half-hour that my shirt-points are beginning to wilt! We will walk over to the doorway, as though we wished to exchange a word with Mortimer, and slip out of the room while the next set is forming. I daresay no one will notice our absence."

"I don't care a rush if they do notice it!" declared Mrs Redgrave, vigorously fanning herself. "People have no business to hold assemblies on such a sultry night as this! They might at least have opened a window!"

"Oh, they never do!" said Desford. "Surely you must know, Emma, that it is only imprudent *young* people who open windows on even the hottest of nights! Thereby causing their elders to suffer all the ills which, I am assured, arise from sitting in a draught, and exposing themselves to even worse dangers. Mortimer, why are you not doing your duty like a man, instead of lounging there and holding up your nose at the company?"

"I wasn't!" said Mr Redgrave indignantly. "The thing is that it's a dashed sight too hot for dancing—and no one thinks anything of it when we old married men don't choose to dance!"

"Quoth the graybeard!" murmured Desford.

40

"Be quiet, wretch!" Emma admonished him. "I won't have poor Mortimer roasted! Recollect that although he is not so very many years older than you he is *much* fatter!"

"There's an archwife for you!" said Mr Redgrave. "If you take my advice, Des, you'll steer wide of parson's mousetrap!"

"Thank you, I mean to! The melancholy sight of you living under the cat's foot is enough to make any man beware!"

Mr Redgrave grinned, but said that Des had hit the nail on the head, adding that he had grown to be a regular Jerry-sneak. Emma knew very well that this inelegant expression signified a henpecked husband, but said with dignity that she didn't understand cant terms. She then said, as both gentlemen laughed, that they were a couple of horrid rudesbys.

"To be sure we are!" cordially agreed her life's companion. "You know, if you mean to take part in this dance, the pair of you, you'd best join the set before it's too late!"

But when he learned that so far from joining the set they were going in search of a little fresh air he instantly said, with considerable aplomb, that having watched Des desperately flirting with Miss Bugle he was dashed well going to see to it that he didn't get the chance to make up to Emma too.

So the three of them passed through the wide double-doors which stood open into the hall. Several people were gathered there, in small groups, most of the ladies fanning themselves, and the gentlemen surreptitiously wiping their heated brows; but Mrs Redgrave had the advantage over them in knowing the geography of the house, and she led her two cavaliers past the stairway to the back of the hall, and through a door which gave access to the gardens. The air was rather more oppressive than it had been during the day, but in comparison to the conditions within the house it was refreshing enough to cause Mr Redgrave to draw a deep breath, and let it go in a vulgar: "Phew!" He then expressed a wistful desire for a cigarillo, but as his wife recognized this as a mere attempt to hoax her into begging him not to do anything so improper as to light a cigarillo at a ball she paid no attention to it, but tucked her hand in his arm, and strolled on to the lawn. The moon was at the full, but was every

41

now and then hidden by clouds drifting across the sky. Summer lightning flickered, and Mr Redgrave said that he wouldn't be surprised if they were in for a storm. A few minutes later a distant rumble made Emma think that perhaps it was time they returned to the ballroom. Her disposition was in general calm, but she had a nervous dread of thunderstorms. Any of her brothers would have scoffed at her fears, but her husband and her cousin were more understanding, and neither scoffed nor tried to convince her that the storm was not imminent.

When they re-entered the house there was no one in the hall, but just as Mr Redgrave softly shut the door into the garden Stonor Bugle came out of the ballroom, and exclaimed: "So there you are! I've been looking for you all over!"

"Oh, dear!" said Emma guiltily. "I hoped no one would notice it if I slipped away for a few minutes! It is *such* a hot night, isn't it?"

He laughed heartily at this. "Ay! Devilish, ain't it? I only wish *I* could sherry off into the garden, but I can't, you know! My mother would comb my hair with a joint-stool if I did! The thing is that old Mrs Barling has been asking for you, ma'am: says she hasn't seen you since time out of mind, and has been peering round the room after you ever since someone told her you was here."

"Oh——! Dear Mrs Barling! I'll come at once!" Emma said, and went back into the ballroom, bearing her reluctant spouse with her.

Stonor followed them, but the Viscount lingered in the hall to adjust his neckcloth, having caught sight of himself in a mirror that hung beside the double-doors into the drawing-room. He was not a dandy; he would have repudiated without hesitation Lady Bugle's assertion that he was a Pink of the Ton; but he was undeniably one of the Smarts, and the glimpse of himself in wilting shirt-points, and a slightly disarranged neckcloth came as a disagreeable shock to him. There was little he could do to restore their starched rigidity to the points of his shirt-collar, but a few deft touches were all that was needed to repair the folds of his neckcloth. Having bestowed these upon it, he turned away, gave his shirt-bands a judicious twitch or two, and was just about to go back into the ballroom when a feeling that he was not alone, as he had supposed himself to be, made him look up, and cast a swift glance round the hall. No one was in sight, but when he raised his eyes towards the upper floor he found that he was being watched by a pair of wondering, innocent eyes which were set in a charming little face, framed by the bannisters through which its owner was looking. He smiled, guessing that it belonged to one of the younger daughters of the house: possibly a member of the schoolroom-party, but more probably one of the nursery-children, and said, as he saw that she was about to run away in evident alarm: "Oh, don't run away! I promise I won't eat you—or tell tales of you to your mama!"

The big eyes widened, in mingled fear and doubt. "You couldn't!" said the lady. "I haven't got a mama! She's been dead for years! I don't think I have a papa either, though that is by no means a certain thing! Oh, don't come up! *Pray* don't come up, sir! They would be so vexed!"

He had mounted half-way up the first flight of stairs, but he paused at this urgent entreaty, saying, between amusement and curiosity: "No mama? But are you not one of Sir Thomas's daughters?"

"Oh, no!" she replied, still in that hushed, scared voice. "I'm not related to him, because being married to my aunt does *not* make him a true uncle—does it?"

"No, no!" he assured her. "It makes him nothing more than an uncle-in-law. But even so I find it hard to believe that he would be cross with you for peeping through those bannisters at the ladies in their smart ball-dresses, and the gentlemen trying to straighten their neckcloths!"

"It isn't *him!*" she said, with an apprehensive look over his head towards the drawing-room. "It's Aunt Bugle, and Lucasta! Oh, pray, sir, go away, before anyone sees you on the stairs, and asks you what you are doing there! You would be obliged to say that you had been talking to me, and that would get me into trouble again!"

His amusement grew, and also his curiosity. "Well, no one is going to see me on the stairs, because I am coming up to further my acquaintance with you, you engaging elf! Oh, don't look so scared! Recollect that I've promised I won't eat you! And talking of eating," he added, remembering his own childhood, "shall I bring you some of the tarts and jellies I've seen laid out for supper? I shall say I want them for my cousin, so you needn't be afraid that anyone will know you ate them!"

She had seemed to be on the point of scrambling to her feet, and beating a hasty retreat, but these words checked her. She stared at him for a moment, and then gave a soft little chuckle, and said: "No, thank you, sir! I had supper hours ago, with Oenone, and Corinna—and Miss Mudford, of course—and my aunt directed the cook to set aside some of the tarts and cakes for the schoolroom supper. So I am not at all hungry. In fact, I'm never hungry, because my aunt doesn't *starve* me! But I am very much obliged to you for being so kind—which I thought you were, the instant you looked up, and smiled at me!"

"Ah, so you are one of the schoolroom-girls, are you?" he said, mounting the rest of the stairs till he stood at the head of the first flight, on the upper hall. "Then I owe you an apology, for I took you for one of the nursery-babies!" He broke off, for she was on her feet, and although the only light illuminating the scene came from the candles burning in the chandelier that hung in the hall below there was enough to show him that she was considerably older than he had supposed.

She smiled shyly up at him, and said: "People nearly always do. It is because I'm such a wretched little dab of a creature, and a severe mortification to me—particularly when I'm amongst my cousins, who are all so tall that I feel a mere squab beside them! At least Lucasta and Oenone and Corinna are tall, and Dianeme is very well grown, so I expect she will be too. Perenna is only just out of leading-strings, so one can't tell about her yet."

Slightly stunned, he said faintly: "Are you sure you have your cousins' names correctly? Did you say *Dianeme*? And *Perenna*?"

"Yes," she answered, with another of her soft chuckles. "You see, when she was very young my aunt was much addicted to

44

poetry, and her papa had a library crammed with old books. That's how she came upon the poems of Robert Herrick. She has the book to this day, and she showed it to me once, when I ventured to ask her why my cousins have such peculiar names. She said she thought them so pretty, and not commonplace, like Maria, and Eliza, and Jane. She wished very much to call Lucasta Electra, but thought it more prudent to name her after her godmama, from whom Lucasta has Expectations. Though I shouldn't think, myself, that anything will come of it," she added, in a reflective tone, "because she's as cantankersome as *old* Lady Bugle was used to be, and she doesn't seem to me even to like Lucasta, or to admire her beauty, which one must own to be unjust, for Lucasta always behaves to her most obligingly, and it must be acknowledged that she *is* beautiful!"

"Very true!" he agreed, his voice grave, but his eyes full of laughter. "And are—er—Oenone and Corinna beautiful too? They should be, with such names as those!"

"Well," she said temperately, "*old* Lady Bugle was for ever telling my aunt that neither of them has beauty enough to figure in London, but I think they are both very pretty, though not, of course, to compare with Lucasta. And as for their names——" She choked on a smothered giggle, and a mischievous gleam shone in her eyes. She raised them to his face, and confided: "Oenone doesn't dislike hers, but Corinna perfectly detests hers, because Stonor discovered the poem called *Corinna's Going a Maying,* and read it to the other boys, so that they instantly took to calling her Sweet Slug-a-bed, and shouting to her outside her door in the morning to Get up, get up for shame, which put her in such a flame that she actually tried to come to cuffs with her papa for having allowed my aunt to saddle her with such a silly, outmoded name. Which was improper, of course, but one can't but sympathize with her."

"No, indeed! And what was her papa's reply to this very just rebuke?" he enquired, much entertained by this artless recital.

"Oh, he merely said that she might think herself fortunate that she hadn't been christened Sappho, and that if it hadn't been for him she would have been. It doesn't sound to me any

45

worse than Corinna, but I believe there was a Greek person of that name who wasn't at all the thing. Oh, *pray* don't laugh so loud, sir!"

He had uttered an involuntary crack of laughter, but he checked it, and begged pardon. He had by this time had time to assimilate the details of her dress and person, and had realized that her figure was elegant, and that her dress had been adapted rather unskilfully from one originally made for a much bigger girl. He also realized, being pretty well experienced in such matters, that it was a trifle dowdy, and that her soft brown ringlets had not enjoyed the ministrations of a hairdresser. It was the fashion for ladies to have their locks cropped and curled, or twisted into high Grecian knots from which carefully brushed and pomaded clusters of curls fell over their ears; but this child's hair fell loosely from a ribbon tied round her head, several strands escaping from it, which gave her a somewhat dishevelled appearance.

Desford said abruptly: "How old are you, my child? Sixteen? Seventeen?"

"Oh, no, I am much older than that!" she replied. "I'm as old as Lucasta—all but a few weeks!"

"Then why are you not downstairs, dancing with the rest of them?" he demanded. "You must surely be out!"

"No, I'm not," she said. "I don't suppose I ever shall be, either. Unless my papa turns out not to be dead, and comes home to take care of me himself. But I don't think that at all likely, and even if he did come home it wouldn't be of the least use, because he seems never to have sixpence to scratch with. I am afraid he is not a very respectable person. My aunt says he was obliged to go abroad on account of being monstrously in debt." She sighed, and said wistfully: "I know that one ought not to criticize one's father, but I can't help feeling that it was just a *little* thoughtless of him to abandon me."

"Do you mean that he left you in your aunt's charge?" he asked, his brows drawing together. "He can't have *abandoned* you!"

"Well, he did," she said. "And it was horridly uncomfortable,

46

I can tell you, sir! I was still at school, in Bath, you see—and I must own that Papa did pay the bills, when he was in funds, and Miss Fletching was very kind, and she never told me that he had stopped doing so until she was obliged to realize that he wasn't going to remember that he owed her for a whole year. She disclosed to me afterwards that for a long time she expected to get a letter from him, or even a visit, for he did sometimes come down to see me. And it seems he had never been very punctual in paying Miss Fletching, so that she was quite in the habit of waiting. And I fancy she had a tendre for him, because she was for ever saying what a handsome man he was, and how particularly affable, and what distinguished manners he had. She was fond of me, too: she said it was because I had lived with her for such a long time, which I had, for Papa placed me in the school when my mama died, and I was only eight years old then, and lived at school all the year round."

"You poor child!" he exclaimed.

"Oh, no!" she assured him. "In the holidays my friends amongst the day-boarders often invited me to their parties, or took me with them on expeditions, and Miss Fletching several times took me to the theatre. I was perfectly happy—indeed, I don't suppose I shall ever be so happy again. But naturally I couldn't remain there for ever, so Miss Fletching was obliged to write to my grandfather. But it so happens that he had disowned Papa years and years before, and he wrote very uncivilly to Miss Fletching, saying that he wanted to know nothing about his ramshackle son's brats, and recommending her to apply to my mama's relations. Which—is how I come to be here."

She ended on a forlorn note, which made Desford say gently: "But you're not happy here, are you?"

She shook her head, but said, with a valiant attempt to smile: "Not very happy, sir. But I do try to be, because I know I am very much obliged to Aunt Bugle for—for giving me a home, when she held Papa in the utmost aversion, and had had a terrible quarrel with my mama when Mama eloped with him, and never forgave her. Which makes it my duty to be grateful to her, don't you think?"

47

"Who is your father?" he demanded, not answering this question. "What is his name? And what is your name?"

"Steane," she replied. "Papa is Wilfred Steane, and I am Cherry Steane."

"Well, you have a very pretty name, Miss Steane!" he said, smiling down at her. "But—Steane? Are you related to old—to Lord Nettlecombe?"

"Yes, he's my grandfather," she said. "Are you acquainted with him, sir?"

"No, I haven't that honour," he replied rather dryly. "I have, however, met your Uncle Jonas, and as I've been credibly informed that he closely resembles his father I am strongly of the opinion, my child, that you are better off with your aunt than you would be with your grandfather! But why should we waste our time talking about either of them? You have told me your name, but it occurs to me that you don't know mine! It is——"

"Oh, I know who you are!" she said. "You are Lord Desford! I knew that when I saw you waltzing with Lucasta. That's why I was looking through the bannisters: you can see this end of the drawing-room from here, you know. I saw you first when you came down the country dance, but I couldn't be positive it was you until I caught a glimpse of you waltzing with Lucasta."

"And then you were positive?" he said, in some amusement. "Why?"

"Oh, because I heard Aunt Bugle tell Lucasta she might waltz if *you* invited her to!" she replied blithely. Then her expression changed swiftly, as some faint sound in the shadows behind her came to her ears, and the wary, frightened look returned to her face. She whispered: "I mustn't stay! That was a board creaking! Please, oh, please go away, and *pray* take care no one sees you going down the stairs!"

She was gone on the words, as noiseless as a ghost; and the Viscount, having assured himself that the coast was clear, walked calmly down the stairs, and went back into the ballroom.

CHAPTER IV

SEIZING ON the excuse offered by her daughter's fear of being driven back to Hazelfield through a thunderstorm, Lady Emborough carried her party off immediately after supper. Lady
Bugle was regretful, but since she was even more frightened of
lightning than was Emma she fully sympathized with her
alarms, and made no effort to delay the departure, prophesying,
when she heard that a storm was brewing, that a great many
others would also leave early: certainly all those faced with a
drive of more than half-an-hour.

The Redgraves took up Edward and Gilbert in their carriage,
and Desford occupied the fourth seat in the Emborough lan-
daulet, sitting beside his uncle, and confronting Lady Emborough and Miss Montsale. For the first few minutes the
ladies discussed the ball, but presently Miss Montsale said that
although she had been prepared to find that Miss Bugle fell
short of the enthusiastic descriptions furnished by Ned and Gil
she had no sooner set eyes on her than she felt that they had
underrated her beauty rather than exaggerated it. "Such great,
sparkling eyes!" she said. "Such a lovely complexion, and such
glorious hair! Oh, I thought she was one of the most beautiful
creatures I've ever seen! Did not you, Lord Desford?"

He was not, like his uncle, drowsing, but he was obviously
abstracted, and she had to repeat her question to recall him
from whatever thoughts were occupying his mind. He said: "I
beg pardon! I wasn't attending! Miss Bugle? Oh, yes, undoubtedly! A dazzling piece of nature!"

"And not just in the common style!"

"By no means!"

"What do you think, Desford? Will she take?" asked Lady
Emborough.

"Lord, yes!"

"Well, I hope she will. I don't like her mother above half,

49

but I do sincerely pity her, for it's no laughing matter to have five daughters to establish creditably when one hasn't a large enough fortune to grease the wheels," she said bluntly. "There's one that ought to be brought out next Season, and so she would be if old Lady Bugle hadn't chosen to die at the most inconvenient time she could! Lucasta might have been engaged by now, which would have made it possible for the next one—I can't remember her name! they all have the most outlandish names!—to have been allowed to try her wings at that little affair tonight, and to have been brought out during the Little Season, this autumn. Not what one would choose, of course, but what's to be done, when the girl is turned seventeen already, and her elder sister has scarcely been seen yet, much less turned-off? And before that unfortunate woman has time to make a recover she'll have the third girl ready for her come-out!"

"Tell me, ma'am!" interposed Desford. "What do you know about Lady Bugle's niece? Have you met her?"

"Why, have *you* met her?" she asked, considerably surprised.

"Yes, I met her tonight," he answered. "But pray don't divulge that to her aunt! She was peeping through the bannisters to watch as much as she could see of the dancing, and I happened to catch sight of her. I thought her one of the children at first, but discovered that she is—all but a few weeks!—as old as her cousin Lucasta. A pretty child, with big, scared eyes, a tangle of brown hair, and a deplorably outmoded and ill-fitting gown."

Lady Emborough tried hard to see his face, but it was too dark inside the carriage for her to distinguish more than its outlines. She said: "Yes, I think I have seen her once. I must own, it astonishes me to learn that she is as old as Lucasta, for —like you!—I thought her a schoolroom miss! A poor little dab of a girl, isn't she? Well, she's the daughter of Lady Bugle's only sister, who ran off with that ne'er-do-well son of old Nettlecombe's. Before your time, but I remember what a scandal it was! Lady Bugle was obliged to take this girl under her roof —oh, a little over a year ago! I forget the rights of it, but I know that I thought it very charitable of her to have done so, when she told me about it."

"Oh, was that how it was?" he said, in an indifferent tone.

"Charitable?" said Miss Montsale. "Why, yes—if the charity was not used as a cloak to cover more mercenary aims!"

"Good God, Mary, what in the world do you mean?" demanded Lady Emborough.

"Oh, nothing, dear ma'am, against Lady Bugle! How could I, when I never met her before tonight? But I have so often seen—as I am persuaded you too must have seen!—the—the indigent female who has been received into the household of one of her more affluent relations, as an act of charity, and has been turned into a drudge!"

"And has been expected to be grateful for it!" struck in the Viscount.

"If," said Lady Emborough awfully, "these remarks refer to my cousin Cordelia's position at Hazelfield——"

"Oh, no, no, no!" Miss Montsale assured her laughingly. "Of course they don't! Lord Desford, *could* anyone suppose Miss Pembury to be a downtrodden drudge?"

"Certainly not!" he responded promptly. "No one, that is to say, who had been privileged to hear her giving handsome set-downs to my aunt! But you are very right, Miss Montsale: I too have seen just what you have described, and I suspect that the child I met tonight may be an example of that sort of charity."

No more was said, for by this time the carriage had drawn up before the imposing portals of Hazelfield House. The ladies were handed down from it; Lord Emborough was roused by his nephew from his gentle slumber; and his sons, springing down from the Redgrave carriage, which drew up a minute later, were indignantly calling upon their pusillanimous sister to own that the storm was still miles distant, and that it had been a great shame to have dragged them away from the ball when (according to them) it had scarcely begun.

Lord Emborough, on entering his house, presented all the appearance of a gentleman no more than half awake, but when

51

he walked into my lady's bedchamber, an hour later, he had emerged from his drowsy mists, and so obviously wished to engage her in private conversation that she dismissed her abigail, who was in the act of fitting a nightcap over her iron-gray locks, and said, as this excellent female curtsied herself out of the room: "Now we can be comfortable, and talk about the party—which I have for long thought to be the best thing about parties, even the finest of 'em! Which the lord knows this wasn't! An insipid evening, wasn't it?"

"It was indeed," he agreed, disposing himself in a cushioned chair, and yawning. "I have never known, my love, why my old friend—as good a man as ever stepped when we were up at Oxford together!—should have chosen to marry—I won't say a smatterer, but a mere miss, which was what we all thought her!"

"Well," said Lady Emborough tolerantly, "I do not say that she is a woman of the first consideration, but it must be acknowledged that she has been a good wife to Sir Thomas, and is an excellent mother. And even you, Emborough, must also acknowledge that Sir Thomas's sense is not superior!"

"No," he agreed, with a melancholy sigh. He then fell silent, but said, after a few moments, somewhat acidly: "I am excessively glad, my dear, that I have never been mortified by the spectacle of *my* wife throwing a daughter at the head of an eligible *parti* in what I can only describe as a positively shocking way!"

"Certainly not!" responded his lady, with unruffled calm. "I hope I have too much rumgumption to do anything so birdwitted. But it must be remembered, my lord, that I have not been cursed with an improvident husband, and five daughters! I promise you, I do most sincerely feel for Lady Bugle, little though I may like her, and perfectly sympathize with her anxiety to achieve a good match for Lucasta as soon as may be possible."

He directed a worried look at her. "Did it seem to you that Desford was strongly attracted to that girl, my love?"

"Not in the least," she replied unhesitatingly.

"Well, I hope you may be right," he said. "It seemed to me that he treated her with very flattering distinction! And it wouldn't do, you know!"

"Of course it wouldn't do, and he knows that as well as we do! Lord, my dear sir, can you suppose that a personable man of birth and fortune who has been on the town for years, and has had I don't know how many girls on the catch for him, don't recognize a lure in no more than the shake of a lambstail? If the mother's odious toadying didn't disgust him, you may depend upon it the coming manners Lucasta assumed did!"

"One would have thought so, but he appeared to me to be quite blatantly flirting with her!"

"To be sure he was!" said her ladyship. "But in my judgment he was very much more interested in Lucasta's little cousin!"

"Good God!" ejaculated Emborough. "Do you mean that scamp's child?—*Wilfred Steane's* daughter?"

His wife burst out laughing, for the look of dismay on his face was comical. "Yes, but there's no need for you to be on the fidgets, I promise you! Recollect that Desford leaves us tomorrow! It is in the highest degree unlikely that he will ever see the girl again; and for my part I wouldn't wager a groat on the chance that he won't have forgotten all about her by the time he reaches London!"

If this was a somewhat exaggerated statement, it is probable that had not Chance intervened Miss Cherry Steane would not have lived for long in the Viscount's memory. But Chance did intervene, and on the very next day.

Since Hazelfield was situated within a few miles of Alton, and he was bound for London, he did not take leave of his hosts until he had consumed a leisurely breakfast. The threatened storm had burst (according to Emma's account) directly over the house in the small hours, but after a violent downpour the weather had cleared, and the Viscount set out on his journey with every expectation of covering the distance in bright sunlight, and of reaching his destination in excellent time to change his dress, and to stroll from his house in Arlington Street to White's Club, where he meant to dine.

At Alton, he joined the post-road to Southampton, and was soon driving through Farnham. It was when he was a few miles beyond this town that Fate took a hand in his affairs.

A female figure, wearing a round bonnet and a gray cloak, plodding ahead, with a slightly dilapidated portmanteau in her grasp, did not attract his attention, but just as his horses drew abreast of her she turned her head, looking up at him, and disclosed the child-like countenance of Miss Cherry Steane. Considerably startled, he uttered an exclamation, and reined in his horses.

"Why, what's amiss, my lord?" demanded Stebbing, even more startled.

The Viscount, slewing round to obtain a second view of Miss Steane, found that the fleeting glance he had cast down at her as his curricle swept past had not deceived him: Miss Steane it most certainly was. He thrust the reins into Stebbing's hands, saying briefly: "Hold 'em! I know that lady!" He then jumped lightly down on to the road, and strode back to meet Miss Steane.

She greeted him with frank delight, and said, in a voice of passionate thanksgiving: "I *thought* it was you, sir! Oh, I am so glad! If you are going to London, would you—would you be so *very* kind as to take me up in your carriage?"

He took the portmanteau from her, and set it down. "What, to London? Why?"

"I've run away," she explained, with a confiding smile.

"That, my child, is obvious!" he said. "But it won't do, you know! How could I possibly aid and abet you to leave the protection of your aunt?"

Her face fell ludicrously; it seemed for a moment that she was going to burst into tears, but she overcame the impulse, swallowing resolutely, and saying in a prim, forlorn little voice: "C-couldn't you, sir? I beg your pardon! I thought—I thought— But it's of no consequence!"

"Will you tell me why you have run away?" he suggested gently.

"I couldn't bear it! You don't *know!*" she said, in a stifled tone.

"No, but I wish you will tell me. I think something must have happened since we talked together last night. Did someone hear you, and tell your aunt?" She nodded, biting her lips. "And she perhaps gave you a scold?"

"Oh, yes! But that's not it! I don't care for mere scolds, but she said such things—and Lucasta too—and all in front of Corinna—and Corinna told the others——" Her voice failed on a sob, and she was quite unable to continue.

He waited until she had in some degree recovered her composure. He thought he had seldom seen a more pathetic picture. Not only was her countenance woebegone, but her shoes and the hem of the duffle cloak which she wore were sadly muddied; several strands of her unruly hair had escaped from the confinement of the round, schoolgirl's bonnet, and strayed across her flushed features; and beads of sweat glistened on her forehead. She looked to be hot, tired, and despairing. For the first of these three ills the duffle cloak was certainly responsible; for the second it was no wonder that she should be tired if she had trudged all the way from her home, carrying a cumbrous portmanteau; but the despair was not to be accounted for so easily: nothing she had said to him on the previous evening had prepared him to find her flying from the security of the only home she seemed to have.

She succeeded in mastering her agitation, and even managed to summon up a gallant, if unconvincing, smile. "I beg your pardon!" she uttered. "It was only because you look so kind, sir, and—and talked to me last night—— But it was wrong of me to ask you to take me up in your carriage. Pray don't regard it! My—my affairs are not your concern, and I shall do very well by myself!"

He ignored the hand she was resolutely holding out to him, but picked up her portmanteau, and said: "We cannot stand talking in the road! I don't promise to take you to London,

55

but at least I'll take you to Farnborough! As I remember, there is a tolerable inn there, where I can procure some refreshment for you, and where we can continue this conversation at our ease. Come along!"

She hung back, searching his face with her wide, scared eyes. "You won't compel me to return to Maplewood, will you?"

"No, I won't do that. What right have I to compel you to do anything? Though it is undoubtedly what I ought to do!"

She seemed to be satisfied with this reply, for she said no more, but went obediently beside him to where his curricle stood. The expression on Stebbing's face when he realized that his master was going to hand into the curricle a Young Person whose unattended state and dowdy raiment clearly denoted that she was not a female of consequence spoke volumes; but he relinquished the reins to the Viscount, without a word, and climbed up into the groom's seat between the springs.

Miss Steane, sinking back against the squabs, uttered a sigh of relief. "Oh, how comfortable this is!" she said thankfully.

"Have you trudged all the way from Maplewood?"

"No, no! I was so fortunate as to have been given a lift to Froyle, in a tax-cart, so I have only been obliged to walk for six or seven miles, and I shouldn't regard that in the least if I weren't burdened with this portmanteau. And I must own I wish my pelisse wasn't quite worn out, so that I might have worn it instead of this dreadful cloak."

"It is certainly not the thing for such a warm day," he agreed.

"No, but I thought I should wear it, in case it comes on to rain, or I felt chilly when the sun goes down."

"When the sun goes down——! You absurd child, you are surely not meaning to continue walking till nightfall?"

"No—at least—Well, I thought I should have been able to travel on the stage-coach, but—but when it reached Alton it was cram-full, and of course I hadn't booked a seat, so I wasn't on the way-bill, and the guard wouldn't take me up. And even if there had been room I found that I hadn't quite enough money to pay for the fare. But I daresay I shall be able to get a lift on a carrier's wagon: they will often take people up, you know,

56

and for no more than a shilling or two. And if I don't I shall go on for as long as I can, and then find a lodging for the night in some respectable farmhouse."

The Viscount's reflections on the sort of reception she was likely to meet at a respectable farmhouse he kept to himself, merely asking her where she proposed to lodge when she did reach London.

"I am going to my grandfather," she replied, a hint of defiance in her voice.

"Indeed! May I ask if he knows it?"

"Well—well, not yet!" she confessed.

He drew an audible breath, and said rather grimly: "Yes, well, we will postpone further discussion until we get to Farnborough, when I must hope to be able to convince you that this scheme of yours won't do, my child!"

"You won't convince me!" she said, betraying signs of agitation. "Oh, pray don't try, sir! It is the only thing I *can* do! You don't understand!"

"Then you shall explain it to me," he said cheerfully.

She said no more, but groped in the folds of her cloak for the pocket which held her handkerchief. He was afraid that she was going to cry, and suffered a moment's dismay. He was not chicken-hearted, but he found himself quite unable to face with equanimity the prospect of driving a lady in floods of tears along a busy post-road. However, she bravely suppressed all but one small sob, and did no more than blow her nose. He was moved to say, for her encouragement: "Good girl!" glancing down at her as he spoke, and smiling.

Of necessity it was a very brief glance, but as he turned his head back again to watch the road he caught a glimpse of the wavering, would-be valiant smile which answered his, and it wrung his heart.

In a few minutes Farnborough was reached, and he had drawn up in front of the Ship. Not many persons patronized this small post-house, so the landlord, who came out to welcome a recognizable member of the Quality, was saddened, but not surprised, when the Viscount, handing Miss Steane into his care, told him that they had stopped only to bait. "Anyone in the coffee-room?" he asked.

"No, sir, no one—not at the moment! But if your honour would wish to partake of refreshment in the private parlour——"

"No, the coffee-room will do very well. Some lemonade for the lady, and cold meat—cakes—fruit—whatever you have! And a tankard of beer for myself, if you please!" He looked down at Miss Steane, and said: "Go in, my dear: I'll be with you in a moment."

He watched her enter the inn, and turned to issue a few instructions to Stebbing, standing at the wheelers' heads. Stebbing received these with a wooden: "Very good, my lord," but the Viscount had taken barely two steps towards the door into the inn before his feelings overcame him, and he said, explosively: "My lord!"

"Well?" said the Viscount, over his shoulder.

"It ain't my place to speak," said Stebbing, with careful restraint, "but being as I've known your lordship ever since you was a little lad, which I taught to ride your first pony—ah, *and* pulled you out of scrapes! and being that——"

"You needn't go on!" interrupted Desford, quizzing him. "I know just what you are trying to say! I must take care I don't fall into yet another scrape, mustn't I?"

"Yes, my lord, and I hope you will—though it don't look to me, the way things is shaping, that you will!"

But Desford only laughed, and went into the inn. The mistress of the establishment had taken Miss Steane upstairs, and when she presently joined his lordship in the coffee-room she had washed her face, tidied her unruly hair, and was carrying her cloak over her arm. She looked much more presentable, but the round dress of faded pink cambric which she wore was rather crumpled, besides being muddied round the hem, and in no way became her. She was looking very grave, but when she saw the chicken, and the tongue, and the raspberries on the table her eyes brightened perceptibly, and she said gratefully: "Oh, thank you, sir! I am very much obliged to you! I ran away before breakfast, and you can't think how hungry I am!"

She then sat down at the table, and proceeded to make a hearty meal. Desford, who was not at all hungry, sat watching her, his tankard in his hand, thinking that for all her nineteen years she was very little removed from childhood. While she ate he forbore to question her, but when she came to the end of her nuncheon, and said that she now felt much better, he said: "Do you feel sufficiently restored to tell me all about it? I wish you will!"

Her brightened eyes clouded, but after a slight hesitation she said: "If I tell you why I've run away, will you take me to London, sir?"

He laughed. "I am making no rash promises—except to carry you straight back to Maplewood if you *don't* tell me!"

She said with quaint dignity, but as though she had a lump in her throat: "I cannot believe that you would do anything so —so unhandsome!"

"No, I am sure you cannot," he said sympathetically. "But you must consider my position, you know! Recollect that all I know at this present is that although you told me last night that you were not very happy I am persuaded you had no intention then of running away. Yet today I come upon you, in a good deal of distress, having apparently reached a sudden decision to leave your aunt. Did you perhaps have a quarrel with her, fly up into the boughs, and run away without giving yourself time to consider whether she had really been unkind enough to warrant your taking such an extreme course? Or whether she too had lost her temper, and had said much more than she meant?"

She looked forlornly at him, and gave her head a shake. "We didn't quarrel. I didn't even quarrel with Corinna. Or with Lucasta. And it wasn't such a sudden decision. I've wished desperately—oh, almost from the moment my aunt took me to Maplewood!—to escape. Only whenever I ventured to ask my aunt if she would help me to find a situation where I could earn my own bread she always scolded me for being ungrateful,

59

and—and said I should soon wish myself back at Maplewood, because I was fit for nothing but a—a menial position." She paused, and, after a moment or two, said rather hopelessly: "I can't explain it to you. I daresay you wouldn't understand if I could, because you have never been so poor that you were obliged to hang on anyone's sleeve, and try to be grateful for a worn-out ribbon, or a scrap of torn lace which one of your cousins gave you, instead of throwing it away."

"No," he replied. "But you are mistaken when you say that I don't understand. I have seen all too many of such cases as you describe, and have sincerely pitied the victims of this so-called charity, who are expected to give unremitting service to show their gratitude for——" He broke off, for she had winced, and turned away her face. "What have I said to upset you?" he asked. "Believe me, I had no intention of doing so!"

"Oh, no!" she said, in a stifled voice. "I beg your pardon! It was stupid of me to care for it, but that word brought it all back to me, like—like a stab! Lucasta said I was well-named, and my aunt s-said: 'Very true, my love!' and that in future I should be called Charity, to keep me in mind of the fact that that is what I am—a charity girl!"

"What a griffin!" he exclaimed disdainfully. "But she won't call you Charity, you know! Depend upon it, she wouldn't wish people to think her spiteful!"

"They wouldn't. Because it *is* my name!" she disclosed tragically. "I know I told you it was Cherry, but it wasn't a fubbery, sir, to say that, because I have always been called Cherry."

"I see. Do you know, I like Charity better than Cherry? I think it is a very pretty name."

"You wouldn't think so if it was your name, and *true!*"

"I suppose I shouldn't," he admitted. "But what did you do to bring down all this ill-will upon your head?"

"Corinna was on the listen last night, when we talked together on the stairs," she said. "She is the most odious, humbugging little cat imaginable, and if you think I shouldn't say such a thing of her I am sorry, but it is true! I was used to think her the most amiable of my cousins, and—and my friend! And even though I did know that she was a shocking fibster, and not in the least above carrying tales against Oenone to my aunt, I never dreamed she would do the same by me! Well—well, there was some excuse for her trying for revenge against Oenone, because Oenone is a very disagreeable girl, and for ever picking out grievances, and trying to set my aunt against her sisters. But——" Her eyes filled with tears, which she made haste to brush away—"she—she had no cause to do me a mischief! But —but she twisted everything I said to you, sir, m-making it seem quite different from what I *did* say! She even said that you wouldn't have come upstairs if I hadn't th-thrown out lures to you! Which I didn't! I *didn't!*"

"On the contrary! You begged me not to come upstairs!" he said, smiling.

"Yes, and so I told them, but neither my aunt nor Lucasta would believe me. They—they accused me of being a—a designing little squirrel, and my aunt read me a scold about g-girls like me ending up in the Magdalen: and when I asked her what the Magdalen is, she said that if I continued to make sheep's eyes at every man that crossed my path I should very soon discover what it is. But I don't, I *don't!*" she said vehemently. "It wasn't my fault that you came up to talk to me last night, and it wasn't my fault that Sir John Thorley took me up in his chaise and so very kindly drove me back to Maplewood, the day he overtook me walking back from the village in the rain; and it wasn't my fault that Mr Rainham came over to talk to me when I brought Dianeme and Tom down to the drawing-room one evening! I did *not* put myself forward! I sat down, just as my aunt bade me, in a chair against the wall, and made not the least push to keep him beside me! I *promise* you I didn't, sir!" Her tears brimmed over, but she brushed them away, and said: "It was nothing but kindness on their parts, and to say that I lured either of them away from Lucasta is wickedly unjust!"

Since he had himself succumbed to the unconscious appeal of her big eyes, and had been moved to compassion by her forlorn aspect, he could readily understand the feelings that had prompted two gentlemen, whom he guessed to be admirers of

Lucasta, to pay her a little attention. He thought, with a sardonic curl of his lips, that Lady Bugle was no wiser than a wet-goose; and wondered how many of Lucasta's court would have paid any attention to her little cousin had Cherry been suitably attired, and treated by Lady Bugle with the affection that lady showed towards Lucasta. Not many, he guessed, for, although she had an innocent charm, she was no more than a candle to the sun of Lucasta's beauty; and if she had been happy she would have roused no chivalrous emotions in any male breast. These reflections, however, he kept to himself, setting himself instead to the task of soothing her agitation, prior to doing what lay within his power to convince her that a return to her house of bondage would be preferable to her present scheme.

With the first of these objects in view, he encouraged her to unburden herself of her wrongs, thinking that to be allowed to pour out her troubles would sensibly allay whatever feelings of hurt and injustice had overset her. He suspected that these might have been exaggerated in her mind by what had obviously been a pulling of caps; but by the time she had been induced to describe what her life had been at Maplewood there was no hint of a smile in his eyes, and no scepticism in his mind.

For she did not answer his questions willingly, and she seemed always to be able to find excuses for the many unkindnesses she had received at Maplewood. Nor did she resent the demands that had been made on her: she felt it was only right that she should repay her aunt's generosity by performing whatever services were required of her; but when she said simply: "I would do anything if only she would love me a little, and just *once* say thank you!" he thought he had never heard a sadder utterance.

It was obvious that Lady Bugle had seen in her not an orphaned niece to be cherished, but a household slave, to be made to fetch and carry all day long, to wait not only on her aunt but on her cousins as well, and to mind the two eldest nursery children whenever Nurse desired her to do so. He suspected that if she had been less docile and less easily dismayed she would have fared better at Maplewood: he had been standing close enough to Lady Bugle on the previous evening to observe her when she approached her husband, and said something pretty sharp to him under her breath. He had not heard what she had said, but that she had issued an order was patent, for Sir Thomas had at first expostulated, and then gone off to do her bidding, and Desford had written her down then and there as one of those overbearing females who would tyrannize over anyone too meek or too scared to withstand her. It had at first surprised him to learn that his brief meeting with Cherry had brought down on her head such a venomous scold, but the more he studied the sweet little face before him the less surprised did he feel that the ambitious mother and daughter should have been so furious to learn that he had been sufficiently attracted by Cherry to have gone upstairs to talk to her. Lucasta was a Beauty, but Cherry was by far the more taking.

While she told her story, at least half of his brain was occupied in trying to think what to do for her. It had not taken long to make him abandon his original intention of restoring her to her aunt, and he wasted no eloquence on attempting to persuade her to agree to such a course. A fleeting notion of placing her in Lady Emborough's care no sooner occurred to him than he banished it; and when he suggested that she should return to Miss Fletching she shook her head, saying that nothing would prevail upon her to make any more demands on that lady's kindness.

"Don't you think you might be very useful to her?" he coaxed. "As a teacher, perhaps?"

"No," she replied. Suddenly her eyes lost their despairing look, and danced mischievously. She giggled, and said: "I shouldn't be in the least useful, and certainly not as a teacher! I am not at all bookish, and although I do *know* how to play on the pianoforte I don't play at all well! I have no aptitude for languages, either, or for painting, and my sums are always wrong. So you see——!"

It was certainly daunting. He could not help laughing, but he said: "Well, now that you've told me all the things you can't do, tell me what you can do!"

The cloud descended again on her brow. She said: "Nothing —nothing of a genteel nature. My aunt says I am only fitted to perform menial tasks, and I suppose that is true. But while I have been at Maplewood I have learnt a great deal about housekeeping, and I know I can take care of sick old ladies, because when old Lady Bugle became too ill to leave her bed there were days when she wouldn't let anyone enter her room except me. And I think she liked me, because though she pinched at me a good deal—she was nearly always as cross as crabs, poor old lady—she never ripped up at me as she did at my aunt, and Lucasta, and Oenone, or accuse me of wishing her dead. So I thought that I could very likely be a comfort to my grandfather. I believe he lives quite alone, except for the servants, which must be excessively melancholy for him. Don't you think so, sir?"

"I should certainly find it so, but your grandfather is said to be a—a confirmed recluse. I have never met him, but if the stories that are told about him are true he is not a very amiable person. After all, you told me yourself that he had written a very disobliging reply to Miss Fletching's letter, didn't you?"

"Yes, but I don't think she asked him to take charge of me," she argued. "She wanted him to pay the money Papa owed her, and I shouldn't wonder at it if she set up his back, for I know, from what Papa has said to me, that he is shockingly clutch-fisted."

"Did your aunt pay her?" he interrupted.

She shook her head, flushing a little. "No. She too said that she wasn't responsible, but because of blood being thicker than water she—she would relieve Miss Fletching by taking me away to live with her. So—so no one has paid for me—yet! But I mean to save every penny I can earn, and *I* shall pay her!" Her chin lifted, and she said: "If my grandfather—if I can see him, and explain to him how it is—surely he won't refuse to let me stay with him at least until I've found a suitable situation?"

The Viscount could not think this likely. No matter how ill-disposed and eccentric Lord Nettlecombe might be, he could scarcely turn away a destitute granddaughter who had no other shelter in London than his house. The probability was that he would take a fancy to her, and if that happened her future would be assured. And if he was such a shabster as to turn her away, he would find he had to deal with my Lord Desford, who would cast aside the deference to his elders so carefully drilled into him from his earliest days, and would counsel the old muck-worm in explicit terms to think well before he behaved in so scaly a fashion as must alienate even the few friends he had, once the story became known, as he, Desford, would make it his business to see that it did.

He did not favour Cherry with these reflections, but got up abruptly, and said: "Very well! I will take you to London!"

She sprang to her feet, caught his hand, and kissed it before he could prevent her. "Oh, thank you, sir!" she cried, gratitude throbbing in her voice, and making her eyes shine through the sudden tears of relief which filled them. "Thank you, thank you, *thank* you!"

Considerably embarrassed, he drew his hand away, and gave her a pat on the shoulder with it, saying: "Draw bridle, you foolish child! Wait until we see how your grandfather receives you before you fly into raptures! If he doesn't receive you, you will have nothing to thank me for, you know!"

He then went away to pay his shot, telling her that he would bring his curricle to the door in a few minutes, and so cut short any further expressions of her gratitude.

But he had still to run the gauntlet of his devoted servitor's disapproval. When he informed Stebbing that he was driving Miss Steane to London, that worthy found himself wholly unable to receive this news in a manner befitting his station, but said forthrightly: "My lord, I beg and implore you not to do no such thing! You'll find yourself in the briars, as sure as check, and it's me as will get the blame for it when his lordship comes to hear of it!"

"Don't be such a gudgeon!" said the Viscount impatiently. "His lordship won't come to hear of it—and if he did the only thing he would blame you for is making such a piece of work about nothing! Do you imagine I'm abducting the child?"

"More likely she's abducting you, my lord!" muttered Stebbing.

The Viscount's eyes hardened; he said coldly: "I allow you a good deal of licence, Stebbing, but that remark goes far beyond the line of what I will permit!"

"My lord," said Stebbing doggedly, "if I spoke too free, I ask your pardon! But I've served you faithfully ever since you was pleased to accept of me as your personal groom, and I couldn't look myself in the face if I didn't make a push to stop you doing something so caper-witted as to carry off this young pers—lady!—the way you're meaning to! You can turn me off, my lord, but I must and will tell you to your head that *I* never seen a young lady which would go off with a gentleman like this Miss Steane is willing to go off with you!"

"Doesn't it suit your sense of propriety? Well, you must bear in mind that you will be sitting behind us, and I give you leave to intervene to protect Miss Steane's virtue from any improper advances I might make to her!" Perceiving that Stebbing was deeply troubled, he relented, and said, laughingly: "There's no need for you to be so hot in the spur, you old pudding-head! All I've engaged myself to do is to convey Miss Steane to her grandfather's house. And if you weren't a pudding-head you would know that her willingness to go with me to London springs from innocence, and not, as you seem to think, from a want of delicacy! Good God, what would you have me to do in this situation? Abandon her to become the prey of the first rakeshame she encounters on the road? A pretty fellow you must think me!"

"No, my lord, I don't think no such thing! But what I do think is that you should take her back where she came from!"

"She won't go, and I have no right to force her to do so." A gleam of humour shot into his eyes; he added: "And even if I had the right I'd be damned if I'd do it! Lord, Stebbing, would *you* drive a girl who was crying her eyes out, in an open carriage?" He laughed, and said: "You know you wouldn't! Put to the horses, and don't spill any more time sermonizing!"

"Very good, my lord. But I shall take leave to say—asking

your pardon for making so bold as to open my budget!—that I never seen you—no, not when you was in the heyday of blood, and kicking up all kinds of conflabberation!—so bedoozled as what you are now! And if you don't end up in the basket—and me with you!—you can call me a Jack Adams, my lord!"

"I'm much obliged to you! I will!" retorted the Viscount.

CHAPTER V

THE VISCOUNT drew up his sweating team two-and-a-half hours later in Albemarle Street, having driven his horses in a spanking style that in anyone but a top-sawyer, which he was, would have been extremely dangerous. Even Stebbing, who had good reason to know that he could drive to an inch, clutched the edge of his seat three times: twice when, on a narrow stretch of the road, he sprang his horses to give the go-by to a slower vehicle, and once when he feather-edged a blind corner without checking; but it was only when they reached the outskirts of London that he allowed himself to utter a gruff warning, saying: "Easy over the pimples, my lord, I do beg of you!"

"What do you take me for?" the Viscount tossed over his shoulder. "A spoon?"

Stebbing returned no answer to this, for while he secretly considered his master to be a first-rate fiddler nothing would have induced him to say so, except when boasting of the Viscount's excellence amongst certain of his cronies at the Horse and Groom. He rarely praised the Viscount's skill to his face; and never when Desford stood in his black books.

Miss Steane, whose spirits had soared from the instant Desford had said that he would convey her to London, enjoyed the journey hugely. She confided to him, with what he thought engaging ingenuousness, that she had never before been driven in a curricle. A gig had hitherto been her only experience of open carriages, and although her cousin Stonor possessed a curricle it was a very shabby affair compared with the Viscount's lightly built and graceful carriage. She thought well of his horses too, and told him so, for which commendation he thanked her with a gravity only very slightly impaired by the quiver of laughter in his voice. They were, in fact, perfectly matched grays, and he had paid so long a price for them as would have confirmed his father (if he had known it) in his belief that his heir was a scattergood.

"You can't think what a high treat this is for me, sir!" she said gaily. "Everything is new! You see, I have never travelled at all since my Papa carried me to Bath, and I don't remember very much about that journey. Besides, we went in a closed coach, and that is *not* the way to see the countryside. This is beyond anything great!"

She chatted away in this artless style, interested in all that met her wondering gaze, continually craning her neck to obtain a better view of a particularly bright garden, or a picturesque cottage, fleetingly seen down a side lane. Such of her conversation as was not concerned with the passing scene was devoted to an earnest discussion with Desford on what ought to be her approach to her grandfather. But when they reached London she became rather silent, a circumstance which made Desford say quizzingly: "Tired, little bagpipe? Not far to go now!"

She smiled, and shook her head: "No, not tired. Has my tongue been running on like a fiddlestick? I beg your pardon! Why didn't you tell me to button my lip? I must have been a sad bore to you."

"On the contrary! I found your conversation most refreshing. Why have you shut up shop? Are you in a worry about your grandfather?"

"A little," she confessed. "I didn't know that London is so big, and—and so noisy, and I cannot help wondering what to do if my grandfather refuses to see me. I wish I had some acquaintance here!"

"Don't fret!" he said reassuringly. "It is in the highest degree unlikely that he will. And if he does I promise I won't desert you! Depend upon it, we shall hit upon some scheme for your relief!"

He spoke lightly, for the more he considered the matter the more convinced did he become that however eccentric Lord Nettlecombe might be he could scarcely be so lost to all sense of propriety as to cast upon the world a granddaughter whose childlike innocence must be obvious to anyone but an incurable

70

lobcock. But when he drew up his weary team outside Lord Nettlecombe's town residence in Albemarle Street such optimistic reflections suffered a severe set-back. Every window of the house was shuttered, and the knocker was off the door: his lordship's eccentricity had not led him to remain in London during the summer months.

"Would your lordship wish me to ring the bell?" enquired Stebbing, in Cassandra-like accents.

"Yes: do so!" the Viscount said curtly.

By this time Miss Steane had had time to assimilate the significance of the closed shutters, and panic seized her. She gripped her hands tightly together in her lap, in a brave attempt to remain calm; and after a few minutes, during which Stebbing vigorously pulled the bell, said, in a voice of would-be carelessness: "It seems that the house has been shut up, d-doesn't it, sir?"

"It does indeed! But I daresay there may be someone left in charge from whom we can discover your grandfather's direction. Try the basement, Stebbing!"

"Begging your lordship's pardon, I don't hardly know how I can do so, being as the area-gate is chained and padlocked." He observed, not without a certain satisfaction, that the Viscount, momentarily at least, was at a non-plus, and relented sufficiently to say that he would enquire at the neighbouring houses. But as one of these had been hired for the summer months by a family whom Stebbing disdainfully described as Proper Mushrooms, and who had no knowledge of Lord Nettlecombe; and the other by an elderly couple whose porter said, with a sniff, that he had seen the old hunks drive off about a week ago, but had no notion where he was going. "My master and mistress don't have nothing to do with him, nor don't any of us in this house have nothing to do with his servants," he stated loftily.

When Stebbing returned to the curricle to report these discouraging tidings, Miss Steane uttered in an anguished whisper: "Oh, what shall I do, what shall I do?"

"Shall I ask at any of the other houses, my lord?"

But the Viscount had had time to think, and he replied: "No.

71

We have wasted enough time, and wherever his lordship may be we can scarcely hope to reach him today. Up with you!" He then turned his attention to his agitated passenger, and said with a cheerfulness he was far from feeling: "Now, why are you shaking like a blancmanger, little pea-goose? To be sure, this mischance has cast a slight rub in our way, but the case isn't desperate, you know!" He set his horses in motion as he spoke, turning them round, and added, with a rueful laugh: "Of course, if we discover that he is drinking the waters in Bath we *shall* be made to look blank, shan't we?"

She paid no heed to this, but repeated: "What shall I do? What *can* I do? Sir, I—I haven't very much money!"

This disclosure was blurted out, and ended in a sob. He replied matter-of-factly: "What you can do, Cherry, is to stop fretting and fuming, and to leave it to me to find a way out of this bumble-bath. I promise you I will, so pluck up!"

"I can't pluck up!" she uttered. "You don't understand! It doesn't curl *your* liver to find yourself alone in this dreadful city, with only a few shillings in your purse, and not knowing where to go, or—Oh, how can you be so unfeeling as to laugh?"

"My dear, I can't help but laugh! Where *did* you pick up that expression?"

"Oh, I don't know, and what does it signify?" she exclaimed. "Where are you taking me? Do you know where there is a Registry Office? I must set about finding a situation immediately! But I shall be obliged to put up for the night—oh, dear, perhaps for several nights, because even if I found a situation at once it can't be supposed that I should be wanted instantly! Unless someone was wanted in a bang, because of some accident, or illness, perhaps, and then——"

"You are forgetting that you would be obliged to provide yourself with a recommendation," he interpolated dampingly.

"Well, I am persuaded Miss Fletching would give me one!"

"No doubt she would, but may I remind you that it will take time to procure one from her?"

She was daunted, but made a quick recover. "Very true! But *you* could recommend me, couldn't you, sir?"

"No," he replied unequivocally.

Her bosom swelled. "I never thought you would be so disobliging!"

He smiled. "I'm not being disobliging. Believe me, nothing could more certainly prejudice your chances of obtaining an eligible situation than a recommendation from me—or any other single man of my age!"

"Oh!" she said, digesting this. A blast on a coach-horn made her flinch, and she said fervently: "How can you bear to live in this odious place, where everything is noise, and bustle, and the streets so full of coaches and carriages and carts that—Oh, pray take care, sir! I *know* we shall collide with something—Oh, look at that carriage, coming out of that street over there!"

"Shut your eyes!" he advised her, amused by her evident want of faith in his ability to avoid accident.

"No!" she said resolutely. "I must learn to accustom myself! Is it always so crowded in London, sir?"

"I am afraid it is often very much more crowded," he said apologetically. "In fact, it is at the moment very empty!"

"And people choose to live here!" she shuddered.

He had turned back into Piccadilly some few minutes earlier, and now checked his horses for the turn into Arlington Street. "Yes. I am one of those very odd people, and I am taking you now to my house, so that you can rest and refresh before we continue our journey."

She said uneasily: "I think I ought not to go to your house, sir. I may be a pea-goose but I do know that it is not the thing for females to visit gentlemen's houses, and—and——"

"No, it is a trifle irregular," he agreed, "but before we go any further there are certain arrangements I must make, and you would scarcely wish to wait in the street, would you? So the best thing I can do is to hand you over to my housekeeper for half-an-hour. I shall tell her that my aunt Emborough placed you in my charge, and that I am taking you to your home, in Hertfordshire."

She asked nervously: "Where—where *are* you taking me, if you please, sir?"

73

"Into Hertfordshire. I am going to ask an old and dear friend of mine to take care of you until I've found your grandfather. Her name is Miss Henrietta Silverdale, and she lives with her mother at a place called Inglehurst. Don't look so scared! I am pretty sure you will like her, and entirely sure that she will be very kind to you."

The curricle had come to a standstill outside one of the smaller houses on the east side of the street, and Stebbing had climbed down, and had gone to the horses' heads. Miss Steane whispered: "It was wrong of me to run away, wasn't it? I know it now, because everything has gone amiss, and—and I have only you to turn to for help in this scrape. But indeed, indeed, sir, I would never have asked you to carry me to London if I had known how it would be!"

He laid his hand over her tightly clenched ones, and said gently: "You are tired, my child, and the world looks black, doesn't it? I can only say to you: *Trust me!* Haven't I told you that I won't abandon you?"

Her hands twisted under his, and clasped it convulsively. She said: "I never meant to be such a charge on you! Oh, pray believe me!"

"Oh, I know you didn't! What *you* don't know is that I don't regard this adventure as a charge: I regard it as a challenge, and am determined to run your grandfather to earth if I have to go to all the watering-places in the land in search of him!" He saw that his butler had opened the door, and was coming towards the curricle, and disengaged his hand, saying: "Ah, here's Aldham! Good-day to you, Aldham! Has Tain arrived yet?"

"Just an hour since, my lord," replied Aldham, beaming fondly upon him, but casting a doubtful glance at his companion. He had known the Viscount since Desford's cradle-days, having been employed at that time as page-boy at Wolversham, from which lowly position he had graduated by slow degrees to that of First Footman, and thence, in one longed-for leap, to the honourable post of butler to his young lordship; and he knew quite as much about him as did Stebbing, and rather more than did Tain, his lordship's excellent valet, who was the only member of the little household in Arlington Street not born and bred at Wolversham. He could have named (had he not been the soul of discretion) every fair Cyprian with whom his volatile master had enjoyed amatory adventures, from the straw damsel who had caught his first, callow fancy, to the high flyer who had almost ruined him; and he had frequently officiated at far from respectable parties in Arlington Street. But he had never known the Viscount to drive up to the door, in broad daylight, with an unattended Young Female sitting beside him. His first impression, that the Viscount had brought home with him a country lightskirt, was dispelled by a second, covert look at Miss Steane: for one thing, she was no lightskirt; and for another the Viscount never seemed to take to very young females. To Aldham's experienced eye she was more like a girl just broken out of the schoolroom—though what the Viscount was doing with any such was a problem beyond his power to solve.

But when he had been favoured with a glib explanation of her presence in the curricle he accepted it without even mental reservation. It was just like my Lady Emborough, he thought, to saddle my lord with a chit of a girl, with instructions to conduct her to her home in Hertfordshire, just as though it had been on the way from Hazelfield to London. And very much embarrassed the young lady was, by the looks of her! So he received her with a fatherly smile, and ushered her into the narrow hall of the house, saying that he would fetch up Mrs Aldham directly to wait upon her.

The Viscount lingered on the flagway to exchange words with the second of his chief mentors and well-wishers, the expression on whose face, compound of sorrow and censure, caused him to say: "Yes, you've no need to look at me like that—as though I didn't know as well as you do that this is a rare case of pickles!"

"My lord," said Stebbing very earnestly, "when I heard you tell Miss you was going to take her into Hertfordshire I was that comfumbuscated I pretty near fell off my seat, because it looked to me like you was going to take her to Wolversham!"

"No, I did think of doing so, but it wouldn't answer," replied the Viscount.

"No, my lord—as I would have taken the liberty of telling your lordship! As I beg leave to do now, for I wouldn't be able to sleep easy in my bed if I didn't, and it don't signify if you choose to turn me off, because——"

"Of course it doesn't signify! You wouldn't go!" retorted the Viscount.

The corners of Stebbing's grim mouth twitched involuntarily, but he refused to be beguiled. He said: "My lord, I've known you do some hey-go-mad things in your time, but you've never till this day done anything so cockle-brained as to make me think you must be short of a sheet! Which I do! My lord, you're never going to take Miss to Inglehurst!"

"But I am," asserted the Viscount. "Unless you can suggest where else I can take her?" He paused, regarding his henchman with mockery in his eyes. "You can't, can you?"

"You hadn't ought to have brought her to London at all!" muttered Stebbing.

"Very likely not, but it's a waste of time to lay that in my dish now! I did bring her to London, and must now abide the consequence. Even you must own that to abandon her here would be the action of a damned ugly customer—which I am not, however hey-go-mad you may think me!" He saw that Stebbing was deeply troubled, and smiled, dropping a hand on his shoulder, and slightly shaking him. "Stubble it, you old rumstick! To whom else should I turn for help in this hobble than to Miss Hetta? Bless her, she's never yet failed me! Good God, *you* should know how often we've rescued one another from scrapes!"

"When you was children!" Stebbing said. "That was different, my lord!"

"Not a bit of it! Stable the grays now, and tell the postilions I shall be needing them to carry me to Inglehurst within the hour. I'll take my own chaise, but I shall have to hire horses: Ockley can be depended on to choose the right type, but warn him that I mean to return tonight. That's all!"

He gave Stebbing no opportunity to utter any further protests, but turned on his heel, and went quickly into his house. Stebbing was left to address his embittered remarks to the weary gray at whose head he was standing before climbing into the curricle and driving it away.

CHAPTER VI

IT WAS past seven o'clock when the Viscount's beautifully sprung chaise reached Inglehurst, for although the journey had taken no more than three hours to accomplish he had not left Arlington Street until after four. Miss Steane, revived as much by the kindly and uncritical attitude of Mrs Aldham (yet another of those born on my Lord Wroxton's wide estates) as by the tea with which she had been regaled, set forth in a tolerably cheerful mood, suppressing as well as she could the inevitable shrinking of a shy girl, who, realizing too late her imprudence, found herself without any other course open to her than to submit to her protector's decree, and to allow him to thrust her into a household which consisted of a widow and her daughter who were wholly unknown to her. She could only hope that they would not resent her intrusion, or think her sunk beneath reproach for having behaved in a manner which she was fast becoming convinced was improper to the point of being unpardonable. Had she been able to think of an alternative to the Viscount's plan she believed she would have embraced it thankfully, even had it been the offer of a post as cook-maid, but no alternative had presented itself to her, and the thought of being stranded in London, with only a few shillings in her purse, and not even the merest acquaintance to seek out in all that terrifying city, was not one she could face.

Something of what was in her mind the Viscount guessed, for although London held no terrors for him, and he had never been stranded anywhere with his pockets to let, neither his consequence nor his wealth had made him blind to the troubles that beset persons less comfortably circumstanced. He might be careless, and frequently rackety, but no one in dire straits had ever appealed to him for help in vain. His friends, and he had many friends, said of him that he was a great gun—true as touch —a right one; and even his severest critics found nothing worse

79

to say of him than that it was high time he brought his carryings on to an end, and settled down. His father did indeed heap opprobrious epithets on him, but anyone unwise enough to utter the mildest criticism of his heir to my lord met with very short shrift. The Viscount was well aware of this; but while he did not doubt his father's affection for him he was far too familiar with the Earl's deep prejudices to introduce Miss Steane into his household. My lord was a rigid stickler, and it was useless to suppose that he would feel any sympathy with a young female who had behaved in a way which he would undoubtedly condemn as brass-faced. My lord's views on propriety were clearly defined: male aberrations were pardonable; the smallest deviation from the rules governing the behaviour of females was inexcusable. He had placed no checks upon his sons, regarding (except when colic or gout had exacerbated his temper) their follies and amatory adventures with cynical amusement, but his daughter had never been allowed, until her marriage, to take a step beyond the gardens without a footman in attendance; and whenever she had gone on a visit to an approved friend or relative she had travelled in my lord's carriage, accompanied not only by her footman and her maid but by a couple of outriders as well.

So the Viscount, not entertaining for more than a very few seconds the notion of conveying his protégée to Wolversham, had, in almost the same length of time, decided to place her in Miss Silverdale's care until he should have run her grandfather to earth, and compelled him to honour his obligations. The only flaw to this scheme which he could perceive was the objection which Miss Silverdale's mama might—and probably would—raise against it; but he had a comfortable belief in Miss Silverdale's ability to bring her hypochondriacal parent round her thumb, and was thus able to set out for Inglehurst without fear of meeting with a rebuff.

However, he did feel that it might be prudent to warn Cherry that Lady Silverdale enjoyed indifferent health, and consequently indulged in rather odd humours, which found expression in fits of the blue-devils, a tendency to fancy herself ill-used, and a marked predilection for enacting what he called Cheltenham tragedies.

She listened to him attentively, and, to his surprise, seemed to derive encouragement from this somewhat daunting description of her prospective hostess. She said, with all the wisdom of one versed in the idiosyncrasies of invalids: "Then perhaps I can be of use in the house! Even Aunt Bugle says I am good at looking after invalids, and although I don't wish to puff myself off I think that is perfectly true. In fact, I have been wondering if I shouldn't seek for a post as attendant to an old, cantankersome lady: I daresay you know the sort of old lady I mean, sir!"

Lively memories of the tyranny exercised by his paternal grandmother over her family and her dependants crossed his mind, and he replied rather grimly: "I do, and can only trust that you will not be obliged to seek any such post!"

"Well," she said seriously, "I own that it's disagreeable to be pinched at for everything one does, but one must remember how much more disagreeable it must be to be old, and unable to do things for oneself. And also," she added reflectively, "if a twitty old lady takes a fancy to one, one becomes valuable to her family. My aunt, and my cousins, were never so kind to me as during the months before poor old Lady Bugle died. Why, my aunt even said that she didn't know how they would go on without me!"

She sounded so much gratified by this tribute that Desford bit back the caustic comment that sprang to the tip of his tongue, and merely said that Lady Silverdale was neither old nor dying; and although she would (in his opinion) wear down the patience of a saint it would be unjust to call her twitty.

When they reached their destination, they were received by Grimshaw, who showed no pleasure at sight of one who had run free at Inglehurst ever since he had been old enough to bestride a pony, but said dampingly that if my lady had known his lordship meant to visit her she would no doubt have set dinner back to suit his convenience. As it was, he regretted to be obliged to inform his lordship that my lady and Miss Henrietta had already retired to the drawing-room.

Too well-accustomed to the butler's habitual air of disparaging gloom to be either surprised or offended the Viscount said: "Yes, I guessed how it would be, but I daresay her ladyship will forgive me. Be a good fellow, Grimshaw, and drop the word in Miss Hetta's ear that I want to see her privately! I'll wait in the library."

Grimshaw might be proof against the Viscount's smile but he was not proof against the lure of a golden coin slid into his hand. He did not demean himself by so much as a glance at it, but his experienced fingers informed him that it was a guinea, so he bowed in a stately way, and went off to perform the errand, not allowing himself to show his disapproval of Miss Steane by more than one look of outraged surprise.

The Viscount then led Miss Steane to a small saloon, and ushered her into it, telling her to sit down, like a good girl, and wait for him to bring Miss Silverdale to her. After that he withdrew to the library at the back of the hall, where, after a few minutes, he was joined by Miss Silverdale, who came in, saying in a rallying tone: "Now, what's all this, Des? What brings you here so unexpectedly? And why the mystery?"

He took her hands, and held them: "Hetta, I'm in a scrape!"

She burst out laughing. "I might have known it! And I am to rescue you from it?"

"And you are to rescue me from it," he corroborated, the smile dancing in his eyes.

"What an unconscionable rogue you are!" she remarked, drawing her hands away, and disposing herself on a sofa. "I can't conceive how I am to rescue you from the sort of scrapes you fall into, but sit down, and make a clean breast of it!"

He did so, telling his story without reservation. Her eyes widened a little, but she heard him in silence, until he reached the end of it, saying: "I would have taken her to Wolversham, but you know what my father is, Hetta! So there was nothing for it but to bring her to you!"

Then, at last, she spoke, shattering his confidence. "But I don't think I can, Ashley!"

He stared incredulously. "But, Hetta——!"

"You can't have considered!" she said. "If I know what your father is you should know just as well what my mother is! Her opinion of your Cherry's exploit wouldn't differ from his by so much as a hair's breadth!"

"Oh, I know that!" he said. "I shan't tell her the true story, stoopid! All I have to do is to say that my Aunt Emborough placed her in my charge, with instructions to deliver her into old Nettlecombe's hands, but owing to his having misread the date —or the letter informing him of it having gone astray—or some such thing—he is still out of town, so that I was at my wits' end to know what to do with the child."

"And what," she enquired conversationally, "will you say when she asks you why you didn't rather place her in your mother's care?"

He took a minute or two to find an answer to this poser, but finally produced, with considerable aplomb: "When I was at Wolversham, little more than a sennight since, I found my father quite out of curl, and Mama in too much of a worry about him to be troubled with a guest."

She drew an audible breath. "You are not only a rogue, Des, but a Banbury man as well!"

He laughed: "No, no, how can you say so? There's a great deal of truth in that part of the story, and you can scarcely expect me to tell your mother that if I were to walk in with Cherry on my arm my poor misguided Papa would instantly leap to the conclusion that I had not only fallen in love with her, but had brought her home in the hope that she would captivate him into bestowing his blessing on precisely the sort of match he most abominates. I daresay she might captivate him, for she's a taking little thing, but hardly to that point!"

"Is she very pretty?" asked Miss Silverdale, keeping her fine eyes on his face.

"Yes, very, I think—even when dressed in cast-off garments which don't become her, and with her hair in a tangle! Enormous eyes in a heart-shaped face, a mouth clearly made for kissing, and a great deal of innocent charm. Not in your style, but I fancy you'll see what I mean when I present her to you. When I first saw her she looked to me to be scared out of her wits—which, half the time, she is, thanks to the Turkish treatment she has endured in her aunt's house—but when she isn't frightened she chatters away in the most engaging fashion, and has the merriest twinkle in her eyes. I think you will like her, Hetta, and I'm pretty sure your mother will. From what I gather she has a positive genius for waiting on—er—elderly invalids!" He paused, scanning her face. It was inscrutable, so, after a moment, he said coaxingly: "Come, now, Hetta! You can't fail me! Good God, I've depended on you all my life! Yes, and if it comes to that, so have you depended on me—and have I ever failed you?"

A gleam of humour shone in her eyes. "You may have rescued me from scrapes when we were children," she said, "but I haven't been in a scrape for years!"

"No, but Charlie has!" he retorted. "You can't deny that I've frequently rescued him, just because you begged me to!"

"Well, no," she acknowledged. "And I can't deny, either, that you have several times given me excellent advice on the management of the estate, but the thing which makes it so very awkward for me to do what you ask this time is that Charlie is at home! And if Miss Steane is so pretty, and so charming, he is bound to fall in love with her, for you know how often he tumbles into love!"

"Yes, and I also know how often he tumbles out of love! When I last saw him he was dangling after a lovely man-trap—thirty if she's a day, and widowed a bare twelvemonth ago!"

"Mrs Cumbertrees," she nodded. "But she has been a thing of the past for weeks, Des!"

"Then he is probably at the feet of some other dasher years older than he is himself. You may take it from me, Hetta, that there's no need for you to be in a worry over the chance that he might take a fancy to Cherry: halflings rarely become nutty upon girls of their own age. In any event, she won't be here long enough for Charlie to form a lasting passion for her! What's he doing here, by the way? I thought he was going to Ireland, with a couple of choice spirits, in search of horses?"

"He was, but he had the misfortune to overturn his new high-perch phaeton three days ago, and broke his head, and his arm, and two of his ribs," said Miss Silverdale, in the voice of one inured to such misfortunes.

"Hunting the squirrel?" asked Desford, with mild interest.

"Very likely, though of course he doesn't say so. He is still confined to his bed, for he was pretty knocked-up, but I don't expect Mama will be able to prevail upon him to remain there for very much longer. He is already fretting to get up, which was why Mama was glad to see Simon drive up—Oh, good heavens! I quite forgot to tell you! I think you would wish to know that Simon has been dining with us, and is now sitting with Charlie! At least, he was when I came away from the drawing-room, but I daresay Mama has drawn him away by this time, for she said that she would only permit him to stay with Charlie for twenty minutes."

"Oh, my God!" ejaculated the Viscount, in accents of the live-liest dismay.

She could not help laughing, but she said severely: "If a stranger heard you, Des, he couldn't be blamed for thinking that you held your little brother in the most unnatural dislike!"

"Well, there aren't any strangers present, and you know well enough that I don't hold him in dislike," said the Viscount im-penitently. "But if ever there was a leaky rattle——! I shall be obliged to see him, I suppose, but if he don't make me grease him handsomely in the fist to keep his tongue about this affair I don't know young Simon!"

She cried shame on him, but in the event he was seen to know his graceless brother better than she did; for when he had talked her into making Cherry's acquaintance, and judging for herself how innocent, and how much to be pitied she was, and had accompanied her to the Green saloon, the unwelcome sight of the Honourable Simon Carrington making himself agreeable to Miss Steane confronted him, and he had no difficulty in inter-

85

preting the sparkling look of mischief with which the Honourable Simon greeted him.

He ignored it, and presented Cherry to Miss Silverdale, saying easily: "I must warn you, Hetta, that I've brought this foolish child to you very much against her will! I strongly suspect that she fears I am handing her over to a dragon!"

Cherry, who had risen quickly to her feet, blushed and stammered, as she dropped a slight curtsy: "Oh, no, no! In—in-*deed* I d-don't, ma'am!"

"Well, if she does think it I shall hold you entirely to blame, Desford," said Miss Silverdale, moving forward, with her hand held out to Cherry, and a smile on her lips. "A pretty picture you must have drawn of me! How do you do, Miss Steane? Desford has been telling me of your adventures, and how you have been quite thrown out by finding that your grandfather is out of town. I can well imagine what your feelings must have been! But I expect Desford will find him very soon, and in the meantime I hope we can make you comfortable at Inglehurst."

Cherry lifted her big eyes, brimming with grateful tears, to Henrietta's face, and whispered: "Thank you! I am so *sorry——!*"

The Viscount, having watched this interchange with satisfaction, transferred his attention to his brother, and demanded, with revulsion: "For God's sake, Simon, what kind of a rig is that?"

Henrietta said laughingly, over her shoulder: "Didn't I tell you, Simon, that Des would utterly condemn it?"

Young Mr Carrington, a very dashing blade, was indeed wearing a startling habit, and the fact that he had the height and the figure to adopt any extravagant mode without appearing grotesque did nothing to recommend the style he had chosen to adopt to his elder brother. He was a goodlooking young man, full of effervescent liveliness, and as ready to laugh at himself as at his fellow-men. His eyes laughed now, as he said solemnly: "This, Des, is the highest kick of fashion, as you would know if you were as dapper-dog as you think you are!" He thrust one foot forward as he spoke, and indicated with a sweep of his hand the voluminous garments which clothed his nether limbs. "The Petersham trousers, my boy!"

"I am aware!" said the Viscount. He raised his quizzing-glass, and through it surveyed his brother from his heels to the inordinately high points of his shirt-collar. These were rivalled by the height of his coat collar, which rose steeply behind his head, and by the gathered and hugely padded shoulders of his coat. The sleeves of his coat were embellished with a number of buttons, those nearest to his wrists being left unbuttoned in a negligent style; and he wore round his neck a very large striped neckcloth. The Viscount, having taken in all these enormities, shuddered, and let his glass fall, saying: "Have you had the infernal brass to sit down to dine with Lady Silverdale in that rig, jackanapes?"

"But, Des, she begged me to do so!" said Simon, deeply injured. "She liked my beautiful new clothes, didn't she, Hetta?"

"I rather think she was stunned by them," Henrietta replied. "And by the time she had recovered from the shock you had flummeried her into inviting you to dine with us—playing off more cajolery than I've been privileged to see in a twelvemonth!"

"Oh come, come!" instantly protested Simon. "It isn't as long as that since you saw me last!"

She laughed, but turned from him to Cherry, who had been listening to this badinage with an appreciative twinkle in her eyes. Miss Silverdale perceived that Desford had spoken no less than the truth when he had described her as a taking little thing, and wondered, with an inexplicable sinking of the heart, if he was more captivated by her than he perhaps knew. Recognizing the tiny pang she felt as the envy of one who was neither little nor taking—besides being past the first blush of youth—of one who was young, and pretty, and little, and very taking indeed, she sternly repressed such ignoble thoughts, smiled at Cherry, and held out her hand, saying: "I must introduce you to my mother, but I am very sure you would wish to put off your bonnet and cloak first, so I shall take you up to my room, while Desford explains to my mother how it comes about that we are to have the pleasure of entertaining you for a little while. You will find Mama in the drawing-room, Des!"

He nodded, and would have followed her out of the saloon immediately had not Simon detained him, with a demand to know whether he meant to spend the night at Wolversham. "No, I am returning to London," he replied. "But I want a word with you before I leave, so don't you go home until we've had a talk!"

"I'll be bound you do!" said Simon, grinning impishly at him. "I won't go!"

The Viscount threw him a speaking glance, and went off to try his own powers of flummery on Lady Silverdale.

He found her engaged, in a somewhat languid fashion, in embroidering an altar cloth, but she pushed the frame aside when he entered the room, and held out a plump hand to him, and saying, in a sweet, failing voice: "Dear Ashley!"

He kissed her hand, retained it in his own for a minute, and set about the task of cajoling her by paying her a compliment. "Dear Lady Silverdale!" he said. "Don't think me abominably saucy!—How is it that you contrive to look younger and prettier every time I see you?"

If she had had the forethought to have provided herself with a fan she would undoubtedly have rapped his knuckles with it, but as it was she was obliged to content herself with giving him a playful slap, and saying archly: "Flatterer!"

"Oh, no!" he returned. "I never flatter!"

"Oh, what a farradiddle!" she said.

He denied it, and she accepted this with a complacency born of the knowledge that she had been, in her heyday, a remarkably pretty girl. Time, and a life of determined indolence, had considerably impaired her figure, but she was generally held to have great remains of beauty; and she had discovered that a *fraise,* or little ruff, admirably concealed a tendency to develop a double chin. A mild attachment to the late Sir John Silverdale had grown, during the years of her widowhood, to proportions which would have astonished that gentleman, and would not have outlived an offer for her hand made by another suitor of birth and fortune. None had come forward to woo the widow, so as much affection as she could spare from herself she had bestowed upon her only son. Such persons who were not intimately acquainted with her believed her to be passionately devoted to her children, which, indeed, she herself believed, but those who had the opportunity to observe her at close quarters were not deceived by her caressing manner: they knew that although she might fairly be said to dote on Charles she had only a tepid affection for Henrietta.

The Viscount was of their number, and he lost no time in enquiring solicitously into the state of Charlie's health, and listening with an air of concern to the description given him of the various injuries Charlie had suffered, of the shock the accident had been to his nerves, and of how serious the repercussions might be if he were not kept perfectly quiet until such time as dear Dr Foston pronounced him to be well enough to leave his room. Since few things interested her more than the ills that could attack the human body, and was one of those who believed that physical disorders lent distinction to those who fell victims to them, the recital took time in the telling, and was further prolonged by an account of the spasms and palpitations she had herself endured ever since she had seen her son's battered body borne into the house on a stretcher. "I fell down instantly in a swoon, for I thought him dead!" she said impressively. "Indeed, they thought *I* was dead, for it was an age before they were able to revive me, and then, you know, I was so much agitated that I couldn't believe dear Hetta was speaking the truth when she assured me Charlie wasn't dead, but in a deep concussion. I've been very poorly ever since, and Dr Foston has been obliged to give me a cordial, besides valerian for my nerves, which are sadly shattered, as you may suppose."

He replied suitably; and after expressing his admiration for the wonderful spirit she showed in bearing up under so prostrating an experience, at last ventured to broach his errand to her. He did it very well, but it was no easy task to gain her consent to his proposal. It was rendered all the more difficult when he disclosed that Cherry was Lord Nettlecombe's granddaughter. She exclaimed at once that she wished to have nothing to do with any member of *that* family. He replied frankly: "I don't blame you, ma'am: who *does* wish to have anything to do with them? But I think your kind heart must be touched by this unfortunate child's plight! If her father isn't dead, he has certainly abandoned her—and without a feather to fly with! She has lately been living with some maternal relations, who haven't used her at all well. So very ill, in fact, that she formed the resolve to claim her grandfather's protection, until such time as she can find employment in some genteel household. So, as I was staying at Hazelfield at the time, my aunt desired me to carry her to London with me, and see her safely deposited in old Nettlecombe's charge. You may conceive of my dismay when we arrived in Albemarle Street to find the house shut up, and none of the neighbours able to give me his lordship's direction! What to do with the girl had me at a stand, until I remembered you, ma'am!"

She interrupted him, demanding: "Is it possible that she is *Wilfred Steane*'s daughter?"

"Yes, poor child! As good as orphaned, even if he should chance to be alive!"

"Desford!" she uttered, groping for her vinaigrette, "I little thought that you, of all people, would be so wanting in conduct as to bring that—that *Creature*'s child to Inglehurst! And how your aunt could—but I always thought poor dear Sophronia strangely freakish! But how she could have supposed that *I* should be willing to befriend the girl——"

"Oh, she didn't, ma'am!" he interposed. "All she asked me to do was to take Cherry to her grandfather. It was I—knowing you much better than my aunt does!—who realized that if there was one person on whom I could depend to shelter this unfortunate girl that person is yourself!" He smiled at her, and added: "Are you trying to hoax me into believing that you are hardhearted enough to repulse her? You won't succeed: I know you too well!"

She plucked uncertainly at the fringe of the silk shawl she wore, eyeing him with resentment. Before she had made up her mind what to say to make him remove Cherry without impairing the vision he had of the saintliness of her own disposition the door opened, and Henrietta came in, leading Miss Steane by the hand.

"Mama, here is poor little Cherry, who has been having a horridly uncomfortable time, as I collect Desford will have told you. She is quite worn down by her troubles, but she *would* have me bring her to you before I tuck her into bed. Now, my dear, you can see for yourself that my mother is no more a dragon than I am!"

"So pleased!" said Lady Silverdale, in a faint voice, and favouring Cherry with a very slight inclination of her head. "Hetta, my love, my cordial!"

Quite dismayed, Cherry whispered: "I should not have come! Oh, I *knew* I should not! I beg your pardon, ma'am!"

Lady Silverdale was a selfish but not an unfeeling woman, and this stricken speech, coupled as it was with a face pale with weariness, considerably mollified her. It was clearly impossible to cast this miserable little girl out of the house, so although she maintained the attitude of one on the brink of sinking into a swoon, and continued to speak in a faint, long-suffering voice, she said: "Oh, not at all! You must forgive me if I leave it to my daughter to show you to your bedroom: I have been very unwell, and my medical attendant warns me that I must avoid all unnecessary exertion. So unfortunate that you should have come to visit us at just this moment! But my daughter will look after you. Pray tell me if there is anything you would wish for! A glass of hot milk, perhaps, before you retire to bed."

"I fancy, ma'am, that she needs something more substantial than a glass of milk," said the Viscount, perceiving that Cherry was looking quite crushed, and most improperly flickering a wink at her.

"Well, of course she does!" said Henrietta. "She is going to have supper as soon as I've tucked her into her bed."

"Oh, thank you!" said Cherry gratefully. "I don't feel I deserve to be given such a treat, but I would very much like it! Aunt Bugle never allowed me to have——"

She broke off in consternation, for these words had had a startling effect on her hostess. At one moment leaning limply back in her chair, and sniffing at her vinaigrette, she suddenly abandoned this moribund pose, sat bolt upright, and said sharply: *"Who* did you say?"

"M-my Aunt Bugle, ma'am," faltered Cherry.

Lady Silverdale's bosom swelled visibly. *"That* woman! she pronounced awfully. "Do you mean to tell me she is your aunt, child?"

"Yes, ma'am," said Cherry, trembling.

"Are you acquainted with her, Mama?"

"We were brought out in the same season!" disclosed Lady Silverdale dramatically. "I beg you will not speak to me of Amelia Bugle! A bouncing, flouncing young female, setting her cap at every single gentleman that crossed her path, and fancying herself to be a beauty, which she was not, for she had a deplorable figure, and a particularly ugly nose, and as for the pretentious airs she gave herself when she caught Bugle, and took to thinking herself the pink of gentility, I laugh whenever I remember them!"

Laughter did not appear to be her predominant emotion, though she did utter a Ha! of withering sarcasm. Henrietta, briefly meeting Desford's dancing eyes, said, with a quivering lip: "We collect, Mama, that she wasn't one of your bosombows!"

"Certainly not! But I remained on common civility terms with her until she had the effrontery to thrust herself before me in a doorway, saying, like the self-important mushroom she was, that she fancied she must take precedence since her husband's baronetcy was an older creation than Silverdale's! After that, of course, I never did more than bow to her, or felt the smallest interest in her. Come and sit down beside me, my dear child, and tell me all about her! I am persuaded she used you shamefully, for I recall that she was never used to waste a particle of politeness on people she considered to be beneath her. You did very right to leave her!"

She patted the place beside her on the sofa invitingly, and

92

Cherry, swiftly recovering from her astonishment, smiled shyly, dropped a little curtsy, and accepted the invitation. The curtsy pleased Lady Silverdale; she was moved to press Cherry's hand, and to say: "Poor child! There! You will not meet with Turkish treatment in *this* house! Is it true that That Woman has *five* daughters?"

Perceiving that her volatile parent was now wholly engrossed by the dreadful fate that had overcome her old rival, Henrietta seized the opportunity thus afforded her to exchange a few words with the Viscount. "Nothing could be more fortunate, could it?" she said, in an undervoice. "I wonder what That Woman really did to make Mama take her in such dislike?"

"Yes, so do I!" he returned. "I depend on you to discover the answer! Clearly, her want of delicacy in claiming precedence in that doorway can only have been the culminating impertinence!"

"I should suppose that they must have been rival beauties," said Henrietta. "But never mind that! We will keep Cherry with us until you have found her grandfather, but what would you have me tell her to do? Should she not write a civil letter to Lady Bugle, informing her that she is at present residing at Inglehurst? I cannot think it right that she should leave her without a word! Lady Bugle cannot be so monstrous as to feel no anxiety about her!"

"No," he agreed reluctantly. "At the same time—Hetta, tell her to write that she has gone to visit her grandfather! Dash it, I must be able to discover where he is in a very few days, and if she mentions Inglehurst she must surely connect me with the business, which will lead her to make enquiries of my Aunt Emborough, and then I *shall* be in the suds!"

"Couldn't you write to Lady Emborough, explaining it all to her?" she suggested.

"No, Hetta, I could not!" he replied. "She doesn't like Lady Bugle, but she don't want to quarrel with her, and she wouldn't thank me for embroiling her in this mingle-mangle!"

"Very true! I hadn't considered that. It shall be as you wish.

Do you mean to rack up here for the night, or are you going to Wolversham with Simon?"

"Neither: I'm going back to London. You can picture me tomorrow, scouring the town to find somebody able to give me Nettlecombe's direction—and in all probability wasting my time! Ah, well! It will be a lesson to me, won't it, not to rescue damsels in distress?"

"Not to venture to cross quagmires without making sure you don't go in over shoes, over boots, at all events!" she said, laughing at him.

"Or at least without making sure that Hetta is there to pull me out!" he amended. He took her hand, and kissed it. "Thank you, my best of friends. I am eternally obliged to you!"

"Oh, fiddle! If you are to drive back to London this evening you had better take leave of your damsel now, because I mean to put her to bed immediately: she's so tired she can scarcely keep her eyes open! I've instructed Grimshaw to set out a supper for you, and you'll find Simon waiting to bear you company."

"Bless you!" he said, and turned from her to bid his protégée farewell.

She got up quickly when she saw him coming towards the sofa, and he saw that she was indeed looking very tired. It was with an effort that she smiled at him, and tried to thank him for his kindness. He cut her short, patted her hand, and adjured her, in avuncular style, to be a good girl. He then promised Lady Silverdale that he would come to take his leave of her as soon as he had eaten his supper, and went off to the dining-room.

Here he found his brother seated sideways at the table, with one elbow resting on it, his long legs, in their preposterous Petersham trousers, stretched out before him, and the brandy decanter beside him. Grimshaw, wearing the expression of one whose finer feelings were grossly offended, bowed the Viscount to his chair and regretted that the dishes laid out before him were of a meagre nature, the lobster and the chickens having been consumed at dinner. Also, he added, in an expressionless voice, the almond cheesecakes, which Mr Simon had been pleased to esteem.

"What he means is that I finished the dish," said Simon. "Devilish good they were too! I wish you will take that Friday-face away, Grimshaw! You've been wearing it the whole evening, and it's giving me a fit of the dismals!"

"I daresay your new rig don't take his fancy," said the Viscount, helping himself to some pickled salmon. "And who shall blame him? It makes you look like a coxscomb. Wouldn't you agree with me, Grimshaw?"

"I should prefer to say, my lord, that it is not a mode which commends itself to me. Nor, if I may be pardoned for putting forward my opinion, one befitting a young gentleman of rank."

"Well, you're out there!" retorted Simon. "It's the very latest style, and it was Petersham who started it!"

"My Lord Petersham, sir," said Grimshaw, unmoved, "is well known to be an Eccentric Gentleman, and frequently appears in a style that one can only call rather of the ratherest."

"And besides which," said Desford, as Grimshaw withdrew from the room, "Petersham is a good fifteen years older than you are, and he don't look like a macaroni-merchant whatever he wears."

"Take care, brother!" Simon warned him. "A little more to that tune and you will find yourself done to a cow's thumb!"

Desford laughed, and surveyed the various dishes before him through his glass. "Shall I? No, really, Simon, those trousers are the outside of enough! However, I didn't come to discuss your clothes: I've something more important to say to you."

"Well, now you put me in mind of it I've something important to say too! It's a lucky chance I dined here tonight. Lend me a monkey, Des, will you?"

"No," responded Desford bluntly. "Or a groat, if it comes to that."

"Quite right!" said Simon approvingly. "One should never encourage young men to break shins! Just make me a present of it, and not a word about this bud of promise you're jauntering about with shall pass my lips!"

"What a stretch-halter you are!" remarked Desford, embarking on a raised pie. "Why do you want a monkey? Considering it isn't a month since the last quarterday it ought to be high tide with you."

"Unfortunately," said Simon, "the last quarter's allowance was, so to say, bespoke!"

"And my father called *me* a scattergood!"

"That's nothing to what he'll call you, my boy, if he gets wind of your little charmer!"

Desford paid no heed to this sally, but directed a searching look at his brother, and asked: "I collect you've been having some deep doings: not let yourself be hooked into any of the Greeking establishments, have you?"

Simon smiled ruefully. "Only once, Des. I may be said to have bought my experience dearly."

"Physicked you, did they? Well, it happens to us all. Is that what brought you home? Wouldn't my father frank you?"

"To own the truth, dear boy, I haven't dared to broach the matter, though that *is* what brought me home. It hasn't yet seemed to me the moment to raise ticklish subjects. His mood is far from benign!"

"No wonder, if he saw you in that rig! What a fool you are, Simon! You might have known it would set him all on end!"

"No, no, how can you suppose me to be so wanting in tact? I clothed myself with the utmost propriety of taste. I even sought to gratify him by wearing knee-breeches for dinner, but knee-breeches have no chance of success against gout. I may add that having been obliged to listen to him cutting at me, you, and even Horace for over an hour this afternoon I seized the opportunity to escape, and very handsomely offered to bear Mama's letter to Lady Silverdale in place of the groom she had meant to send with it. She felt it behoved her to write to enquire after Charlie. Did Hetta tell you that the silly cawker has knocked himself up?"

Desford nodded. "Oh, yes! How bad is he?"

"Well, he looks as sick as a horse, but they seem to think he's going on pretty prosperously. Now, about that monkey, Des!"

96

"I'll give you a cheque on Drummond's—on one condition!"
Simon laughed. "I won't breathe a word, Des!"

"Oh, I know that, codling! My condition is that you throw those clothes away!"

"It will be a sacrifice," said Simon mournfully, "but I'll do it. What's more, if there's any little thing you think I might be able to do for you in your present very odd situation I'll do that too."

"Much obliged to you!" said Desford, rather amused, but touched as well. "There isn't anything—unless you chance to know where old Nettlecombe has loped off to?"

"Nettlecombe? What the devil do you want with that old screw?" demanded Simon, in considerable astonishment.

"My bud of promise, as you call her, is his granddaughter, and I've charged myself with the task of delivering her into his care. Only when we reached London we found he had gone out of town, and shut up his house. That's why I brought her here."

"Good God, is she a Steane?"

"Yes: Wilfred Steane's only child."

"And who the deuce may he be?"

"Oh, the black sheep of the family! Before your time! Before mine too, if it comes to that, but I remember all the talk that went on about him, and in particular the things Papa said of him, and every other Steane he had ever heard of! Which is why I don't want him to get wind of Cherry!"

"Is that the girl's name?" asked Simon. "Queer sort of a name to give a girl!"

"No, her name is Charity, but she prefers to be called Cherry. I met her when I was staying at Hazelfield. I don't propose to take you into the circumstances which led me to bring her to London in search of her grandfather, but you may believe I was pretty well forced to do so. She was living with her maternal aunt, and being so shabbily treated that she ran away. I met her trying to walk to London, and since nothing would prevail upon her to let me take her back to her aunt what else could I do but take her up?"

"A regular Galahad, ain't you?" grinned Simon.

"No, I am not! If I'd dreamed I should be dipped in the wing over the business I wouldn't have done it!"

"You would," said Simon. "Think I don't know you? What, by the way, did the black sheep do to cause a scandal?"

"According to my father, just about everything, short of murder! Nettlecombe cast him off when he eloped with Cherry's mother, but what forced him to fly abroad was being found out in Greeking transactions. Took to drinking young 'uns into a proper state for plucking, and then fuzzed the cards."

Simon opened his eyes very wide. "Nice fellow!" he commented. "What has become of him?"

"Nobody seems to know, but since nothing has been heard of him for some years he is generally thought to be dead."

"Well, it's to be hoped he is," said Simon. "If you don't mind my saying so, dear boy, the sooner you palm the girl off on to her grandfather the better it will be. You haven't a tendre for her, have you?"

"Oh, for God's sake——!" Desford exclaimed. "Of course I haven't!"

"Beg pardon!" murmured Simon. "Only wondered!"

CHAPTER VII

BEFORE THE brothers parted that evening Simon had
tucked into his pocket the Viscount's cheque, and had asked
him in a soft, mischievous voice if he meant to go to Newmarket, for the July Meeting. The Viscount answered that he
had meant to go, but now saw little hope of it. "Ten to one I
shall still be hunting for Nettlecombe," he said. "But if you are
going I rather fancy I can put you on to a sure thing: Mopsqueezer. Old Jerry Tawton earwigged me at Tatt's last week,
and he's in general a safe man at the corner."

Simon gripped his hand, smiling warmly at him, and said:
"Thank you, Des. Dash it, you *are* a trump!"

Slightly surprised, Desford responded: "What, for passing
on Jerry's tip? Don't be such a gudgeon!"

"No, not for that, and not even for this," said Simon, patting his pocket. "For not reading me any elder-brotherly jobations!"

"Much heed you would pay to them if I did!"

"Oh, you never know! I might!" Simon said lightly. He
picked up his hat, and set it at a rakish angle on his fair locks.
He hesitated for a moment, and then said: "I shall go back to
London tomorrow, and shall be fixed there until I go to Newmarket. So, if you do find yourself in a hobble, and think I
might be able to help, come round to my lodgings, and—and I'll
do my best for you!" He added, returning to his insouciant
manner: "You've no notion how nacky my best is! Goodbye,
dear boy!"

The Viscount left Inglehurst some twenty minutes later relieved of at least one of his worries. Lady Silverdale, thanks
largely to her dislike of Lady Bugle, and in some measure to
Cherry's modest demeanour, seemed inclined to look favourably
upon her uninvited guest. It was perhaps fortunate that she
did not think Cherry more than passably pretty. "Poor child!"

she said. "Such a pity that she should be a little dab of a thing, and dress so dowdily! Hetta, my love, it would be only kind, I think, to make her rather more presentable; and I have been wondering whether, if you gave her that green cambric which we decided was not the colour for you, she might make herself a dress. Just a simple round dress, you know! And she must have her hair cropped, for I cannot endure untidy heads."

Henrietta being very willing to encourage her parent in these charitable schemes the Viscount took his leave of both ladies, and went away feeling that, at least for the present, her hostess would treat Cherry kindly.

When he left the house Cherry was sunk in profound slumber, from which the noise of his chaise-wheels under her window, and the trampling of hooves on the gravel, did not even disturb her dreams. She was so tired after the exertions and the agitations of the day that she hardly stirred until one of the housemaids came in to draw back the curtains round her bed, expressing, as Cherry opened her drowsy eyes and stretched like a kitten, the hope that she had slept well, and informing her that it was a beautiful morning. In proof of this statement she drew back the window-blinds, making Cherry blink at the sudden blaze of sunlight that flooded the room. Cherry sat up with a jerk, remembering all the events of the previous day, and asked to be told what time it was. Upon hearing that it was eight o'clock, she gave a gasp of dismay, and exclaimed: "Oh, goodness! Then I must have slept for twelve hours! However did I come to do such a thing?"

The housemaid, perceiving that she was about to scramble out of bed, told her that there was no need for her to hurry herself, since my lady never came downstairs to breakfast, and Miss Hetta had given orders that she was not to be disturbed until eight o'clock. She then set a burnished brass can of hot water down beside the little corner washstand, begged Miss to ring the bell if there was anything else she required, and went away, pausing in the doorway to say that breakfast would be served in the parlour at ten o'clock.

Cherry was left to take stock of her surroundings. She had

100

been too much exhausted when Hetta had put her to bed to pay much heed to them, the only things which had impressed themselves on her having been very soft pillows, and the most comfortable bed in which it had ever been her lot to lie; but now, hugging her knees, she stared about her in awe and wonderment. She thought it the most elegant bedchamber imaginable, and would have been amazed had she known that Lady Silverdale was most dissatisfied with the hangings, which she said had faded so much that they now looked detestably shabby. Her ladyship had also detected a slight stain on the carpet, where some careless guest had spilt some lotion. But Cherry did not notice this, or that the hangings were faded. Miss Fletching's Seminary for Young Ladies had been furnished neatly but austerely; and at Maplewood Cherry had shared a room with Corinna and Dianeme, who were not considered by their mama to be old enough to justify the expenditure of any more money on them than was strictly necessary. Consequently, their room was furnished with a heterogeneous collection of chairs and cupboards which had either been judged too shabby for the rooms where they had originally stood, or bought dog-cheap in a saleroom. And even Aunt Bugle's bed was not hung with curtains of silk damask, thought Cherry, almost fearfully stroking them.

She slid out of bed, and made a discovery: someone had not only unpacked her portmanteau, but had also ironed the creases out of the two dresses she had brought with her. This seemed to her such a dizzy height of luxury that she almost supposed herself to be still asleep and dreaming.

When she entered the breakfast-parlour, conducted to it by Grimshaw at his most stately, she found Henrietta making the tea, and was greeted by her in so kind and friendly a way that she lost the terror with which Grimshaw had inspired her, and said impulsively: "I think I was so stupid last night that I didn't tell you how very, very grateful I am to you, and to Lady Silverdale, for being so excessively kind to me! Indeed, I don't know how to thank you enough!"

"Nonsense!" said Henrietta, smiling at her. "I lost count of

101

the times you thanked me last night! I think it was the last thing you said, when I blew out the candle, but as you were three parts asleep I might be mistaken!"

By the time they rose from the table Henrietta had succeeded in charming Cherry out of her nervous shyness, and had won enough of her confidence to make her feel sincerely sorry for her. It was plain that she had not been encouraged to confide in her aunt; and although she spoke affectionately of Miss Fletching Henrietta did not think that their relationship had been closer than that of kind and just mistress, and grateful pupil. Cherry answered her questions with a good deal of reserve, and seemed at first to expect to be snubbed; but when she realized that she stood in no such danger she became very much more natural, and chatted away as easily as she had done on her journey to London. But much persuasion was needed to prevail upon her to accept the length of green cambric, and when she did at last yield, it was on condition that she should be allowed to pay for it—not with money, but with service. "I have been used to being employed," she assured Henrietta. "So *pray*, Miss Silverdale, tell me what you would wish me to do!"

"But I don't wish you to do anything!" objected Henrietta. "You are our guest, Cherry, not a hired servant!"

"No," said Cherry, flushing, and lifting her determined chin. "It is only your kindness which makes you say that, and—and it gives me such a warm *feel* in my heart that I couldn't be happy if you didn't permit me to make myself useful here. I can see, of course, that you have a great many servants, but there must be hundreds of things I could do for you, and for Lady Silverdale, that perhaps you would not ask the servants to do! Running errands—fetching things—searching for things you have mislaid—darning holes in your stockings—oh, all the things which I daresay you do for yourselves, and think a dead bore!"

Since Henrietta had yet to discover anything her parent would hesitate to ask her servants to do for her she could not help laughing, but she naturally did not tell Cherry why she laughed. All she said was: "Well, I'll do my best to oblige you, but I think it only right to warn you that if you encourage me to shuffle off every dull task it is my duty to perform you will rapidly turn me into the most indolent, selfish creature imaginable!"

"No. That I know I *couldn't* do!" said Cherry, mistily smiling at her.

She spent most of the morning happily engaged in cutting out the green cambric, and tacking the pieces together. In this she had the expert assistance of Miss Hephzibah Cardle, my lady's own dresser, whose spinsterish form and acidulated countenance could have led no one to suppose that she combined a rare talent for turning her mistress out complete to the last feather with a jealous adoration of that singularly unappreciative lady. Her services to Miss Steane were proffered with extreme reluctance, and would not have been proffered at all if her ladyship had not commanded her to do what she could to give Miss Steane a new touch. Professional pride overcame less admirable feelings, and even led her (to save my lady the expense of sending for her own hairdresser, she said) to trim Miss Steane's unruly locks into a more manageable, and very much more becoming style, which won for her one of my lady's rare encomiums. But although nothing could have been more prettily expressed than Cherry's gratitude for her kind offices she could not like her. She found only one sympathizer in the household: Mrs Honeybourne, the stout and goodnatured housekeeper, might declare that Miss was a sweet young lady; the maids and the two footmen, and even the cross-grained head-gardener smiled indulgently upon her, but Grimshaw regarded her with dislike and suspicion. He and Miss Cardle were convinced that she was an artful humbugger, bent on insinuating herself into my lady's and Miss Hetta's good graces by palavering them, and playing off all manner of cajoleries. "If you was to ask me for my opinion, Miss Cardle," he said portentously, "I should feel myself bound to say that I consider she is cutting a wheedle. And what I think of my Lord Desford's conduct in foisting her on to my lady is something I wouldn't demean myself by divulging."

Happily for Cherry's peace of mind the punctilious civility with which both these ill-wishers treated her precluded her from realizing how bitterly they resented her presence at Inglehurst. Within three days of her arrival she had lost her apprehensive look, and was unfolding shy petals in the warmth of a hitherto unknown approval. To be greeted with a smile, when she entered a room; to be addressed as "dear child" by Lady Silverdale; to be fondly scolded by that lady for running an unnecessary errand; to be encouraged by Miss Silverdale to roam about the grounds at will; and to be treated as though she had been an invited guest, and not the unwanted incubus she felt herself to be, were such hitherto unexperienced circumstances that she was passionately anxious to repay her kind hostesses by every means that lay within her power. It did not take her more than a day to realize that there was little she could do for Henrietta, but much she could do for Lady Silverdale; and since she had never previously encountered Lady Silverdale's like she did not for a moment suspect that that lady's plaintive voice and caressing manner concealed a selfishness and a determination to have her own way far more ruthless than the cruder methods employed by Aunt Bugle. Where Lady Bugle would have imperiously commanded her to go in search of something she had mislaid, and reward her, when she brought the object to her, by wondering what in the world had taken her so long to find it, Lady Silverdale would initiate the search by saying, at the outset: "Oh dear, how stupid of me! I've lost my embroidery-scissors! Now, where can I have left them? No, no, dear child! Why should *you* suffer for *my* carelessness?" And when Cherry, after an exhaustive search, found the missing scissors, and presented them, Lady Silverdale would say: "Oh, Cherry, you dear child! You shouldn't have troubled yourself!"

It was small wonder that she should blossom under such treatment, and think no task too laborious or too irksome to be performed for so amiable a benefactress. She had never been so happy in her life; and Henrietta, realizing this, forbore to intervene. She did, however, drop a gentle hint in Cherry's ear that Lady Silverdale's disposition was a trifle uncertain, and depended largely on how she happened to be feeling, the state of the weather, or the shortcomings of her domestic staff. It was by no means unknown for her to take sudden dislikes to persons whom she had previously, and just as suddenly, taken into the warmest favour; and while such capricious fits seldom lasted for very long they made life extremely uncomfortable for their victim.

Cherry listened to this, and nodded wisely, saying that old Lady Bugle had been subject to just such distempered freaks. "Only her crotchets were worse, because she wasn't at all kind, or amiable, even at her best, which dear Lady Silverdale *is!* Indeed, I think she and you are the kindest people I have ever met!"

This was said with a glowing look. Henrietta could only hope that her parent's sunny mood would outlast Cherry's visit.

It was three days before Sir Charles Silverdale was allowed to leave his bedchamber, and it was plain to his mother and his sister that he was much more shaken by his accident than he would admit. He insisted on coming downstairs but when, leaning heavily on his valet, he reached the library he was only too glad to stretch himself out on the sofa, and even to drink the cordial his mama pressed upon him. He was a handsome youth, but his features were too often marred by his expression, which was inclined to be petulant, and even, when he could not have his own way, or anything went amiss, sullen. In temperament, as in looks, he was very like his mother; but owing to the circumstance of his having been bereft of a father at an early age, and grossly indulged by his doting mama, all the faults which he had inherited from her were exaggerated. He had a good deal of charm; an ease of manner which made him generally an acceptable guest; and a reckless daring which won him the admiration of a number of like-minded young gentlemen. His servants liked him, for although he was quite as exacting as his mother, and very much more selfish, he had inherited her genius for making his most outrageous demands appear to be the merest requests; and because he always thanked them, with the sweetest of smiles, expressed contrition for any out-

105

burst of temper, and gave them leave of absence whenever he foresaw no need of their services, he was thought to be very goodnatured. His hare-brained exploits were regarded by them with indulgence, as being the natural conduct to be expected of any high-spirited young gentleman; and his carelessness was excused on the score of his youth. Only his sister, whose natural fondness for him did not prevent her from recognizing his faults, had said once, when exasperated by some example of churlishness, that since he seemed to have a number of friends it was to be supposed that he reserved his bad temper for his family, conducting himself with propriety everywhere that lay beyond the bounds of his home; and since this caustic comment had drawn down upon her the instant wrath and longlasting reproaches of her mother, she had never repeated the offence.

She had looked forward to her brother's emergence from his sickroom with misgiving, knowing his susceptibility, and well-aware that the smallest tendency on his part to flirt with Cherry would transform Lady Silverdale, in the twinkling of a bedpost, from a benevolent protectress into an inveterate enemy. But she discovered that Desford had been right: the dashing Mrs Cumbertrees might be a thing of the past, but Sir Charles's taste still ran to ladies of opulent charms and vast experience. He had no interest in ingénues, and his only comment, on meeting Cherry, must have allayed any alarm felt by his anxious parent. In fact, she felt none, and quite agreed with him when he said: "What a snippety thing she is, Mama! A regular go-by-the-ground! I wonder Des should have troubled himself with her."

Mr Cary Nethercott wondered too, but, being a simple, straightforward man, he accepted what was indeed the true explanation without question, and without difficulty. "One can only honour his lordship for his conduct in such a difficult situation," he said, adding with a faint smile: "And hope that one would have had the strength of mind to have behaved in the same way, had one been in his place!"

"I expect you would have!" Henrietta returned, smiling. "It was a very sad case, you know—sadder than the poor child

106

revealed to Desford, I am afraid. Only a monster could have left her to her fate!"

He agreed, but said gravely: "But what is to become of her? So young, and so friendless—for *you* cannot continue to be responsible for her—or, I don't doubt, Lord Desford expect it of you."

"No, of course he doesn't. He has merely left her at Inglehurst while he discovers her grandfather's whereabouts. Though whether Lord Nettlecombe will be willing to receive her into his household I can't but think extremely doubtful."

"I am not acquainted with his lordship—except by reputation."

"Nor am I, but if only half the tales told of him are true he must be the most disagreeable, clutchfisted old man imaginable! I can but hope that he may be moved by Cherry's plight —even take a fancy to her, which wouldn't be wonderful, for there is something very attaching about her, and she has the sweetest of dispositions."

"She is certainly a very taking little thing," he concurred. "One doesn't like to think of her becoming a slave to such a purse-leech as Lord Nettlecombe is said to be." He paused, frowning, and tapping his finger on the table. "What does she mean to do if Nettlecombe doesn't acknowledge her?" he asked abruptly. "Has she considered that possibility?"

"Oh, yes! She has the intention—the very firm intention!— of seeking a post in some genteel household."

His frown deepened. "What kind of a post? As governess? She must be too young to fill such a position!"

"Not only too young, but quite unqualified for it," said Henrietta. "She thinks she could instruct children just out of the nursery, but I hope I may have convinced her that such a situation would be no improvement on the conditions she endured in her aunt's establishment. The other notion she has is to seek employment with an elderly invalid. She says—and I believe her!—that although she is not bookish she does know how to deal with what she calls cantankersome old ladies. Well, my own mama may not be old, and God forbid I should call her

107

cantankersome, but it must be owned that—that she has odd humours! I daresay you know what I mean?" He bowed, looking gravely at her. "Yes. Well, I can only say that I have never known anyone who knew better how to keep her pleased and happy!"

"Other than yourself?" he suggested.

"Oh, good God, no!" she said, laughing. "I'm no hand at it, I promise you! I haven't enough patience! But Cherry has. And she has more sympathy than I fear I shall ever have with hypochondriacs! Does that shock you? Forget I said it!"

He shook his head. "Nothing you did me the honour to confide to me could shock me," he said simply. "What shocks me is knowing that you are aware of the imaginary nature of Lady Silverdale's aches and ills. Forgive me if I am expressing myself badly! I'm not ready of tongue, and find it hard to put my thoughts into words! But it has always seemed to me that you believed her to be in failing health, in which case your devotion to her was a natural thing, making it an impertinence for anyone to pity you, or—or to presume to think of rescuing you!"

He stopped, reddening, as he perceived in her expressive eyes as much amusement as surprise. When she spoke, her words acted on him like a douche of cold water, for she said, on a quiver of laughter: "Well, so I would suppose, sir! Good God, is it possible that you think me an object for pity, or that I need to be rescued? What a very odd notion you must have of me—and, indeed, of my poor mama! She may sometimes be tiresome, but I assure you she is as much attached to me as I am to her. I am perfectly happy, you know!"

"Forgive me!" he muttered. "I said too much!"

"Why, of course!" she said, smiling at him. "The truth is that you are too romantical, my friend, and should have lived when gentlemen of your cut used to ride out to rescue some damsel in distress. What a vast number of them there seem to have been, by the way! While as for the dragons and giants and ogres who held the damsels in thrall, when you consider how many of them were slain by the rescuing knights, you must be

108

forced to the conclusion that the country was positively infested with them!"

He could not help laughing, but he shook his head, saying: "You are always so humoursome, Miss Hetta, that one can't but be diverted by your jokes. Are you *never* serious?"

"Well, not for very long at a time!" she replied. "I fear I am like Beatrice, and was born to speak all mirth and no matter! But come, we were discussing little Cherry's situation, not mine! She really is a damsel in distress!"

"Hers is indeed a hard case," he said heavily.

"Yes, but I have every hope that it won't be long before she receives an offer!"

"From Lord Desford?" he interrupted, watching her face closely.

"From Desford?" she exclaimed involuntarily. "Good God, no! At least, I most sincerely hope not! It would never do!"

"Why do you say that? If he has fallen in love with her——"

"My dear sir, I daresay Desford must be the last man to forget what he owes to his name, and his family! What in the world do you imagine Lord Wroxton would say to such a match?"

"Do you mean to say that Lord Desford will marry to oblige his father?" he demanded.

"No, but I am very sure he won't marry to disoblige him!" she said. "When I said that I hoped it wouldn't be long before she received an offer I meant that if we can but introduce her into some household where she will be expected to help to entertain the visitors I have little doubt that she *will* receive an offer—perhaps several offers!—from perfectly respectable suitors, to whom her father's reputation won't signify a button."

"You must permit me to say, Miss Hetta, that her father's reputation ought not to signify to any man who loved her!"

"Yes, that is all very well," she said impatiently, "but you cannot expect a Carrington to ally himself to a Steane! It isn't even as if they were of the true nobility! Lord Nettlecombe is only the second baron, you know, and his father, from all I have heard, was a very rough diamond."

109

"A man need not be contemptible because he was a rough diamond."

"Very true!" she retorted. "He might be an admirable person! But unless I have been quite misinformed he was certainly not that! There is bad blood in the Steanes, Mr Nethercott, and although it hasn't come out in Cherry, who knows but what it might show itself in her children?"

"If these are your sentiments, Miss Hetta, I must wonder at it that you dared to expose your brother to the risk of falling in love with her!" he said, in a quizzing tone, but with a grave look.

She responded lightly: "Yes, and I must own that I had the strongest misgivings! But Desford said that there was no need for me to tease myself over that, because it wouldn't happen. He says that boys of Charlie's age seldom fall in love with girls no older than they are themselves, but languish at the feet of dashing man-traps. And he was perfectly right, as he by far too often is!—Charlie thinks poor Cherry a very mean bit! Which is a good thing, of course, but I do trust that by the time he is old enough to think of settling down he will have outgrown his taste for dashing man-traps!"

"Is that Lord Desford's opinion?" asked Mr Nethercott, unable to keep a sardonic note out of his voice.

It passed her by. She said, wrinkling her brow: "I don't think I ever asked him, but I'm very sure it would be, because, now you put me in mind of it, I recall that the first females he ever dangled after were years older than he was himself, and not at all the sort of women anyone but a confirmed noddicock would have dreamt of asking to marry him. And that, you know, Desford never was, even in his most ramshackle days!"

Her eyes lit with reminiscent amusement as she spoke, but a glance at Mr Nethercott's face informed her that he did not share her amusement, so she very wisely brought their tête-à-tête to an end, by getting up from her chair, and inviting him to go with her to the library, where Charlie, still confined largely to the sofa, would be delighted to enjoy a comfortable cose with him.

CHAPTER VIII

IN THE meantime the Viscount was being afforded ample opportunity to regret his chivalry. He spent the day following his return to Arlington Street in a number of abortive attempts to discover Lord Nettlecombe's whereabouts, even (though with extreme reluctance) going to the length of overcoming his strong dislike of Mr Jonas Steane, and calling at his house in Upper Grosvenor Street. But Mr Steane, like his father, had gone out of town; and although he had not left his house entirely empty the ancient caretaker who was at last induced to respond to the summons of a bell pulled with enough vigour to have broken the wires, and to a crescendo of knocks, was unable to give Desford any more precise information than that Mr Steane had taken his family to Scarborough. No, he disremembered that he had ever been told the exact direction of his lodgings: all he knew was that the servants had been given a fortnight's holiday, but would be back again at the end of the following week, with orders to give the house a proper clean-up before the family returned to it. No, he hadn't never heard that Lord Nettlecombe had gone off to Scarborough too, but if anyone was to ask him he'd be bound to say he didn't think he had, being as he was at outs with Mr Steane. Finally, with the praiseworthy intention of assisting the Viscount, he said that he wouldn't wonder at it if Mr Steane's lawyer knew where he was to be found; but as he was unable to furnish Desford with the lawyer's name, misdoubting that no one had ever told him what it was, being that it wasn't no concern of his, the suggestion that Desford should seek him out was not as helpful as he plainly believed it to be.

It was at the end of a singularly unrewarding day, when the Viscount sat down to dine in solitary state in his own house, that his deeply sympathetic butler, distressed by his master's sad lack of appetite, and extremely harassed expression, racked his

111

own brains, and was suddenly inspired to present him with the most promising advice of any that had yet been proffered. He said, as he refilled the Viscount's glass: "Has it occurred to your lordship that Lord Nettlecombe may have retired to his country seat for the summer months?"

The Viscount, who had been lost in gloomy consideration of the difficulties which confronted him, looked up quickly, and ejaculated: "Good God, what a fool I am! I'd forgotten he had one!"

"Yes, my lord," said Aldham, placing a cheesecake before him. "I have only a few minutes ago remembered it myself. So while you were partaking of your first course I took the liberty of consulting the *Index to the House of Lords,* which I recalled having seen on your lordship's bookshelves, and although this volume is ten years old I fancy the information it contains may still be relied upon. It states that Lord Nettlecombe's country seat is situated in the County of Kent, not far from Staplehurst. One cannot suppose that it will be difficult to find, for it is known as Nettlecombe Manor."

"Thank you!" said the Viscount warmly. "I am very much obliged to you! Indeed, I don't know where I should be without you! I'll post off to Staplehurst tomorrow morning!"

He did so, demanding his breakfast at an unfashionably early hour, so that his chaise had gone beyond the stones before such members of the ton who still remained in London had emerged from their bedchambers. His postilions had no difficulty at all in locating Nettlecombe Manor, for a few miles before Staplehurst was reached a signpost pointed the way to the house. It was approached by a narrow lane, bordered by high, straggling hedges, and with grass growing between the wheel-ruts. This did not hold out much promise that my Lord Nettlecombe's house would justify the description of it as a "Country seat", but it was found to be, if not a mansion, quite a large house, set in a small park, and approached by a short carriage-drive, which led from a pretty little lodge, and showed signs of having undergone extensive weeding operations. When the chaise drew up before the main entrance, and the Viscount jumped lightly down from it, he saw that the house was being repaired, a circumstance which, as he later said acidly, should have been enough to inform him that whoever was residing in the house he was not Lord Nettlecombe.

This was soon proved to be the case. My lord had hired the house to a retired merchant, whose wife, he informed Desford, had been mad after what he called a grand Country Place for years. "Mind you, my lord," he said, with a fat chuckle, "what *she* set her heart on was a swapping big house, like Chatsworth, or some such, but I told her to her head that ducal mansions was above my touch, even if his grace was wishful to hire it, which, so far as I am aware of, he ain't. All to one, it took pretty nigh on two years before we found this place, and I was so sick and tired of jumbling and jolting all over the country to look at houses that wasn't one of them what we wanted, nor what they was puffed off to be by the agents, that when I saw this place I'd have hired it, even if I hadn't taken a fancy to it, which I own I did. Of course I saw in no more than a pig's whisper that there was a lot wanted doing to it, but, lord, I said to myself, it'll give me something to do when I retire from my business, and if I don't have anything to do it's likely I'll get to be as blue as megrim. What's more, I was able to drive a bargain with his lordship's man of business, though not," he added, with a darkling look, "as good a one as I'd have driven if I'd known what I know now about the house! Well, if you're one of his lordship's friends, sir, I wouldn't wish to say anything unbecoming, but you wouldn't credit the way everything's been let go to rack and ruin!"

"I'm not one of his friends, and I do credit it!" Desford said promptly, before Mr Tugsley could continue his discourse. "I have a—a matter of business to discuss with him, and hoped I might find him here when I called at his London house, and discovered that he had gone out of town. If you know where he is to be found I should be very much obliged to you if you would furnish me with his direction."

"Well, that I can't do, but I *can* tell you his lawyer's name, *and* his direction, so if you'll do us the honour to step into the next room, which Mrs T. calls the Green Saloon, but which to my way of thinking is just a parlour, and partake of a morsel of refreshment, I'll go and see if I can't find it for you."

The Viscount thanked him, but would have declined the offer of hospitality had he not perceived that Mr Tugsley's feelings would be hurt by a refusal. He never willingly wounded the susceptibilities of his social inferiors, so he accompanied his host into the adjoining room, bowed to Mrs Tugsley just as though (as she later informed her husband) she had been a duchess, and even endured, with an air of courteous interest, twenty minutes of her somewhat overpowering conversation, during which time he drank a glass of wine, and ate a peach. The table was loaded with dishes, but he contrived to refuse them all without giving offence, saying (with perfect truth) that although he couldn't resist the peach, he never ate a nuncheon.

It was plain that Mrs Tugsley had social ambitions, and her efforts to impress him led her to ape what she supposed to be the manners of the haut ton, and to interlard her conversation with the names of a number of titled persons, generally describing them as "such a sweet creature!" or "a perfect gentleman", and trying to convey the impression that she was well-acquainted with them. The Viscount responded with easy civility, and allowed no trace either of disgust or boredom to appear in his demeanour, but he was thankful when Mr Tugsley returned, bearing a slip of paper on which he had transcribed the name and direction of Lord Nettlecombe's lawyer. This he handed to Desford, recommending him not to let the old huckster burn him. Mrs Tugsley begged him not to talk in such a vulgar way, and wondered (with a minatory frown at him) whatever his lordship must be thinking of him. But Desford laughed, and said that he was much obliged to Mr Tugsley for the warning, adding that if Lord Nettlecombe's man of business was as hardfisted as he was himself he must be a very neat article indeed.

He parted from the Tugsleys at long last on the best of good terms, and neither of them suspected that he had been chafing to get away from Nettlecombe Manor for the greater part of an hour. There could be little hope of his reaching London before

114

Mr Crick had shut up his office, and, since the following day would be Sunday, none at all of his being able to consult Mr Crick until Monday.

In the event it was not until Monday afternoon that he interviewed Mr Crick, for when he drove to that practitioner's office early in the morning it was to be met by the intelligence that Mr Crick had been summoned to attend another of his clients. The apologetic clerk who informed Desford of this circumstance was unable to say when he would return to his office, but he did not think it would be before noon. He asked, with another of his deprecatory bows, if my lord would wish him to desire Mr Crick to call in Arlington Street, to learn his pleasure; but the Viscount, to whom it would not have occurred to visit his own, and his father's, man of business, unhesitatingly refused this offer, saying that the matter on which he wished to see Mr Crick was merely to discover from him the present whereabouts of Lord Nettlecombe. "And that," he added, with his pleasant smile, "I daresay *you* may be able to tell me!"

But it was immediately apparent that this information the clerk was either unable or unwilling to disclose, so there was nothing for it but to withdraw, leaving his card, and saying that he would return later in the day.

"Which," said Stebbing, as he resumed his place beside the Viscount in the tilbury, "will give this Crick plenty of time to play least-in-sight."

"I wish to God you'd come out of the sullens!" retorted Desford, in some exasperation. "You've been glumping ever since we left Hazelfield, and I'm sick of it! Why the devil should he want to play least-in-sight?"

"That's more than I can tell, my lord, but what the both of us knows is that he's my Lord Nettlecombe's man of business, and if my lord ain't cut his stick I'm a bag-pudding! Which I ain't!"

"You may not be a bag-pudding, but you're one of the worst surly-boots it has ever been my ill-fortune to encounter!" said Desford roundly. "I know very well what made you turn knaggy, but what I do not know is what business it is of yours if I choose to lend my aid to Miss Steane, or to any one else!"

115

Chastened by the Viscount's most unusual severity, Stebbing muttered an apology, but since the Viscount cut short his subsequent stumbling attempt to excuse himself by saying curtly: "Very well, but don't let it happen again!" he did not venture to speak again until Arlington Street was reached, when, as he received the reins from his master, he asked with unprecedented humility at what hour my lord wished his tilbury to be brought to the door for his second visit to the City.

"I shan't need it again: I'll take a hack," replied Desford.

"Very good, my lord," said Stebbing woodenly. "It is just as your lordship pleases, of course. Though if you prefer to drive yourself, you could take young Upton with you, in my place."

Neither this speech, nor his expression, could have led any uninitiated person to suppose that he passionately desired to be reconciled with his master, but the Viscount was not uninitiated, and he relented, well-aware that Stebbing's gruffness and frequent attempts to scold and bully him sprang from a very real regard for him; and that to take the under-groom in his place would be to wound him to the heart. So, after eyeing him sternly for a moment, he laughed, and said: "Don't try to play off your tricks on me, you old humbugger! Think I don't know you? Bring it round at two o'clock!"

Stebbing was so much relieved by this sure sign that the Viscount was no longer angry with him that when he again took his place beside him in the tilbury he comported himself with such anxious civility that the Viscount, if he had not known that such unnatural subservience was unlikely to last for long, would have adjured him to abandon it. In fact, it showed signs of deserting him when the Viscount handed the reins to him outside the grimy building in which Mr Crick had his office, saying that he expected to be with him again in a very few minutes. He then said that he was sure he hoped his lordship would find Mr Crick, and demanded to know what his lordship was meaning to do if he didn't find him. But the Viscount only laughed, and walked into the building.

The clerk bowed him into Mr Crick's room, where he was received by that practitioner with the greatest civility. Mr Crick begged him to be seated; he apologized for having been absent from his office that morning; but he did not furnish him with Lord Nettlecombe's direction. He said that he was fully conversant with my lord's affairs, and did not doubt that if my Lord Desford would condescend to divulge the nature of the business he wished to discuss with my lord he would be able to deal with it.

"What I wish to discuss with him is not a business matter," said the Viscount. "It is private, and personal, and can only be answered by himself."

He spoke perfectly pleasantly, but there was an underlying note of determination in his voice which did not escape Mr Crick, and appeared to discompose him. He coughed genteelly, and murmured: "Quite! Exactly so! Naturally I understand. . . . But I assure your lordship that you need have no hesitation in disclosing it to me. A delicate matter, I apprehend? You might not be aware—perhaps I should tell you that my client honours me with his entire confidence."

"Yes?" said the Viscount politely.

Mr Crick fidgeted with the pounce-box, straightened a sheet of paper, and finally said: "He is—er—quite a *character,* my lord, if I may so put it!"

"I'm not—yet!—acquainted with him, but I have always understood him to be a deuced odd fish," agreed the Viscount.

Mr Crick uttered a little titter, but said it wouldn't become him to agree, though he was bound to own that Lord Nettlecombe had some rather odd ways. "He has become quite a recluse, you know, and almost never receives anyone, except Mr Jonas Steane—and not even him at present." He sighed, and shook his head. "I regret to say that he and Mr Steane had a difference of opinion a few weeks ago, which resulted in his lordship's going off to Harrowgate, and leaving me with instructions to deal with any matters that might arise during his absence. He stated in—in what I may call unequivocal terms that he did not wish to see Mr Steane, or, in fact, *anyone,* or to receive any communications whatsoever—even from me!"

117

"Good God, he must be short of a sheet!" exclaimed the Viscount.

"No, no, my lord!" Mr Crick said hastily. "That is, not if you mean to say that he's *deranged,* which, I collect, *is* your meaning! He has a—a somewhat untoward disposition, and has what I venture to say are some rather odd humours, but he is very shrewd—oh, very shrewd indeed!—in all worldly matters! Extremely long-headed, or, as he would say himself, *up to all the rigs!*" He tittered again, but, as the Viscount remained unresponsive to this evidence of Lord Nettlecombe's humour, changed the titter into a cough, and said, with a confidential drop of his voice: "His—his eccentricities derive, I believe, from the unfortunate circumstances of his *private* life, which has not, alas, been a happy one! It would be improper in me to expatiate on this subject, but I need not scruple to tell your lordship (for it is common knowledge) that his marriage was not attended by that degree of connubial bliss which one has so frequently known to soften a somewhat harsh disposition. And the very unsteady character of his younger son was a source of great pain to him— oh, *very* great pain! One had hoped that he would find consolation in Mr Jonas Steane, but, unfortunately, he did not care for Mr Jonas's wife, so that his relationship with Mr Jonas has sometimes been a trifle strained, though there has never been any serious quarrel between them, until—But more I must not say on that head!"

"My dear sir," interrupted the Viscount, who had been growing perceptibly impatient during this monologue, "do, pray, let me make it plain to you that I am not concerned with Lord Nettlecombe's marital troubles, or with his quarrels with his sons! All I wish to know is where, in Harrowgate, he is to be found!"

"Oh dear, oh dear, did I say that he was in Harrowgate?" asked Mr Crick, looking dismayed.

"You did, so you may just as well give me his exact direction," said the Viscount. "That will save me the trouble of enquiring for him at every hotel, inn, or lodging-house in the place, which, I promise you, I shall do, if you persist in withholding his direction!"

"My lord, I don't know his direction!"

The Viscount's brows drew together. He said incredulously: "You don't know it? How is this possible? You have told me that you are wholly in his confidence!"

"Yes, yes, I am!" averred Mr Crick, apparently on the verge of bursting into tears. "That is to say, I know why he has chosen to go away, but he would not tell me where he meant to stay, because he said he didn't wish to be troubled with any business while he was away. He did me the honour to say that he was confident I could settle any matter that might come up without referring it to him. May I venture to suggest to your lordship that you should wait until he returns to London—which, according to my information, he will do next month——"

"Why, certainly!" said the Viscount affably, rising from his chair, and picking up his hat and gloves. "You may suggest anything you please, Mr Crick! I am sorry you are unable to furnish me with Lord Nettlecombe's direction, and I won't waste any more of your time. Oh, no! pray don't trouble to escort me to the door! I can very well find the way out!"

But this Mr Crick would by no means permit him to do. He darted across the room to hold open the door for his distinguished visitor, bowing even more deeply than his clerk had done, and followed him down the dusty stairs, begging first his pardon and then his understanding of the delicacy of his own position as the trusted confidant of a noble client. The Viscount reassured him on both heads, but left him looking more harassed than ever. His last words, as Desford was about to mount into his tilbury, were that he hoped nothing he had said had given a wrong impression! Lord Nettlecombe had gone to try what the Harrowgate Chalybeate would do for his gout.

"Don't tease yourself!" Desford said, over his shoulder. "I won't disclose to his lordship that it was you who let slip the information that he had gone to Harrowgate!"

He then took his seat in the tilbury, recovered the reins from Stebbing, and drove off at a brisk trot, saying abruptly: "Didn't my father go to Harrowgate once—oh, years ago, when he was first troubled by the gout! I was still up at Oxford, I think."

Stebbing took a minute or two to answer this, frowning in an effort of memory. Finally he said: "Yes, my lord, he did. But, according to what I remember, he came home within a sennight, not liking the place. Unless it was Leamington he took against." His frown deepened, but cleared after another few moments, and he said: "No, it wasn't Leamington, my lord— though the waters never did him any good. It was Harrowgate right enough. And those waters didn't do him any good neither —not but what there's no saying that they wouldn't have done him good if he'd drunk more than one glass, which tasted so bad it made him sick."

The Viscount grinned appreciatively. "Poor Papa! Who shall blame him for going home? Did he take you there?"

"Me, my lord?" said Stebbing, shocked. "Lor', no! In them days I was only one of the under-grooms!"

"I suppose you must have been. What a pity! I hoped you might know the place, for I don't. Oh, well, we'd best stop at Hatchards, and I'll see if I can come by a guide-book there!"

"My lord, you're never going to go all that way just to find Miss's grandpa?" exclaimed Stebbing. "Which—if you'll pardon the liberty!—don't seem to be a grandpa as anyone would be wishful to find!"

"Very likely not—indeed, almost certainly not!—but I've pledged my word to Miss Steane that I will find him, and—damn it, my blood's up, and I will *not* be beaten!"

"But, my lord," expostulated Stebbing, "it'll take you four or five days to get there! It's above two hundred miles away: that I *do* know, for when my lord and her ladyship went there, they were five days on the road, and Mr Rudford, which was his lordship's valet at that time, always held to it that it was that which set up his lordship's back so that he wouldn't have liked the place no matter what!"

"Good God, you don't imagine, do you, that I mean to go in the family travelling-carriage? What with four people in the carriage, the coachman, and I'll go bail a couple of footmen outside, and a coach following, chuck-full of baggage, besides the rest of my father's retinue, I'm astonished they weren't a sen-

120

night on the road! I shall travel in my chaise, of course, taking Tain, and one portmanteau only, and changing horses as often as need be, and I promise you I shan't be more than three days on the road. No, don't pull that long face! If I can post to Doncaster in two days, which you know well I have frequently done, I can certainly reach Harrowgate in three days—possibly less!"

"Yes, my lord, and possibly more, if you was to have an accident," said Stebbing. "Or find yourself with a stumbler in the team, or maybe a limper!"

"Or founder in a snowdrift," agreed the Viscount.

"That," said Stebbing coldly, "I didn't say, nor wouldn't, not being such a cabbage-head as to look for snowdrifts at this time o'year. But if you was to drop the high toby, who's to say you won't find yourself foundering in a regular hasty-pudding?"

"Who indeed? I'll bear it in mind, and take care to stick to the post-road," promised his lordship.

Stebbing sniffed, but refrained from further speech.

Desford was unable to find a guide-book of Harrowgate at Hatchard's shop, but he was offered a fat little volume, which announced itself to be a Guide to All the Watering and Sea-bathing Places, and contained, besides some tasteful Views, numerous maps, town-plans, and itineraries. He bore this off for perusal that evening, hoping to discover in the chapter devoted to the amenities of Harrowgate a list of the hotels and lodgings there. But although almost a dozen inns received favourable notice neither High nor Low Harrowgate appeared to boast of any establishment comparable to the hotels to be found at more fashionable watering-places; nor was any lodging-house mentioned. As he read what the unknown author had to say about the place, and pictured his father there, he was torn between appreciative amusement, and a strong wish that he himself were not obliged to go there. The very first paragraph was daunting, for it stated that because Harrowgate possessed "in a superior degree" neither the attraction of being fashionable, nor beauty of scenery, it was chiefly resorted to by valetudinarians. No doubt feeling that he had been rather too severe, the author bestowed some temperate praise on the situation of High Harrowgate, which he described as exceedingly pleasant, and commanding an extensive prospect of the distant country. But as, in the very next paragraph, he referred to the "dreary common" on which both High and Low Harrowgate were built, and to "the barren wolds of Yorkshire", it seemed safe to assume that the place had not taken his fancy. Which, thought Desford, flicking over the pages which dealt with the qualities and virtues of the wells, and reading the passage headed Customs and Accommodations, was not to be wondered at. He could almost feel the hairs rising on his scalp when he read that one of the advantages enjoyed by visitors to Harrowgate was that the narrow circle of their amusements drew them into "something like family parties"; but when he read that the presence of the ladies sitting at the same board as the gentlemen excluded any rudeness or indelicacy, he began to chuckle; and when, on the next page, he learned that one of the advantages of mixing freely with the ladies was the sobriety it ensured—to which the author acidly added that to this the waters contributed "not a little", he laughed so much that it was several moments before his vision was sufficiently clear to enable him to read any more. However, he did read more, and although he found no mention of a pump room, he did learn that there was an Assembly Room, and a Master of Ceremonies, who presided over the public balls; a theatre; two libraries; a billiard-room; and a morning lounge in one of the new buildings, called the Promenade; which made it seem probable that he would experience no very great difficulty in discovering where he could find Lord Nettlecombe.

But what he found very difficult to understand was why Lord Nettlecombe, who, so far from enjoying the company of his fellow men and women, had for years spurned even his oldest acquaintances, should have elected suddenly to spend the summer months where, according to the author of the Guide, repasts (served in the long rooms of the various inns) were "seasoned by social conversation"; and where "both sexes vied with each other in the art of being mutually agreeable". It was possible, of course, that the circumstance of the expenses of living and lodging being moderate might have attracted his cheese-paring lordship; but this advantage must surely have been off-set by the cost of so long a journey. The Viscount, as he took his candle up to bed, wondered if Nettlecombe had travelled north on the common stage, but abandoned this notion, feeling that the old screw could not be such a shocking lickpenny as that. He might, with perfect propriety, have travelled on the Mail coach, but although this was much cheaper than hiring a private chaise it was by no means dog-cheap, particularly when two places would have to be booked. Lord Nettlecombe might not travel in the rather outmoded state favoured by Lord Wroxton, but it was inconceivable to Desford that he could have gone away on a protracted visit without taking his valet with him. The thought of his high and imposing father's regal progress to Harrowgate, and his very brief stay there, made Desford begin to chuckle again. He must remember, he told himself, to ask Poor Dear Papa, at a suitable moment, for his opinion of Harrowgate.

Tain, his own extremely accomplished valet, had received without a blink the news that his lively young master meant to leave almost at crack of dawn for an unfashionable resort in Yorkshire; and when further told that he must pack whatever was strictly necessary into one portmanteau, he merely said: "Certainly, my lord. For how many days does your lordship mean to stay in Harrowgate?"

"Oh, not above two or three!" replied Desford. "I shan't be attending any evening-parties, so don't pack any ball-toggery."

"Then one portmanteau will be quite sufficient for your lordship's needs," said Tain calmly. "Your dressing-case may go inside the chaise, and I shall not pack your Hessians, or any of your town-coats. I fancy they would be quite ineligible for wear in Those Parts."

That was all he had to say about the projected expedition, either then or later; and Desford, who had had several years' experience of his competence, never so much as thought of asking him whether he had packed enough shirts and neckcloths, and had found room for a change of outer raiment.

For his part, Tain showed not the smallest surprise at what he might have thought to be a very queer start, or betrayed by look or word that he was well aware of the Viscount's purpose in going post-haste to Harrowgate, when his intention had been to attend the races at Newmarket. He had not yet seen Miss Steane, but he knew all about her meeting with the Viscount, for he stood on very friendly terms with both the Aldhams, and had contrived, without showing a vulgar curiosity unbecoming to a man of his consequence, to discover from them quite as much as they knew, and many of Mrs Aldham's conjectures on the probable outcome of the adventure. On these he withheld judgment, feeling that he knew my lord far more intimately than they did, and having yet to see in him any of the signs of a gentleman who had fallen head over ears in love. He did not discuss the matter with Stebbing, not so much because it would have been beneath a gentleman's gentleman to hob-nob with a groom, but because he was as jealous of Stebbing as Stebbing was of him.

Before he went to bed, the Viscount wrote a brief letter to Miss Silverdale, informing her that he was off to Harrowgate, where he was reliably informed Nettlecombe was to be found, but hoped to be back again in not much more than a sennight's time, when he would come to Inglehurst immediately, to tell her how his mission had prospered, *or,* he added, *if it has not prospered, to discuss with you what were best to do next for that unfortunate child. I should think myself the biggest rascal unhung to have foisted her on to you, my best of friends, if I were not persuaded that she must have made you like her.*

This missive he gave to Aldham on the following morning, telling him to send it by express post to Inglehurst. He then climbed into his chaise, and set forward on the long journey into Yorkshire.

CHAPTER IX

THE VISCOUNT suffered no delays on his journey, and might have reached Harrowgate at the end of the second day had it not occurred to him that to arrive without warning at a watering-place in the height of its season would probably entail a prolonged search for accommodation, and that the late evening was scarcely the time to prosecute this. So he spent the second night at the King's Arms, in Leeds, leaving himself with only some twenty more miles to cover. He was an extremely healthy young man, and since he spent a great part of his time in all the more energetic forms of sport it was hard to tire him out, but two very long days in a post-chaise had made him feel as weary as he was bored. The chaise was his own, and very well-sprung, but it was also very lightly built, which, while it made for speed, meant that it bounded over the inequalities of the road in a manner not at all conducive to repose. Midway through the second day he remarked to Tain that he wished he could exchange places with one of the post-boys. Quite shocked, Tain said incredulously: "Exchange places with a *post-boy*, my lord?"

"Yes, for he at least has something to do. Though I daresay I shouldn't care to be obliged to wear a leg-iron," he added reflectively.

"No, my lord," said Tain, primly. "Certainly not! A very unbecoming thing for any gentleman to do!"

"Also uncomfortable, don't you think?" suggested Desford, gently quizzing him.

"I have never worn one, my lord, so I cannot take it upon myself to venture an opinion," replied Tain, in chilly accents.

"I must remember to ask my own wheel-boy," said Desford provocatively.

But Tain, refusing to be drawn, merely said: "Certainly, my lord," leaving Desford to regret that it was he and not Stebbing who was sitting beside him. Stebbing would undoubtedly have entered with enthusiasm into a discussion, embellishing it with some entertaining anecdotes illustrative of the advantages and disadvantages attached to a postilion's career.

However, the regret vanished when the Viscount remembered how valuable Tain's services became from the instant that he climbed down from the chaise, and entered whatever posting-house his employer had chosen to honour with his patronage on this or any other journey. In some mysterious way known only to himself he could transform the most unpromising bedchamber into an inviting one in no more than a flea's leap, as the saying was; to lay out a change of raiment for his master; to make such arrangements for his comfort as Desford would not have thought it necessary to command, if left to manage for himself; to press out the creases in his coat; to launder his neckcloth and his shirt; to procure extra candles; and to overawe the domestic staff into bringing up hot water to my lord's room without delay as soon as he himself demanded it. Stebbing might be a more amusing companion during a tedious journey, but none of Tain's arts was known to him, as the Viscount realized, and acknowledged, when, as Tain drew the curtains round his bed that evening, he murmured: "Thank you! I only wish you may have ensured your own comfort half as well as you have ensured mine!"

He did not reach Harrowgate until shortly before noon on the following morning, because although he had had the intention of setting forward on the last few miles of his journey at eight o'clock Tain had quite deliberately refrained from rousing him until an hour later, saying mendaciously, but with complete sangfroid, that he had misunderstood his instructions. What he did not say was that when he had softly entered the room at six o'clock he had found the Viscount sunk in a profound sleep from which he had not had the heart to rouse him. He guessed, judging by his own experience, that my lord had spent the first part of the night under the lingering impression that he was still bowling and bounding and swaying over the road, and had only slept in uneasy snatches until overcome by exhaustion. As this guess was correct, and Desford was still feeling both sleepy and battered, the excuse was received with a prodigious yawn, accompanied by nothing more alarming than a sceptical glance, and a rather thickly uttered: "Oh, well——!"

Revived by an excellent breakfast, Desford shook off his unaccustomed lassitude, and resumed his journey. It was a day of bright sunshine, with just enough wind blowing off the moors to make it invigorating, and under these conditions he saw Harrowgate at its best, and was much inclined to think that his anonymous Guide had maligned the place. The Low Town did not attract him, but the situation of High Harrowgate, which lay nearly a mile beyond it, was as pleasant as the Guide had grudgingly described. On a clear day—and this was a very clear day—York Minster could be seen in the distance, with the Hambleton hills beyond; and to the west the mountains of Craven. Besides the race course, the theatre, and the principal Chalybeate, High Harrowgate possessed a large green, which was one of its most agreeable features, and round which three of its chief hotels stood, a great many shops, and what bore all the appearance of being a fashionable library. "Come now!" exclaimed Desford cheerfully, as the chaise drew up at the Dragon. "I don't consider this a dreary place at all, do you, Tain?"

"Your lordship has not yet seen it in bad weather," responded Tain unencouragingly. "I should not myself choose to sojourn here on a dull day, when the prospect would no doubt be shrouded in mist."

Neither the Dragon nor the Granby had a room to spare, but the Viscount was more fortunate at the Queen's, where, after a hurried colloquy with his spouse, conducted in an urgent whisper, the landlord was happy to inform his lordship that he had just one room vacant—indeed, one of his best rooms, looking out on to the green, which he was only able to offer because the gentleman who had booked it had unaccountably failed to honour his contract. He then escorted Desford upstairs to inspect it, and, on its being approved, bowed himself out, and hurried downstairs again, first to order a couple of menials to carry up the gentleman's baggage to No. 7, and then to inform his flustered wife that if Mr Fritwell *should* happen to show his front Jack (the hope of his house) would have to give up his room to him,

127

and bed down over the stables. Upon her venturing to expostulate he silenced her by saying that if she thought he was going to turn away a well-breeched swell, travelling in a chaise-and-four, and attended by his valet, merely to avoid offending old Mr Fritwell, who was more inclined to argue over the reckoning than to drop his blunt freely, she was the more mistaken.

Little though he knew it, the Viscount was indebted to Tain's entrance upon the scene, bearing his dressing-case, for the landlord's decision to sacrifice old Mr Fritwell. The landlord was sharp enough to recognize after one look at his lordship that a member of the Quality had walked into the inn, and—after a second, shrewd, glance at the cut of his lordship's coat, the intricate folds of his neckcloth, and the gloss on his top-boots—no country squire, but a London buck of the first head; but it was Tain's arrival which clinched the matter. Unknown ladies and gentlemen travelling without their personal servants found it hard to obtain accommodation at any of the best inns in Harrowgate, valets and abigails apparently being regarded by the landlords as insurances against the possibility of being choused out of their due reckonings.

The Viscount had not thought it necessary to acquaint the landlord either with his name or his rank, but this was a foolish omission speedily rectified by Tain, far better versed in such matters than his master. Instead of following immediately in the Viscount's wake, he awaited the landlord's return at the foot of the stairs, and proceeded with quelling civility to make known to him my lord's requirements. By the time he had reached the stage of warning the landlord not, on any account, to permit the Boots to lay a finger on my lord's footwear, he had succeeded in so much enlarging his master's consequence that it would not have been surprising if the landlord had believed himself to be entertaining, if not a Royal prince, at least a Serene Highness.

As a result of these competent, if top-lofty, tactics, he was able to inform the Viscount, when he presently rejoined him in No. 7, that he had ventured to bespeak a private parlour for him, and to arrange with the landlord for his dinner to be served there. The Viscount, who was standing by the window, watching the various persons passing below, replied absently: "Have you? I thought it not worth while to ask for one since I don't expect to be here above a couple of nights, but I daresay you're right. You know, Tain, the place *is* full of valetudinarians! I've never seen so many people hobbling along on sticks in my life!"

"Exactly so, my lord!" said Tain, beginning swiftly to unpack the contents of the dressing-case. "I have myself seen three of them enter this house, one of them being an elderly lady of what one must call a garrulous disposition. I formed the opinion that if she were to subject your lordship to a description of her sufferings and of the cure which she is undergoing you would be hard put to it to maintain even the appearance of civility."

"Then you were certainly right to procure a private parlour for me," said the Viscount, laughing.

Leaving Tain to unpack his portmanteau, he sallied forth to continue his search for Lord Nettlecombe. He had already enquired for him at the Dragon and the Granby, without meeting with anything but blank looks, and head-shakings, so, as the Chalybeate, under its imposing dome, lay on the opposite side of the green he thought he might as well make that his first port of call. If Lord Nettlecombe had come to Harrowgate for his health's sake it seemed likely that he must by now have become a familiar figure there. But none of the attendants seemed to have heard of his lordship, the most helpful amongst them being unable to do more than suggest that he should be sought at the Tewit Well, which was the second of the two Chalybeates, situated half-a-mile to the west of the principal one.

Desford strode off, glad to be able to stretch his legs after having been cooped up for so many hours, but although he enjoyed a brisk walk it ended in another rebuff, accompanied by a recommendation to try the Sulphur Wells, at Lower Harrowgate, and the information that although the Lower town was a mile distant by road it was no more than half-a-mile away if approached "over the stile". But as the directions given to him on how to reach the stile were as vague as such directions too often are, Desford decided to enquire at the inns

129

and boarding-houses in High Harrowgate, before extending his search to the Lower town.

He very soon discovered that although Harrowgate was described by the Guide as consisting of two scattered villages this was another of that anonymous author's misleading statements: no village that Desford had yet seen contained so many inns and boarding-houses as High Harrowgate. At none of those he visited was he able to obtain any news of his quarry, and by the time a church clock struck the hour of six, at which unfashionable time dinner was served at all the best inns, he was tired, hungry, and exasperated, and thankfully abandoned, for that day, his fruitless search.

When he reached the Queen he was considerably surprised by the respect with which he was greeted, the porter bowing him in, a waiter hurrying forward to discover whether he would take a glass of sherry before he went upstairs to his parlour, and the landlord breaking off a conversation with a less favoured guest to conduct him to the stairs, informing him on the way that dinner—which he trusted would meet with his approval —should be served immediately, and that he had taken it upon himself to bring up a bottle of his best burgundy from the cellar, and one of a very tolerable claret, in case my lord should prefer the lighter wine.

The reason for these embarrassingly obsequious attentions was soon made plain to the Viscount. Tain, relieving him of his hat and gloves, said that he had ventured to order a neat, plain dinner for him, consisting of a Cressy soup, removed with a fillet of veal, some glazed sweetbreads, and a few petit pâtés, to be followed by a second course of which prawns, peas, and a gooseberry tart were the principal dishes. "I took the precaution, my lord," he said, "of looking at the bill of fare, and saw that it was just as I had feared: a mere ordinary, and not at all what you are accustomed to. So I ordered what I believe you will like."

"Well, I am certainly hungry, but I couldn't eat the half of it!" Desford declared.

However, when he sat down to table he found that he was

hungrier than he had supposed, and he ate rather more than half of what was set before him. The claret, though not of the first growth, was better than the landlord's somewhat slighting description of it had led him to expect; and the brandy with which he rounded off the repast was a true Cognac. Under its benign influence he began to take a more hopeful view of his immediate prospects, and to consider what his next move should be. He decided that the best thing he could do would be to visit first the Sulphur Well, and next, if he failed to come by any intelligence of Lord Nettlecombe's whereabouts there, to discover the names and directions of the doctors practising in Harrowgate.

The experiences of the first wearing day he had spent in his search for Nettlecombe prevented him from feeling either surprise or any marked degree of disappointment when his enquiries at the Sulphur Well were productive of nothing more than regretful headshakes; but he was a trifle daunted when presented with a list of the Harrowgate doctors: he had not thought that so many medical men were to be found in so small a spa. He betook himself to the Crown, to study the list over a fortifying tankard of Home Brewed; and, having crossed off from it those who advertised themselves as Surgeons, and consulted a plan of both High and Low Harrowgate, which he had had the forethought to buy that morning, set out on foot to visit the first of the Lower town's practitioners which figured on the list. Neither this member of the Faculty, nor the next on his list, numbered Lord Nettlecombe amongst his patients, but just as the Viscount was contemplating with disgust the prospect of spending the rest of the day in what he was fast coming to believe was an abortive search, fortune at last smiled upon him: Dr Easton, third on the list, not only knew where Nettlecombe was lodging, but had actually been summoned to attend him, when his lordship had suffered a severe attack of colic. "As far as I am aware," he said, austerely regarding Desford over the top of his spectacles, "his lordship has not removed from that lodging, but since he has not again sought my services I do not claim him as a patient. I will go further! Should he again request my attendance upon him I should have no hesitation in recommending him to consult some other physician more willing than I am, perhaps, to being told that his diagnosis is false, and to having his prescription spurned!"

Resisting an absurd but strong impulse to offer Dr Easton an apology for Nettlecombe's rudeness, Desford took his leave, saying that he was much obliged to him, and assuring him, with a disarming smile, that he had all his sympathy.

It transpired that Nettlecombe's lodging was in one of the larger boarding-houses in the Lower town. It has an air of somewhat gloomy respectability, and was presided over by an angular lady whose appearance carried the suggestion that she must be in mourning for a near relation, since she wore a bombasine dress of sombre hue, without frills, or lace, or even a ribbon to lighten its sobriety. Her cap was of starched cambric, tied tightly beneath her chin; and as much of her hair as was allowed to be seen was iron-gray, and smoothed into bands as severe as her expression. She put Desford forcibly in mind of the dame in the village that lay beyond Wolversham who terrified the rural children into good behaviour and the rudiments of learning; and he would not have been in the least surprised to have seen a birch-rod on the high desk behind which she stood.

She was talking to an elderly couple, whose decorous bearing and prim voices exactly matched their surroundings, when Desford entered the house, but she broke off the conversation to direct a piercing look of appraisal at him, which made him feel that at any moment she would tell him that his neckcloth was crooked, or demand to know if he had washed his hands before venturing into her presence. His lips twitched, and his eyes began to dance, upon which her countenance relaxed, and, excusing herself to the elderly couple, she came towards him, saying, with a slight bow: "Yes, sir? What may I have the honour to do for you? If it is accommodation you are seeking, I regret I have none to offer: my house is always fully booked for the season."

"No, I don't want accommodation," he replied. "But I believe you have Lord Nettlecombe staying here. Is that so?"

Her face hardened again; she said grimly: "Yes, sir, it *is* so!"

It was apparent that the presence of Lord Nettlecombe in her house afforded her no gratification, and that Desford's enquiry had caused whatever good opinion she had formed of himself to wither at birth. When he requested her to have his card taken to my lord she gave a small, contemptuous sniff, and without deigning to reply, turned away to call sharply to a waiter just about to enter the long room: "George! Conduct this gentleman to Lord Nettlecombe's parlour!"

She then favoured the Viscount with a haughty inclination of her head, and resumed her conversation with the elderly couple.

Amused, but also a trifle ruffled by this cavalier treatment, Desford was on the verge of telling her that when he had handed her his card he had intended it to be taken to Lord Nettlecombe, not laid on her desk, when it occurred to him that perhaps it would be as well not to give his lordship the opportunity to refuse to see him, so he suppressed the impulse to give this ridiculously uppish creature a set-down, and followed the waiter up the stairs, and along a corridor. The waiter, whose air of profound gloom argued a life of intolerable slavery, but was probably due to the pain of flat feet, stopped outside a door at the end of the corridor, and asked what name he should say, and, upon learning it, opened the door, and repeated it in a raised, indifferent voice.

"Eh? What's that?" demanded Lord Nettlecombe wrathfully. "I won't see him! What the devil do you mean by bringing people up here without my leave? Tell him to go away!"

"I fear you will be obliged to do that yourself, sir," said Desford, shutting the door upon the waiter, and coming forward. "Pray accept my apologies for not sending up my card! It was my intention to have done so, but the formidable lady belowstairs thought otherwise."

"That damned pigeon-fancier!" ejaculated his lordship

133

fiercely. "She had the curst impudence to try to diddle me! But I'm no pigeon for her plucking, and so I told her! Gullcatcher! Slip-gibbet! Nail!" He broke off suddenly. "What do you want?" he snarled.

"A few words with you, sir," said the Viscount coolly.

"Well, I don't want to talk to you! I don't want to talk to anyone! If your name's Desford you must be old Wroxton's son, and he's no friend of mine, I'll have you know!"

"Oh, I do know it!" responded the Viscount, laying his hat, his gloves, and his malacca cane down on the table.

This indication that he meant to prolong his visit infuriated Nettlecombe so much that he said, in a kind of scream: "Don't do that! Go away! Do you want to send me off the hooks? I'm a sick man! Worn to the bone with all the worry and trouble I've had! Burnt to the socket, damn it! I won't have strangers thrust in on me, I tell you!"

"I'm sorry you are in such indifferent health," said Desford politely, "I will try not to tax your strength, but I have a duty to discharge which closely concerns you, and I believe——"

"If you've come from my son Jonas you've wasted your time!" interrupted Nettlecombe, his pale eyes sharp with suspicion.

"I have not," said Desford, his calm voice in marked contrast to Nettlecombe's shrill accents. "I have come on behalf of your granddaughter."

"That's a damned quibble!" instantly exclaimed his lordship. "Jonas may take care of his brats himself, and so you may tell him! I wash my hands of the whole brood!"

"I am not speaking of Mr Jonas Steane's daughters, sir, but of your younger son's only child."

My lord's bony hands clenched the arms of his chair convulsively. "I have no younger son!"

"From what I have been able to discover I fear that that may be true," said Desford.

"Ha! Dead, is he? And a good thing if he is!" said Nettlecombe viciously. "He's been dead to me for years, and if you think I'll have anything to do with any child of his you're mistaken!"

"I do think it, and I am persuaded that I'm not mistaken, sir. When you have heard in what a desperate situation she has been left I cannot believe that you will refuse to help her. Her mother died when she was a child, and her father placed her in a school in Bath. Until a few years ago, he paid the necessary fees, though not always, I fancy, very punctually, and from time to time he visited her. But the payments and the visits ceased——"

"I know all this!" interrupted Nettlecombe. "The woman wrote to me! Demanded that *I* should pay for the girl! A damned insolent letter I thought it, too! I told her to apply to the girl's maternal relations, for she wouldn't get a groat out of me!"

"She obeyed you, sir, she applied to Lady Bugle, but I don't think she got a groat out of her either," said Desford dryly. "Lady Bugle, perceiving an opportunity to provide herself with an unpaid servant, took Miss Steane to her home in Hampshire, under an odious pretence of charity, for which she demanded a slavish gratitude, and unending service, not only for herself, but for every other member of her large family. Miss Steane's disposition is compliant and affectionate: she had every wish in the world to repay her aunt for having given her a home, and uncomplainingly performed every task set before her, from hemming sheets, or running errands for her cousins, to taking charge of the nursery-children. And I daresay she would still be doing so, perfectly happily, had her aunt treated her with kindness. But she did not, and the poor child became so unhappy that she ran away, with the intention of appealing to you, sir, for protection."

Nettlecombe, who had listened to this speech with a scowl on his brow, punctuating it with muttered comments, and fidgeting restlessly in his chair, burst out angrily: "It's no concern of mine! I warned that scoundrelly son of mine how it would be if he didn't mend his ways. He made his bed, and he must lie on it!"

"But it is not he who is lying on it," said the Viscount. "It is his daughter who is the innocent victim of her father's misdeeds."

"You should read your Bible, young man!" retorted Nettlecombe on a note of triumph. "The sins of the fathers shall be visited on the children! What about *that,* eh?"

A pungent reply sprang to the Viscount's lips, but it remained unuttered, for at that moment the door opened, and a middle-aged and buxom woman sailed into the room, saying in far from refined accents: "Well, this *is* a surprise, to be sure! When that old Tabby downstairs, which has the impudence to call herself *Mrs* Nunny, just as though a rabbit-pole like she is ever had a husband, told me my lord had a gentleman visiting him you could have knocked me down with a feather, for in general he don't receive, not being in very high force. Though we shall soon have him quite rumtitum again, shan't we, my lord?"

My lord responded to this sprightly prophecy with a growl. As for Desford, the newcomer's surprise was as nothing to his, for she spoke as though she were well-acquainted with him, and he knew that he had never before seen her. He wondered who the devil she could be. Her manner towards Nettlecombe suggested that she might be a nurse, hired to attend him during recuperation from some illness but a stunned look at the lavishly plumed and high-crowned bonnet set upon her brassy curls rapidly put that idea to flight. No nurse wearing such an exaggeratedly fashionable bonnet would ever have been allowed to cross the threshold of a sick-room; nor would she have dreamt of arraying herself (even if she could have afforded to do so) in a purple gown with a demi-train, and trimmed with knots of ribbon.

His blank astonishment must have shown itself in his face, for she simpered, and said archly: "I have the advantage of you, haven't I? You don't know who I am, but I know who *you* are, because I've seen your card. So my lord don't have to tell me."

Thus put pointedly in mind of his social obligations Lord Nettlecombe said sourly: "Lord Desford—Lady Nettlecombe.

And you've no need to look like that!" he added, as Desford blinked increduously at him. "My marriage doesn't have to meet with your approval!"

"Certainly not!" said Desford, recovering himself. "Pray accept my felicitations, sir! Lady Nettlecombe, your servant!"

He bowed, and finding that she was extending her hand to him took it in his, and (since she clearly expected it) raised it briefly to his lips.

"However did you find us out, my lord?" she asked. "Such pains did we take to keep it secret that we'd gone off on our honeymoon! Not that I'm not very happy to make your acquaintance, for I'm sure we couldn't have wished for a more amiable bride-guest, neither of us!"

"Don't talk such fiddle-faddle, Maria!" said Nettlecombe irascibly. "He's not a bride-guest! He didn't know we were married when he forced his way in here! All he wants to do is to foist Wilfred's brat on to me, and I won't have her!"

"You are mistaken, sir!" said the Viscount icily. "I have not the smallest wish to see Miss Steane in a house where she is not welcome! My purpose in coming to visit you is to inform you that she—your granddaughter, let me remind you!—is entirely destitute! Had I not been with her when she found your house shut up she must have been in a desperate case, for she has no acquaintance in London, no one in the world to turn to but yourself! What might have become of her I leave to your imagination!"

"She had no business to run away from her aunt's house!" Nettlecombe said angrily. "Most unbecoming! Hoydenish behaviour! Not that I should have expected anything better from a daughter of that rake-shame I refuse to call my son!" He turned towards his bride. "It's Wilfred's brat he's talking about, Maria: you remember how vexed I was when some brass-faced schoolkeeper wrote to demand that I—*I!*—should pay for the girl's schooling? Well, now, if you please——" He broke off, his gaze suddenly riveted to the shawl she was wearing draped across her elbows. "That's new!" he said, stabbing an accusing finger at it. "Where did it come from?"

"I've just purchased it," she answered boldly. She still smiled, but her smile was at variance with the determined jut of her chin, and the martial gleam in her eyes. "And don't try to bamboozle me into thinking you didn't give me leave to buy myself a new shawl, because you did, and this very morning, what's more!"

"But it's *silk!*" he moaned.

"Norwich silk," she said, smoothing it complacently. "Now, don't fly into a miff, my lord! You wouldn't wish for me to be seen about in a cheap shawl, such as anyone could wear, not when I'm your wife!"

There was nothing in his expression to encourage her in this belief; and as he complained mournfully that if she meant to squander his money on finery he would soon be ruined, and added a reproachful rider to the effect that he had expected his marriage to be an economy, Desford very soon found himself the sole, and wholly disregarded, witness to a matrimonial squabble. From the various things that were said, he gathered, without much surprise, that Lord Nettlecombe had married his housekeeper. Why he had done so did not emerge; the reason was to be revealed to him later. But it was plain that in the rôle of housekeeper my lord's bride had proved herself to be as big a save-all as he was himself; and that once she had him firmly hooked she had lapsed a little from her former economical habits. And, watching her, as she contended with her lord, always with that firm smile on her lips and that dangerous gleam in her eyes, he thought that it would not be long before my lord would be living under the cat's foot, as the saying was. For a moment he wondered whether it might be possible to enlist her support, but only for a moment: my Lady Nettlecombe was concerned only with her own support. There was not a trace of womanly compassion in her eyes, and no softness beneath her determined smile.

The quarrel ended as abruptly as it had begun, my lady suddenly recollecting Desford's presence, and exclaiming: "Oh, whatever must Lord Desford be thinking of us, coming to cuffs like a couple of children over no more than a barley-straw?

138

You must excuse us, my lord! Well, they do say that the first year of marriage is difficult, don't they, and I'm sure my First and I had many a tiff, but no more than lovers' quarrels, like this little breeze me and my Second has just had!" She leaned forward to fondle her Second's unresponsive hand as she spoke, and adjured him, in sugared accents, not to put himself into a fuss over a mere shawl.

"I don't give a rush for what Desford thinks of me!" declared Nettlecombe, two hectic spots of colour burning in his cheeks. "Cocky young busy-head! Meddling in my affairs!"

"Oh, no!" Desford interposed. "Merely bringing your affairs to your notice, sir!"

Nettlecombe glared at him. "Wilfred's daughter is no affair of mine! It seems to me she's *your* affair, young man! Ay, and it seems to me there's something very havey-cavey about this! How did you come to be with her when she called at my house? Tell me that! It's my belief you ran off with her from her aunt's house, and now you're trying to be rid of her! Well, you're blowing at a cold coal! No man has ever contrived to put the change on *me!*"

Desford turned white with anger, and for an instant such an ugly look blazed in his eyes that Nettlecombe shrank back in his chair, and his spouse rushed forward, and dramatically commanded the Viscount to remember her lord's age and infirmities. It was unnecessary. The Viscount had already regained control over his temper, and although he was still pale with wrath, he was able to say in a level voice: "I do not forget it, ma'am. His lordship's infirmities seem to have affected his brain, and God forbid I should call a lunatic to account! If I allowed myself to follow my own inclinations I should leave this house immediately, but I am not here for any purpose of my own, but solely on behalf of an unfortunate child, who has no one but him to turn to, and so must suffer him to insult me with what patience I can muster!"

Nettlecombe, who had been scared out of his ungovernable fury, muttered something that might have been an apology, and

139

added, in a querulous tone: "Well, it *does* sound havey-cavey to me—and so it would to anyone!"

"It is not, however. I did not *run off* with Miss Steane from her aunt's house. Even if I were such a loose screw as to run off with any girl, you can hardly suppose that I could possibly do so after barely half-an-hour's conversation with her! I encountered her, the day after my one meeting with her, trudging along the post-road to London, quite unattended, and carrying a heavy portmanteau. I pulled up my horses, of course, and tried to discover what had led her to take such an imprudent —indeed, such an improper step! I shall not weary you with what she was induced to tell me: I will merely say that she was in great distress, and by far too young and inexperienced to have the least idea of what might be the disastrous consequences of her rashness. Her one thought was to reach *you,* sir—believing in her innocence that you would help her! Since you haven't hesitated to throw the grossest of insults at my head, I need not scruple to tell you that I didn't share her belief! I did what I could to persuade her to let me drive her back to her aunt's house, but I failed. She begged me instead to take her to London. We reached your house in the late afternoon, by which time I had seen enough of her to make me feel that no one, least of all a grandparent, could be hardhearted enough to turn her from his door. And in spite of the intemperate things you have said I still think that had you been at home, and had seen her, you must have taken pity on her. But you were not at home—which was almost as big a facer for me as it was for her! In the circumstances, I thought the best thing I could do was to take her to a very old friend of mine, and leave her in her charge until I could discover your whereabouts, and put her case before you. I trust I have now done so to your satisfaction."

"There's only one thing she can do. She must return to her aunt," said Nettlecombe. "*She* took the girl away from school, so it's *her* responsibility to look after her, not mine!"

"That's just what I was thinking!" nodded the lady.

"It is a waste of time to think it, ma'am: she won't go. I daresay she would liefer hire herself out as a cook-maid!"

140

"Well, and why shouldn't she?" demanded her ladyship, bristling. "I'm sure it's a very respectable calling, and there's plenty of chances for her to rise higher, if she has her wits about her, and gives satisfaction!"

"What have you to say to that, sir?" asked the Viscount. "Could you stomach the knowledge that your granddaughter was earning her bread as a servant?"

Nettlecombe uttered a brutal laugh. "Why not? I *married* one!"

This declaration not unnaturally took Desford's breath away. He found himself bereft of words; but on my lady it had quite another effect. She rounded on Nettlecombe, and said in a trembling voice: "I was never a servant of yours, and well you know it! I was your lady-housekeeper, and I'll thank you to remember it! The idea of you casting nasty aspersions at me! Don't you dare do so never no more, or you'll hear some homespeaking from me, my lord, and so I warn you!"

He looked a little ashamed, and more than a little apprehensive, and said hastily: "There, don't take a pet, Maria! I didn't mean it! The thing is that Desford has nettled me into such a flame that I hardly know what I'm saying. Not but what—However, let it rest! I'll give you a new bonnet!"

This offer led to an instant reconciliation, my lady even going so far as to embrace him, exclaiming: *"That's* more like my dear old Nettle!"

"Yes, but I'll go with you to choose it, mind!" said his lordship warily. "And as for Wilfred's brat, if you think you can palaver me into taking her into my house, Desford, I'll tell you once and for all I won't do it!"

"I don't think it. What I beg leave to suggest to you, sir, is that you should make her an allowance: enough to enable her to maintain herself respectably. Not a fortune, but an independence."

But this proposal made Nettlecombe's eyes start alarmingly in their sockets, with as much incredulity as dismay. He said in a choked voice: "Squander my money on that little gypsy? Do you take me for a cabbage-head?"

141

He received prompt support from his bride, who advised him strongly not to let himself be choused out of his blunt. She added, with great frankness, that for her part she had no notion of raking and scraping to save his blunt for him only to see it thrown away on a hurly-burly girl who had no claim on him. "It's bad enough for you to be obliged to grease Jonas's wheels," she said, "and when I think of the way he's behaved to me, trying to get you to turn me off, let alone coming the nob over me, it turns me downright queasy to think of him, and that niffy-naffy wife of his, living as high as coach-horses at *our* expense!"

The Viscount picked up his hat and gloves, and said contemptuously: "Very well, sir. If money means more to you than reputation there is nothing further to be said, and I'll take my leave of you."

"It does!" snapped Nettlecombe. "I care nothing for what anyone says of me—never have cared! And the sooner you take yourself off the better pleased I shall be!"

But the Viscount's words had made the bride look sharply at him, a shade of uneasiness in her face. She said, in a blustering manner: "I'm sure there's no reason why anyone should blame my lord! No one ever blamed him for disowning the girl's father, and he was his son!"

The Viscount, who had not missed that swift, faint look of uneasiness, replied, slightly raising his brows: "Well, that is not quite true, ma'am. It was acknowledged that he had been given great provocation, but a number of people considered that he had acted in a—let us say, in a way that was unbecoming in one who was not only a father, but a man of rank."

"Balderdash!" ejaculated Nettlecombe, flushing. "How do *you* know what anyone thought? You were in the schoolroom!"

"You must have forgotten, sir, that my father was one of those who did blame you," said the Viscount gently. "And—er—made no secret of his disapproval!"

As Lord Wroxton's disapproval had found expression in giving Nettlecombe the cut direct in full view of some dozen members of the ton, it was not surprising that the angry flush on

142

Nettlecombe's face deepened to a purple hue. He snarled: "Much I cared for Wroxton's opinion!" but his fingers curled themselves into claws, and he glared at Desford as though he would have liked to fix those claws round his throat.

"Furthermore," pursued Desford relentlessly, "whatever excuses might be found for your treatment of your son, none can be found for your behaviour towards his orphaned daughter, who is innocent of any fault, but is to become not only the victim of her father's improvidence but also of her grandfather's rancour!"

"Let 'em say what they choose! I don't care a button *what* they say!"

"They won't know anything about it!" said my lady. "My lord don't go about much nowadays, so——" She stopped, staring at Desford, who was smiling in a very disquieting way.

"Oh, yes, they will know, ma'am!" he said. "I pledge you my word the story will be all over town within a sennight!"

"Jackanapes! Rush-buckler!" Nettlecombe spat at him.

But at this point my lady quickly intervened, begging him not to fret himself into a fever. "It won't do to act hasty!" she urged. "You may not care for what people say of you, but it's my belief it's me as will be blamed! Even your friends have behaved very stiff to me, and I don't doubt but what they'd say it was my doing you wouldn't have anything to do with this girl, and that won't suit *me,* my lord, and no amount of argufying will make me say different!"

"And it won't suit me to waste my money on the girl! Next you'll be telling me it's my duty to buy her an annuity!"

"No, I shan't. It isn't to be expected that you should, nor that you should pay her an allowance, for who's to say when you might find it inconvenient to be obliged to shell out the ready—pay the allowance, I mean? I don't hold with allowances: it makes anyone fidgety to have a thing like that coming due every quarter. No, I've got a better notion in my noddle—better for the girl too! What she wants, poor little thing, is a home, and that's what you *can* give her, and without being purse-pinched. So why don't you write to her, and offer to take

143

her into the family? I'll see to it she don't worrit you, and she won't worrit me either. In fact, the more I think of it the more I feel I should *like* to have her. She'll be company for me."

"Take Wilfred's brat into the family?" he repeated, almost stunned.

She patted his hand. "Well, my lord here is in the right of it when he says it ain't her fault she's Wilfred's brat. I declare I feel downright sorry for her! And if it's expense you're thinking of, Nettle, I shouldn't wonder at it if she turned out to be an economy, because it wouldn't be an extra mouth to feed, for you know I paid off Betty before we left London, thinking it was a sinful waste of money to keep a girl just to mend the linen, and wash the chandeliers, and the best china, and lend old Lattiford a hand with the silver, and that. Mind you, it's a bigger waste of money keeping a butler that's as old and infirm as what he is, but you'd have to pension him off if you sent him packing, so while he *can* work it's best for us to keep him."

Nettlecombe, who had listened to her in gathering exasperation, said explosively: "No, I tell you! I won't have her in my house!"

"Allow me to set your mind at rest!" said Desford. "You will most certainly not have her in your house, sir! I didn't help her to escape from one slavery only to pitchfork her into another!"

He strode towards the door, ignoring a plea from my lady to wait. She followed him into the corridor, begging him not to take her lord's tetchiness amiss, and assuring him that he might rely on her to bring him round. "The thing is," she said earnestly, "that he's out of sorts, poor dear gentleman, and no wonder, with all the kick-up there's been, thinking he was going to lose me, because that shabster, Jonas, had the impudence to set it about that I was setting my cap at him, which I never did, nor thought of! All I thought of was to make him comfortable, which I promise you I did! What's more, I was the most saving housekeeper he'd ever had! But when that Jonas took to saying I was a man-trap, and warning his pa against me—*well!* I was obliged to tell his lordship I must leave at the term, because

I've got my good name to think about, haven't I? So his lordship made me an Offer, which is all the good Master Jonas got out of trying to be rid of me!" She ended on a triumphant note, but as the Viscount was wholly unresponsive, tightened her hold on his sleeve, and said ingratiatingly: "And as for making his granddaughter a *slave,* you quite mistook my meaning, my lord! I'm sure I wouldn't ask her to do anything I wouldn't do myself—yes, and have done, times out of mind! Not that I was born to it, mind you! Oh, dear me, no! I often think my poor father would have turned in his grave if he'd lived to see the straits I was reduced to, him having been cheated out of his inheritance, like he was, and my First losing his fortune, and leaving me without a souse, which is why I was forced to earn my own bread as best I could. No one knows better than me what it means to step down from one's rightful station, so if you was thinking Miss Steane would be a *servant* in her grandpa's house you're quite beside the bridge, my lord! She'll have a good home, and not be asked to do anything any genteel girl wouldn't be expected to do to help her ma!"

"You are wasting your breath, ma'am," he replied, inexorably removing her hand from his sleeve, and continuing his progress towards the stairs.

Baffled, she delivered a Parthian shot. "At any hand," she said shrilly, "you can't say it was me that wouldn't offer the girl a home!"

CHAPTER X

FOR SEVERAL minutes after he left Lord Nettlecombe's lodging the Viscount seethed with anger, but by the time he was half-way to the High town this had diminished, and the comical side of the late interview struck him, so forcibly that the sparkling look of wrath in his eyes vanished, and the hardened lines about his mouth relaxed. As he recalled some of the things which had been said he began to chuckle; and when he pictured the scenes which must have goaded Nettlecombe to marry the most economical housekeeper he had ever employed he found that he was within ames-ace of positively liking the vulgar creature.

He wished very much that there was someone with him to share the joke: Hetta, for instance, whose sense of the ridiculous was as lively as his own. He would tell her all about if, of course, but recounting an absurd experience was not the same as sharing it. It was to be hoped she didn't make the mistake of marrying that prosy fellow whom he had found dangling after her at Inglehurst, for he wouldn't suit her at all: he was just the kind of slow-top to ask her in a puzzled voice what she meant when she made a joke. Come to think of it, none of Hetta's suitors—and, lord, how many of them there had been!—had ever seemed to him worthy of her: queer that such an intelligent girl should be unable to recognize at a glance men who were quite beneath her touch! Recalling her numerous suitors he could not bring to mind one whom he had liked. There had been several dead bores amongst them; at least two bladders, who never stopped gabbing; and any number of men who were, in his opinion, very poor sticks indeed.

These reflections had led his mind away from the immediate problem confronting him, but the recollection of it soon recurred, and put an end to any desire in him to laugh at the failure of his mission, or to speculate on the strange vagaries of females. A less determined man might have felt that he had been tipped a settler, and have thrown his towel into the ring, but the Viscount had a streak of strong determination running through his easy-going nature, and he had no intention of being beaten on this, or any other, suit. He had certainly suffered a set-back, so what he must now do was to think of some other way of providing for Cherry's future well-being. None immediately occurred to him. He wondered what she was doing, whether she was happy at Inglehurst, or whether she was too anxious to be happy; and realized with a slight sense of shock that it was now nine days since he had left her there.

Had he but known it, Cherry was blissfully happy, and only now and then thought about her future. She had fitted into her surroundings as though she had lived at Inglehurst all her life; and she seemed to take as much pleasure in making herself useful to her hostesses as in the small parties Lady Silverdale gave to her neighbours. Indeed, Henrietta thought that she took more, for her disposition was retiring, and her shyness tied her tongue, so that when she was seated at the dinner-table beside a stranger her conversation was inclined to be monosyllabic. Henrietta ascribed this to Lady Bugle's treatment. She had relegated the poor child to the background, and had so systematically impressed upon her that she was far less important than her cousins, and must never put herself forward as though she thought herself their equal, that it had become second nature to her. Henrietta hoped that she would overcome her almost morbid shrinking from strangers for such excessive shyness was, in her view, a handicap to any penniless female obliged to make her own way in the world. It was unfortunate, too, that she was noticeably more ill-at-ease with the various young gentlemen who visited the house than with their fathers. However, once she became acquainted with them she grew less self-conscious, and chatted to them quite naturally. With Sir Charles, and young Mr Beckenham, she was soon on friendly terms; but she treated Tom Ellerdine, who showed a disposition to make her the object of his youthful gallantry, with marked reserve. Henrietta could not help feeling that it was a pity.

Lady Silverdale did not agree. "For my part," she said, "I

think her a very pretty-behaved girl. I own, my love, it quite astonishes me that she is not in the least pert, or *coming,* as so many girls are nowadays, for one never expected a Steane to be so well-conducted, and her mama was not at all the thing. Not that I ever knew her, because she eloped with Wilfred Steane out of the schoolroom, you know, which shows the most shocking want of delicacy, and just what one would expect in any sister of that Bugle woman!"

"Dear Mama, I am perfectly ready to join you in abusing Lady Bugle, but that is going too far!" expostulated Henrietta laughingly. "She is a horrid creature, but I'm persuaded that she is quite boringly respectable!"

"Good gracious, Hetta, how you do take one up!" Lady Silverdale complained. "You know very well what I mean! She's an excessively underbred woman, and that, you will allow, dear little Cherry is not! I think it remarkable that she shouldn't be, for we all know what the Steanes are like, and although I never heard anything said against the Wissets they did *not* move in the first circles. I believe old Mr Wisset was an attorney, or something of the sort. And when you consider that Cherry has had no other home than her aunt's house it has me in a puzzle to know how she came by her pretty, modest manners. She certainly cannot have learnt them from Amelia Bugle!"

"No, I fancy she must have learnt them from Miss Fletching," said Henrietta. "From what Cherry has told me, she must be an excellent woman—and it is to Mr Wilfred Steane's credit that he placed Cherry in her school, even if he did forget to pay the bills!"

"Well, it may be so," acknowledged Lady Silverdale, reluctant to perceive any saving grace in Mr Wilfred Steane's character, "but for my part I should rather suppose that he chose the first school that hit his eye. And I am much inclined to think that Cherry's manners spring from her disposition—so very amiable and obliging, and with such delicacy of principle! —than from any lesson Miss Fletching could have taught her. You know, dearest, how very rarely I take a fancy to anyone, but I own I have taken a strong fancy to Cherry, and shall miss her sadly when she leaves us. Indeed, if Nettlecombe refuses to adopt her, which wouldn't surprise me in the least, because he was always known to be as close as wax, and has become positively *freakish* of late years—I have a very good mind to keep her here!"

Henrietta, who knew well, not how rarely her mama took fancies to people, but how frequently she did, and how inevitably she discovered that she had been mistaken in the character of her latest protégée, was startled into exclaiming: "Handsomely over the bricks, Mama, I do beg of you! You have only known Cherry for a sennight!"

"I have known her for nine days," replied her ladyship, with dignity. "And I must request you, Hetta, not to employ vulgar slang when you are talking to me! Or to anyone, for it is not at all becoming in you! I have not the remotest conjecture what *handsomely over the bricks* may signify, but I collect that you have heard Charlie say it, and I must tell you that you are very ill-advised to copy the things young men say."

"Oh, don't blame Charlie, ma'am!" Henrietta said, her eyes alight with laughter. "It is what Desford says, when he thinks I am about to do something rash! But I should not have said it to you, and I beg your pardon! In—in unexceptionable language, I hope that you will consider carefully before you come to any decision about Cherry."

"Naturally I shall do so," said Lady Silverdale. "You may be sure of *that!*"

Henrietta was anything but sure of it, but she said no more, knowing that few things were more likely to goad Lady Silverdale into precipitate action than opposition from herself. Upon reflection she realized that she ought to have been prepared for the announcement which had startled her into uttering the slang phrase which had offended her mama's chaste ears for she had watched Cherry winning more and more approval, and had several times heard Lady Silverdale say that she couldn't conceive how she had ever contrived to exist without "our sweet little sunbeam". Well, there was nothing surprising in that: still less was it surprising that Lady Silverdale should be enjoying Cherry's visit, for Cherry was always ready to do whatever her kind hostess wished, and happily ran errands, unravelled tangled embroidery silks, went for tediously slow walks with her round the gardens, accompanied her on sedate drives in her landaulette, read aloud to her, and listened with unfeigned interest to her store of very dull anecdotes. These duties had hitherto fallen to Henrietta's lot, and although she had performed them cheerfully they had bored her very much, and none of them more than listening to reminiscences which had been told her many times before, and reading aloud absurdly romantic and adventurous novels, for which form of literature Lady Silverdale had an incurable passion. But three days after Cherry's arrival at Inglehurst Henrietta contracted a slight cold, which made her throat too sore for reading aloud, and she had suggested that Cherry might take her place until she had recovered from her trifling indisposition. She had apologized to Cherry for saddling her with a task which she feared she would think abominably dull, but Cherry had said that indeed she wouldn't think it dull, and the wonder was that she didn't. At least, it seemed wonderful at the outset, but it was soon brought home to Henrietta that Cherry's literary taste exactly matched Lady Silverdale's. Never having been permitted by Miss Fletching to read novels, she was instantly entranced by the specimen Henrietta gave her, entering into all the hapless heroine's alarms, adoring the hero, hating the villain, uncritically accepting every extravagance of the plot, and eagerly discussing with Lady Silverdale how the story would end. Almost as absorbing did she find the *Mirror of Fashion,* a monthly periodical to which Lady Silverdale subscribed, and was ready to pore over it for as long as Lady Silverdale pleased. It had to be admitted that with all the advantages of a pretty face, engaging manners, and sweetness of disposition, one attribute had been denied her: she was regrettably lacking in intellect. Henrietta thought that when the ingenuousness of youth left her she would be as foolish as Lady Silverdale (though probably not as indolent), and a sad bore to any man of superior sense, for she was interested only in trivialities and domestic matters, and had very little understanding of wider issues. To

151

Henrietta, who possessed considerable force of mind, this made her no more companionable than a small child would have been, but it suited Lady Silverdale admirably, and would possibly suit some other elderly and rather silly lady just as well. But what a bleak prospect for an affectionate girl, crying out to be loved and cherished! Henrietta sighed over it, but could see no other solution to the problem of her future, if Nettlecombe refused to acknowledge her. The realization that her mother had taken it into her head to keep Cherry with her seriously dismayed her. No dependence could be placed on Lady Silverdale's continuing to dote on the girl: at any moment she might take her in dislike; and even if she did not do that she would almost certainly find her an irksome burden when the family removed to London, which they always did in the spring, and she became engaged in too many social activities to have the smallest need of any other attendant than her dresser. In London, Cherry would inevitably be regarded as that tiresome Extra Female, the bane of all hostesses, and could count herself fortunate if the sudden indisposition of one of the invited ladies led to her inclusion in some of her ladyship's dinner-parties. To suppose that Lady Silverdale's matchmaking instincts would prompt her to find a suitable husband for Cherry was to indulge fancy far beyond the bounds of probability: they were concentrated on her daughter, whose obstinate spinsterhood constituted almost the only flaw in her otherwise carefree existence. In a year or two she would no doubt be seeking a bride for her adored son, but at no time would she think it incumbent upon her to find a mate for Cherry.

The thought of her brother caused Henrietta to feel a twinge of uneasiness. It had not occurred to Lady Silverdale that he might seek distraction in his enforced stay at Inglehurst by pursuing an à suivie flirtation with Cherry, but Henrietta laboured under no delusions about him, and she knew that he had begun to look far more favourably upon Cherry than when he had first seen her. He no longer spoke contemptuously of her as a snippety-thing, but had described her to at least two of Lady Silverdale's morning visitors as a taking little puss. Henrietta did not for a moment suppose that he had any serious intention in mind; and she had a shrewd suspicion that Cherry's friendly manner towards him rose from a very proper wish to avoid offending the suscepti- bilities of his mother and sister, and not at all from a desire to encourage his advances. She had at first been very shy of him, but that, naturally, had worn off, as she became better acquainted with him, and it was not many days before she was able to take him very much for granted, behaving towards him with little more ceremony than she would have used towards an elder brother. She fetched and carried for him, and sought to divert him by playing cribbage and backgammon and draughts with him, or even such infantile games as span-counters, in which his superior skill was counterbalanced by his inability to use his right hand. She did these things because she was sorry for him, and anxious to help his mother and sister to keep him amused; but although she enjoyed playing such games and was young enough to be intent on proving herself a match for him, Henrietta did not think that she liked him very much. That made Henrietta sigh again. Not that she wanted Cherry to fall a victim to Charlie's lures, but she did wish that Cherry were not so in- different to every young man she met, for her indifference, coupled as it was with a tongue-tied shyness, did not make her appear to advantage. The only men with whom she was natural and at ease were nearly all of them old enough to have fathered her; or, if not quite so middle-aged, too old to be considered as possible suitors, at all events. She certainly liked Desford, but although in years he was only ten years her senior, in experience he was at least twenty years older; and Henrietta believed (and hoped) that she regarded him in the light of a protector, not as a possible suitor. Cary Nethercott, and Sir James Radcliffe had also won her liking, but both these kindly gentlemen were in their thirties, which was probably why she didn't retire into her shell when they came to Inglehurst, but chatted away to them in the most natural style imaginable. She even told Mr Nethercott all about the lurid romance she was reading to Lady Silverdale, when she was seated beside him at dinner one evening. Henrietta heard her doing it, and was moved to silent admiration of the good-nature which made him listen with apparent interest to the tangled story that was being described to him.

As for Charlie, she had little doubt that if some dashing beauty were to come within his ken he would have no thoughts to spare for Cherry. Unfortunately, there were no dashing beauties living in the vicinity, and very few unattached young females of any description. Whether it was unfortunate that his particular cronies, none of whom hailed from Hertfordshire, were either disporting themselves at Brighton, or had retired to their parental homes in distant parts of the country, to recover from the ravages to their constitutions and purses caused by too many sprees, jollifications, and revel-routs, was a moot point. Lady Silverdale was for ever saying that if only two or three of his friends lived within visiting-distance they could have ridden over to entertain him; and she even went so far as to suggest to him that he should invite one of them to spend a week or two at Inglehurst. He spurned the notion, saying ungraciously that his friends would think it curst flat to be stuck down in the country with nothing to do all day, and nothing to enliven the evenings but short whist, or half-guinea commerce. Having uttered this disagreeable speech, he found that his sister had raised her eyes from her book and was steadily regarding him from under lifted brows. He coloured, and begged his mother's pardon, saying: "I didn't mean to be uncivil, ma'am, but you don't understand how it is! I mean—oh, dash it, how could it be possible to invite anyone to visit me when I can't ride, or drive, or play billiards, or—or *anything?*"

Lady Silverdale saw the force of this argument; but as she continued to regret it for the next twenty minutes Henrietta could hardly blame Charlie for dragging himself up from the sofa, and walking out of the room.

She was sorry for him, but she had suspected long since that his haggard appearance and slow recovery from his injuries were due not so much to his accident, but to the dissipated life he had been leading, in the company of those choice spirits who, in her private opinion, belonged to a fast, rackety set, and were rapidly ruining his character. The suspicion had been confirmed by the

154

Squire, who had visited him two days after his accident, and had told her bluntly that it was just as well that the young ram-stam *had* knocked himself up. He was one of Charlie's trustees, and had been intimately acquainted with both him and his sister all their lives, and he saw no need to mince his words. He said that what Charlie wanted was a long repairing lease. "Been going the pace, m'dear: only have to look at him to know that! I warned your mother he was too callow to be let loose on the town, but all she would do was to talk gibble-gabble about not keeping him tied to her apron-strings, and having complete confidence in him, and a lot more to that tune. 'All very well,' I told her, 'if the boy's father were alive, or he had elder brothers, or a *male* guardian, to tell him how he should go on, and warn him against the things no female knows anything about, but——' Oh, well! No use crying over spilt milk, so I'll say no more. Though how your father, as shrewd a man as ever I knew, could have allowed her ladyship to bamboozle him into appointing her to be Charlie's guardian—Well, well, my tongue runs away with me, but you're a sensible girl, Hetta, and you won't take it amiss! We must hope that this latest bit of folly will have taught Charlie a lesson!" He refreshed himself with a pinch of snuff, and added, in a heartening tone: "No reason why he shouldn't turn out to be as good a man as his father! Most codlings take time to find their feet, y'know, Hetta! Best thing for him would be to get himself buckled to a nice girl! He's been philandering after dashing women of fashion, but there's no harm in that! He don't have petticoat affairs with straw damsels, and you may take it from me that's true, for I've had my eye on him, ever since he set up for himself in London!"

"What can I do, Sir John?" she asked straitly.

"Can't do anything!" he answered, restoring his snuff-box to the capacious pocket of his riding-coat. "Just try what you can to keep him amused, so that he don't run off before he's in better point than he is now!"

With this piece of advice she had to be satisfied, but she found it almost impossible to follow. The only things that amused Charlie were the country-sports which he was debarred from

155

pursuing, and almost every variety of gaming. To do him justice, he enjoyed, for their own sake, such games as offered a challenge to his skill, but Henrietta, who played a good game at chess, had so little card-sense that it bored him to play with her. Cherry, on the other hand, had neither the desire nor the ability to master the intricacies of chess, but she possessed a certain quickness which enabled her to grasp the rules and the objects of any card game he taught her, and to play well enough to make him declare that it wouldn't be long before she became a dashed dangerous opponent.

"Such a good thing, dearest!" Lady Silverdale confided to her daughter. "At last we have hit upon something that keeps him tolerably well entertained! Gentlemen, you know, always like to *instruct* one, but they are much inclined to be vexed when people like you and me, my love, show no aptitude, or, at any hand, don't instantly comprehend what they tell us. What a fortunate circumstance it is that dear little Cherry has a turn for cards! I declare I am positively grateful to Desford for having brought her to me!"

But two days later Cherry's star suffered a temporary eclipse, when the most longstanding of Lady Silverdale's cicisbeos was so ill-advised as to beg her to bestow on him one of the roses she was carrying into the house. With playful gallantry he insisted that she should put it into his buttonhole with her own fair hands, saying that it would smell the sweeter. Since she regarded him in the light of a grandparent, which indeed he was, she complied with his requests, but could not help giggling a little at the fulsome compliment he had paid her. Lady Silverdale, on the other hand, was not amused; and for an anxious moment Henrietta feared that Cherry's popularity had already come to an end. Happily, Lady Silverdale's faithful admirer had the wit to say (after one look at her stiffening countenance) that he was glad Cherry had gone into the house, because he never knew what to say to chits of her age, adding, as he sat down again on the rustic seat beside my lady: "Now we can be comfortable together, my lady!" This mollified her so much that instead of scolding Cherry she merely warned her not to encourage strange gentlemen to flirt with her. But even this mild reproof made startled tears spring to Cherry's eyes as she exclaimed in trembling accents: "Oh, no, no! Indeed I didn't! I thought he was being kind to me because you had asked him to be, ma'am!" She added imploringly, as the tears coursed down her face: "Don't be vexed with me! Pray don't be vexed with me, dear, dear Lady Silverdale! I can't bear you to be displeased with me, for I wouldn't displease you for the world, after all your goodness to me!"

Much touched by this speech, Lady Silverdale melted completely, to the extent of shedding a few tears herself; and within the hour told her dresser, when that jealous spinster uttered a sly criticism of Cherry, that she was a nasty, ill-natured creature, and if she ever again dared to speak of Miss Steane as *That* Miss Steane she would find herself turned off without a character. Upon which, Cardle too burst into tears, but as this display of sensibility was accompanied by lamentations that her own virtues should go unrecognized, and a pious hope that my lady would learn before it was too late who were her real friends, Lady Silverdale was easily able to refrain from succumbing to her own tendency to become lachrymose upon the smallest provocation. She accepted an apology from Cardle, but with chilly dignity; and immediately went off to tell Henrietta that Cardle was growing to be intolerably bumptious, and that if it weren't for the circumstances of her being such an excellent dresser she would be much inclined to get rid of her. Henrietta knew, of course, that nothing would prevail upon her to put this threat into execution, but her mother's account of the painful scene which had taken place, made her heart sink. Nothing, she thought, could have more surely increased Cardle's jealousy of one whom she persisted in believing to be her rival. She embarked on the task of peace-making, soothing her ruffled parent by agreeing that Cardle was detestably uppish, but saying that she was so devoted to her mistress that she resented it if even Mama's own daughter dared to perform any service for her which she regarded as her sole prerogative. "Do, pray, say something kind to her, Mama, when she puts you to bed to-

157

night! She'll cry herself to sleep, if she thinks you are still angry with her!"

These tactics succeeded very well with Lady Silverdale, but Henrietta failed to induce any softening of Cardle's heart towards Cherry. Not even a casual reference to the probability that Cherry's visit would soon come to an end had the least effect on Cardle. "And the sooner the better, miss!" she said tartly. "*One* thing's certain! The day my lady invites her to *live* here is the day I leave this house! I pity you, Miss Hetta, having your nose put out of joint by that designing little hussy, and being taken in by her coaxing ways, every bit as much as my poor deluded mistress is! And it's no good telling me I've got no business to say she's a designing hussy, which I wouldn't have presumed to do if you hadn't opened the subject, for I know what I know, and I hope and pray you won't regret your kindness to her!"

Henrietta went down to dinner fervently hoping, for her part, that Desford's return from Harrowgate would not be long delayed.

In fact, it was delayed for longer than the Viscount had anticipated, for his journey south was not attended by the good fortune which had made his northward journey so speedy. A series of mishaps befell him, the most serious of which, the loss of a tyre, kept him kicking his heels for a day and a half, this accident occurring on the first day out from Harrowgate, which happened to be a Saturday, midway between Chesterfield and Mansfield. By the time the chaise bumped its way into Mansfield it was too late for the necessary repair to be effected, and on the Sunday the premises of both the wheelwright and the blacksmith were found to be closed: the one because its owner was a stern opposer of Sunday Travel; the other because the smith had gone off to spend the day with his married sister. It was not until Monday morning was merging into Monday afternoon that a new tyre was fitted to the wheel, and the Viscount was able to proceed on his way. And then (proving to him his belief that his luck had run out) one of his wheelers went dead lame, so that his progress to the next post-house more nearly resembled a funeral cortège than the swift journey of a gentleman of wealth and fashion. What with this, and several minor hindrances, it was four days before he reached Dunstable, where he decided to put up for the night, since there were still almost thirty miles to cover to Inglehurst, and he had no wish to arrive there long after the dinner-hour.

So it was not until a fortnight after he had deposited Cherry at Inglehurst that Henrietta, a little before noon, was at last gratified by having him ushered into her presence. Grimshaw announced him, in a sepulchral voice, and she started up out of her chair in front of the writing-desk, exclaiming impulsively: "Oh, Des, I am so thankful you've come at last!"

"Good God, Hetta, what's amiss?" he demanded, brought up short in his advance across the room.

"Nothing!—that is to say, I *hope* nothing, but I am much afraid that things are beginning to go amiss." He had taken her hands in his, and kissed them both, and was still holding them in his strong clasp, but she gently drew them away, and said, scanning his face: "Your errand hasn't prospered, has it?"

He shook his head. "No. Nettlecombe has become an April-gentleman!"

Her eyes widened. *"Married?"* she asked incredulously.

"That's it: leg-shackled to his housekeeper—oh, I beg her pardon! his *lady*-housekeeper!"

"Ah!" she said, with a twinkle of perfect comprehension. "No doubt she told you so herself!"

He grinned at her. "No, she told Nettlecombe, when *he* told me that he had married his cook. She said she would thank him to remember it, too, and I don't doubt he will. Oh, Hetta, you can't think how much I longed for you to be present at that interview! You must have laughed yourself into stitches!"

She moved to the sofa, and sat down, patting the place beside her. "Tell me!" she invited.

He did tell her, and she appreciated the story just as he had known she would. But he ended on a sober note, when, having described the final scene, in the corridor, he paused for an instant, before saying abruptly: "Hetta, I *could* not thrust that unfortunate child into such a household!"

"No," she agreed, her own brow as troubled as his. "Only— Des, what is to be done with her? Mama said, a week ago, that if Nettlecombe repudiated her she had a good mind to keep her here, but—it wouldn't do—I *know* it wouldn't do! It is always the same when Mama takes a violent fancy to anyone! At first she thinks the new treasure perfect, and then she begins to perceive faults in her—and even when they are quite trivial faults she exaggerates them in her mind, and—which is worse!—remembers them, and adds them on to the next error her wretched favourite falls into!"

"Good God, has it come to that? Poor Cherry!"

"No, no, not yet!" she assured him. "But she has begun to criticize her—oh, not unkindly! merely noticing little innocent habits, or tricks of speech, and saying that she wishes Cherry would rid herself of them. And that odious woman of hers is so jealous of Cherry that she never loses an opportunity to drop poison into Mama's ears. So far, she hasn't succeeded in turning Mama against poor Cherry, but I own to you, Des, that I can't persuade myself that——"

"Don't tease yourself!" he interrupted. "There can be no question of Cherry's remaining here! I never for a moment had such a solution to the problem in my mind. I had hoped to have left her with you only for a very few days, but I didn't discover Nettlecombe's whereabouts until Monday of last week, and even when I did discover that he had gone to Harrowgate I couldn't induce his man of business to divulge his exact direction, and was obliged to spend the better part of two days scouring the town for him."

"Oh, poor Des! No wonder you are looking so tired!"

"Am I? Well, if I am it's only because I had the most devilish journey up from Yorkshire," he said cheerfully. "No sooner did we get over one check than we fell into another, which is why I'm so late showing my front, as Horace would say. However, I've had time to decide what I had best do for Cherry—and that's the most urgent matter I want you to consider, my best of friends!"

The door opened. "Mr Nethercott!" announced Grimshaw.

Cary Nethercott trod into the room, but checked at sight of the Viscount, and said: "I beg pardon! Grimshaw must have misunderstood me! I enquired for Lady Silverdale, and he ushered me into this room, where—where I can only trust that I am not intruding, Miss Hetta!"

"Not at all," she responded, rising, and shaking hands with him. "You have already met Lord Desford, haven't you?"

The gentlemen exchanged bows. Mr Nethercott said painstakingly that he had indeed had that pleasure, and the Viscount said nothing at all. Mr Nethercott then explained he had ridden over to bring Lady Silverdale his copy of the last number of the *New Monthly Magazine,* which contained an interesting article which he had mentioned to her ladyship on the occasion of his last visit, and which she had expressed a desire to read.

"How very kind of you!" said Henrietta. "She has gone for a stroll in the shrubbery, with Miss Steane."

"Oh, then I will take it to her myself!" he said, his cheeks slightly reddening. "I shall hope to see you again presently, Miss Hetta!" He then said: "Your servant, sir!" and bowed himself out of the room.

The Viscount, who had been eyeing him with disfavour, hardly waited for the door to be shut before demanding: "Does that fellow *live* at Inglehurst, Hetta?"

"No," replied Henrietta calmly. "He lives at Marley House."

"Well, he seems to be here every time *I* come to visit you!" said the Viscount irritably.

She wrinkled her brow, and, after apparently cudgelling her memory, said, with a wholly spurious air of innocence: "But had you met him before you came to visit us on your way to Hazelfield?"

The Viscount ignored this home-question, and said: "I wonder which of us he thought he was hoaxing with his gammon about the *New Monthly?* Lord, what a fimble-famble!" He did not resume his seat, but glanced frowningly down at Henrietta,

161

and said, with unaccustomed asperity: "I can't conceive why you —No, never mind! What were we saying when that fellow interrupted us?"

"You were about to tell me what you have decided will be the best thing to do for Cherry," she replied. "The most urgent question to be considered—or, rather, which you wish me to consider."

"Yes, so I was. There are other things I should wish to talk about, but until I've provided for her Cherry must be my only concern."

"Provided for her?" she repeated, her eyes lifting quickly to his face.

"Yes, of course. What else can I do but try to establish her comfortably? It was no doing of mine when she ran away from Maplewood, but when I drove her to London I became responsible for her: there's no getting away from that, Hetta! Good God, what a shabster I should be if I abandoned her now!"

"Very true. What scheme have you in mind?" she asked. "I have thought that—that marriage is the only answer to the problem, only—her parentage, and her want of fortune must stand in the way—don't you think?"

He nodded, but said: "Not in the way of a man who fell in love with her, and had no need of a rich wife. But that's for the future: my concern is for the immediate present. I'm going to Bath, to try if I can persuade Miss Fletching to help Cherry. Has she spoken to you about her? She was at Miss Fletching's school, and talked to me about her on the way to London, saying how kind she had been."

"Yes, indeed she has, and most affectionately, but when I suggested to her that she might return to that school, as a teacher, rather than hire herself out as a companion, she said Miss Fletching would have offered her that position if she had had enough learning, or enough skill on the pianoforte to teach music. Only she hadn't. And I am afraid, Des, that that is true. Her only skill is in stitchery. She has the most amiable disposition in the world, but she is not at all bookish, you know. If Miss Fletching were to offer to take her I am very sure she

162

would refuse, because she feels herself to be under a heavy obligation to her already."

"I know she does. And if I were to pay Miss Fletching the debt that is owing to her——"

"No, Desford!" Henrietta said stringently. "You mustn't do that! She is by far too proud to countenance such a thing!"

"Not, surely, if she supposed I had prevailed upon Nettlecombe to tip over the dibs!"

"If she believed you she would write to thank him."

"I should tell her that he had paid Miss Fletching on condition that she neither wrote to him nor attempted to see him ever again. It is exactly what he *would* say, too!"

She smiled, but shook her head. "It won't do. Only consider what an uncomfortable situation she would be in if ever it became known that you had paid Miss Fletching to give her a home! You must consider your own situation as well: you would compromise yourself as much as Cherry. You know what all the tattle-boxes would say! And it is useless to suppose that the secret wouldn't leak out, because you may depend upon it that it would."

The smile was reflected in his eyes, but he said ruefully: "I've wondered about that. I hoped you would tell me I was being absurd—but I had a pretty shrewd notion you wouldn't! You're right, of course. So I shall lay the whole case before Miss Fletching, and ask her if she knows of anyone residing in Bath who would be glad to employ Cherry. There must be scores of elderly invalids there: whenever I've visited the place it has always seemed to me to teem with decrepit old ladies! And if she must seek such a post I think Bath would be the best place for her. She would have Miss Fletching to turn to, and I know she has other acquaintances in the town whom she would be able to visit."

The tiny crease vanished from between her brows; she exclaimed: "Yes, that would be the very thing for her! But not, Des, if *you* recommend her to a prospective employer!"

"I thought it wouldn't be long before you made me stand the roast, my sweet wit-cracker," he observed appreciatively. "How fortunate it is that you should have warned me—such a slow-top as I am!"

She laughed. "No, no, not a *slow-top,* Ashley! But dreadfully imprudent when you take one of your quixotic notions into your head!"

"Lord, Hetta, you must have windmills in your own head! I've never done such a thing in my life! Now, stop funning! If I'm to post off to Bath tomorrow, I've precious little time to waste—and, all things considered, I fancy it will be as well if I leave from here before Cherry comes in. I should be obliged to tell her what I mean to do, and if she didn't try to stop me, but liked the scheme, I don't wish to raise what might prove to be a false hope."

"But she's bound to know that you've been here!" protested Henrietta. "What am I to say to her, pray?"

"Tell her that I called here, but was unable to stay more than a few minutes, because I have an urgent appointment in London, and only broke my journey to tell her that although I couldn't bring old Nettlecombe up to scratch I haven't abandoned her, but—but have now hit upon a fresh plan for her relief. Which I didn't disclose to you, for fear it might not come to anything!"

"Banbury man!"

"No. I do fear it may come to nothing! By the by, has Lady Bugle tried to make her return to Maplewood?"

"No—and that puts me in mind of something I must tell you! Lady Bugle doesn't know where she is, because when I suggested to Cherry that she should write to her she became so much agitated that I let the matter drop. But I should warn you that although Lady Bugle doesn't know she's here she does know that you had something to do with her flight. And that brings me to another thing I must tell you. Lord and Lady Wroxton know she is at Inglehurst."

"Oh, my God!" he ejaculated. "As though I hadn't enough to deal with! Who was the tale-pitcher who carried that news to Wolversham?"

"My dear Ashley, you cannot, surely, have forgotten how inevitably the smallest piece of news flies round the county!

Steward's gossip, but in this case it reached Wolversham by way of one of the chambermaids, who is the daughter of our head groom. Lady Wroxton gave her leave to come to Inglehurst, on the occasion of her parents' silver wedding—and *so* you can wish for no further explanation!"

He was regarding her intently. "That's not the whole story, is it?"

"No, not quite. Lord and Lady Wroxton visited us two days ago."

"If my father undertook a drive of sixteen miles, either his gout has spent itself, or he must have supposed me to be on the verge of disgracing him!" interjected the Viscount.

"Well, he was walking with a stick, but I think he *is* much improved in health," said Henrietta, forgiving this rude interruption for the sake of the balm it applied to her sorely troubled heart. "They came to enquire after Charlie—at least, that was what Lord Wroxton told Mama—but their real purpose, I am very sure, was to discover the truth of the story they had heard. I didn't have much conversation with Lord Wroxton, but your mama made an excuse to take me apart, and she asked me, without any roundaboutation, to tell her if it was true that you had brought Cherry here, and, if so, why you had done so. She said that I need not scruple to open my budget to her, because she was very sure that you had a good reason for having done so. Des, I do like your mama so much!"

"Yes, so do I," he agreed cordially. "She's a right one! What did you tell her?"

"I told her the truth, exactly as you told it to me. And she then disclosed to me that she had received a letter from your aunt Emborough, saying that Lady Bugle had called upon her, demanding to know what *you* had done with Cherry. It seems that one of her daughters—I can't recall her name, but I know it was most extraordinary——"

"They all have extraordinary names—all five of 'em!"

"Good gracious! Well, this one seems to have been on the listen when you talked to Cherry, that night at the ball; and when it was discovered that Cherry had run away, she put it into

Lady Bugle's head that she had gone off with you! How Lady Bugle can have believed such a nonsensical story I can't conceive, but apparently she did, and at once drove over to Hazelfield to demand of Lady Emborough what were your intentions! Lady Emborough wrote to your mama that she had laughed to scorn the idea that you had had anything to do with Cherry's flight, and had assured Lady Bugle that so far from stealing Cherry away from Maplewood at dawn you had been eating breakfast at Hazelfield at ten o'clock. But she also wrote that she was burning to know whether you *had* had anything to do with Cherry's escape, because she recalled that it had seemed to her that you were much more interested in Cherry than in her cousin, who is a singularly beautiful girl."

"Lucasta," he nodded. "I was, but never mind that! My aunt wrote to my mother, you say. She hasn't divulged any of this to my father, has she?"

"No, and your mother hasn't shown him her letter. But it was he who first heard the local tittle-tattle, and I have a very shrewd notion that it was he who insisted on coming to visit us, to discover how true it was. Or, rather, that your mama should do so! You know what he is, Des!"

"None better! He would think it beneath him to betray the least interest in the exploits of his sons—to anyone, of course, but the sons themselves!"

"Exactly so!" she said, with a twinkle. "Most fortunately, this visit was paid when Mama was feeling particularly pleased with Cherry, for having found a lace flounce which was thought to have been thrown away years ago, so I am quite certain she must have spoken of her to Lord Wroxton with the warmest approbation!"

"Did he see Cherry?"

"Yes, certainly he did—but whether he liked her or not I don't know! He was perfectly civil to her, at all events."

"That's nothing to judge by," said Desford. "He would be, even if he had taken her in dislike. Well, there's nothing for it: I shall have to sleep at Wolversham tonight, which means a further delay. I'm sorry for it, Hetta, but you see how I'm fixed, don't you? I don't ask you if you are willing to keep Cherry here for a few more days, because I know what your answer would be. Bless you, my dear!" He possessed himself of her hands, and again kissed them, and with no more words took his departure.

CHAPTER XI

THE VISCOUNT'S reception at Wolversham was unexpectedly benign. It did not surprise him that Pedmore should greet
him with a beaming smile, and say, as he relieved him of his hat
and his gloves: "Well, my lord, this *is* a pleasant surprise!" because he knew that Pedmore held him, and both his brothers,
in deep affection; but he smiled a little wryly when Pedmore
said: "His lordship *will* be pleased to see you, sir! My lady is
taking her afternoon rest, but you will find his lordship in the
library. Will you be making a long stay, my lord?"

"No: only one night," the Viscount replied. "Will you give
orders for the housing of the post-boys? But of course you will!"

"Of *course* I will, my lord!" said Pedmore fondly.

The Viscount, having assured himself, by a swift glance at the
Chippendale mirror which hung in the hall, that the folds of his
neckcloth had not become disarranged, or his shining locks
ruffled—two possibilities certain to incur censure from his father
—trod resolutely towards the double-doors which opened into
the library. He paused for a moment before entering the room,
bracing himself to face what he felt sure (in spite of Pedmore's
encouraging words) would be a pretty sulphurous reception; but
when Lord Wroxton looked up from the journal he was perusing
to see who had come into the room he said nothing more alarming than: "Ha! Is that you, Desford? Glad to see you, my boy!"

Admirably overcoming his astonishment, the Viscount crossed
the floor to the wing-chair in which my lord was sitting, duti-
fully kissed the hand which was held out to him, and said, with
his attractive smile: "Thank you, sir! For my part, *I* am very
glad to see *you,* with your foot out of cotton at last! Are you in
as plump currant as you look to be?"

"Oh, I'm in pretty good point!" said his lordship boastfully.
"The last time I saw you you said I was all skin and whipcord,

jackanapes, but damme if you didn't nick the nick! It'll be a long trig before you step into my shoes!"

"So I should hope!" retorted the Viscount. "Don't try to bamboozle *me* into thinking you're in your dotage, and are likely to stick your spoon in the wall at any moment, because I know to a day how old you are, sir!"

The Earl, apostrophizing him as an impudent whipster, told him that if he thought he could talk in such an improper style to his father he would very soon learn how mistaken he was; but he was secretly rather pleased, as he always was (except when his temper was exacerbated by gout) when any of his sons showed themselves to be full of what he called proper spunk. So, having, for form's sake, read the Viscount a brief scold, he bade him sit down, and tell him what he had been doing since he was last at Wolversham.

"That's what I've come to do," said the Viscount. "And since I've no more liking for beating about the bush than you have, sir, I'll tell you at once that I've driven over from Inglehurst, where I learned of your visit there."

"I thought as much!" said the Earl. "Come to beg me to help you out of this scrape you've got yourself into, have you?"

"No, nothing of that sort," responded Desford. "Merely to give you a round tale, which—since I understand you learned by way of the backstairs of Cherry Steane's presence at Inglehurst, and that it was I who took her there—I'm tolerably certain you haven't yet heard."

"I'm well aware of that!" said his father, his eyes kindling. "And before you say any more, Desford, let me tell you that I set no store by servants' gossip—least of all when it concerns any of my sons!"

The Viscount smiled at him. "Of course you don't, sir. But it did send you to Inglehurst to discover what I *had* been doing to give rise to such gossip, didn't it? I don't blame you: it must have seemed to you that I was up to my chin in some devilish havey-cavey doings. Hetta could have told you why I placed Cherry in her care, but she says you didn't ask her any questions at all."

170

"Do you imagine that I would ask her, or anyone else, prying questions about my sons?" demanded the Earl, bristling. "Upon my word, Desford, if that's the opinion you hold of me you have gone your length!"

"I know you far too well, Papa, to hold any such opinion," replied the Viscount imperturbably. "For which reason I've thought it best to open the whole budget to you myself."

"Then cut line and do so!" commanded his father sternly.

Thus encouraged, Desford disclosed to him, in unvarnished terms, the history of the past two weeks. The Earl listened to him in silence, and with a frown drawing his brows together over his hard, piercing eyes. It did not relax when the Viscount came to the end of his recital, but all he said was: "In the briars, aren't you?"

"I may be in the briars," retorted Desford, "but I'm not at Point Non-Plus, sir, believe me!"

The Earl grunted. "What do you mean to do if this school-dame you talk about don't come up to scratch?"

"Try a fresh cast!"

The Earl grunted again, and his frown deepened. After a long pause, during which he bore all the appearance of being engaged in a struggle with himself, he said, as though the words were being forced out of him: "You're of age, you're independent of me, you can please yourself, but—I beg of you, Desford, don't think yourself obliged, in honour, to marry the girl!"

The Viscount said gently: "I don't think it, sir, for I have in no way compromised her. But I do think that I am bound, in honour, to befriend her."

His father nodded, but said, in sudden exasperation: "I wish to God you had left Sophronia's house an hour earlier!"

"Well," said Desford, with a twisted smile, "between ourselves, sir, so do I! At least—No, I don't wish it, when I think of what might have befallen that pretty, foolish child if I hadn't overtaken her on the road. But I certainly wish I hadn't accepted my aunt's invitation to stay at Hazelfield!"

"No good ever yet came from crying over spilt milk, so we'll leave that! You've got yourself into a rare bumble-bath, but it might have been worse." He pulled his snuff-box out of his pocket, and helped himself to a pinch. He then said abruptly: "I've met the girl. I don't scruple to own to you that I went over to Inglehurst for that purpose, and I'm glad I did, for I saw at a glance that she isn't the sort of highflyer *you* dangle after."

Desford laughed. "Pray, sir, how do you know what sort of highflyers I dangle after?"

"I know more than you think, my boy!" said his lordship, grimly pleased with himself. "When I first heard of this business, I was afraid you'd lost your head over the girl, and meant to become riveted to her. You wouldn't have taken a lightskirt to the Silverdales. And if you were meaning to become a tenant-for-life you wouldn't have brought her here, for you know well I'd do my utmost to prevent your marrying into *that* family! Another possibility was that she'd snared you—Yes, yes, I know you've plenty of rumgumption, but wiser men than you have been trapped by designing females! To tell you the truth, I was prepared to buy her off, but I cut my wisdoms before you were born, and it didn't take me more than a couple of minutes to realize that she was nothing but a schoolroom miss—pretty enough, but not your style of female, and damned shy into the bargain! So now, Desford, perhaps you'll have the goodness to tell me why you didn't bring her here, instead of planting her on Lady Silverdale?"

The Viscount, who had foreseen that this question would sooner or later be shot at him, flung up a hand, in the gesture of a fencer acknowledging a hit, and said, with a comical look of guilt: "Peccavi, Papa! I didn't dare to!"

His father gave a crack of laughter, which he instantly suppressed, saying: "I suppose I must consider it *some* comfort that in spite of your faults you are at least honest! I collect you dared not bring her here for fear that I might be so lost to all sense of propriety as to have driven the pair of you out of the house. Much obliged to you, Desford!"

"Papa, how *can* you rip up at me so unkindly?" said Desford reproachfully. "I thought nothing of the sort—as well you know! —but I did think that it would make you as cross as crabs if

172

I saddled you and Mama with Wilfred Steane's daughter. If you tell me that I was wrong, I have nothing to do but to beg your pardon for having so wickedly misjudged you—but *was* I wrong, sir?"

The Earl eyed him in fulminating silence for several minutes, but at last replied, in the voice of one driven into the last ditch: "No, damn you!"

"If I'm honest," said Desford, smiling at him, "it's an inherited virtue, sir!"

"Mawworm!" said his lordship, concealing under this opprobrious word his gratification. "Don't think you can flummery *me!*" He then palliated his severity by saying, after a reflective moment: "Well, well, I don't mean to pinch at you, so we'll say no more on *that* head! All I will say is that if you find yourself at the end of your rope over this business come to me! I may be outdated, and gout-ridden, but I still know one point more than the devil!"

"Several points more than the devil, sir!" said Desford. "I should most certainly come to you if I reached the end of my rope."

His lordship nodded, apparently satisfied, for the next thing he said was: "To think of old Nettlecombe's having fallen into parson's mousetrap at his time of life! Did you say that he'd married his housekeeper?"

Thus it came about that when Lady Wroxton entered the library half-an-hour later she found father and son on the best of good terms. Indeed, the first sound she heard when she opened the door was a shout of laughter from Desford, to whom his father was describing, in highly coloured terms, what had been his own experiences in Harrowgate. She was not very much surprised, for she had considerable faith in Desford's ability to deal with his father, and she knew that however violently her lord might deny the imputation, Desford was the son nearest to his heart.

My lord greeted her genially, saying: "Ah, here you are, my lady! Now, come in, and tell Desford if I wasn't poisoned by those stinking waters at Harrowgate!"

173

"Well, they certainly made you extremely sick," she said. "But you only drank a very small quantity, you know, and there's no saying that they wouldn't have done you good if only we could have prevailed upon you to persevere." As she spoke, she warmly embraced Desford, who had risen at her entrance, and had crossed the floor towards her, to put his arms round her in a breath-taking hug. She kissed him, but pinched his chin as well, saying, as she looked lovingly up into his handsome face: "So now you've turned into a knight-errant, I hear! What next will you do, dearest?"

He laughed, but my lord said that he forbade her to give the boy a scold. "He has made a clean breast of the affair to me, my love, and I have said all that was necessary, so there's an end to it! No one," he added, with absolute conviction, "can say that I am one to ride grub!"

"No, my dear," she said gravely, but with Desford's smile lurking in her eyes. She let Desford lead her to a chair, and gave his hand a little squeeze before she let it go, and said: "I had a comfortable cose with Hetta, Ashley, and I collect, from what she told me, that your protégée is a very amiable and well-conducted girl, which, I own, surprised me, and makes me think her mama must have had more delicacy of principle than one would have supposed—recalling the circumstances of her marriage—for Wilfred Steane had no principles at all. It seems that Lady Silverdale has taken a great fancy to her, and is much inclined to invite her to stay at Inglehurst, but Hetta thinks it will not answer."

"I know she does, ma'am, and I agree with her."

"A pity," she said, in her calm way. "However, I daresay Hetta is right. So what do you mean to do with the poor little creature?"

He told her what his plan was, and she accepted it, merely saying that if any other recommendation of Cherry to a possible employer than Miss Fletching's was needed, she would be very happy to supply it. After that no more was said on the subject, my lord demanding to know what she thought of old Nettle-combe's being trapped into marriage by his housekeeper, and bidding Desford tell her all about his Harrowgate adventures.

Nothing occurred to mar the harmony of the evening, and when his lordship said goodnight to Desford outside his bedroom, he was in perfect charity with him, partly because he was so much relieved to know that his heir was not contemplating matrimony with the daughter of a man whom he had no hesitation in saying was the greatest rascal he had ever known, and partly because he had succeeded in winning two out of the three rubbers of picquet he had played with him.

Before he left for London on the following day Desford was able to have some private conversation with his mother, while Lord Wroxton was engaged with his bailiff. She took him to see the improvements she had made in the rose-garden, and as they strolled down the walks together he asked her, lifting a quizzical eyebrow at her, whether he had her to thank for the welcome accorded to him by his father.

"No, no, Ashley! I didn't utter a word in your defence!" she assured him. "Indeed, I said I would never have believed it of you, and was never more shocked in my life!"

"What a *very* sure card you are, Mama!" he said appreciatively. "In fact, I did owe my pardon to you!"

She smiled, but shook her head. "You may always be sure of his pardon, my dear, however much you may have vexed him. But perhaps you might not have won it as quickly if I had been so gooseish as to have tried to plead your cause, for nothing, you know, makes Papa more obstinate than opposition, and he *was* very angry. You'll own that he can scarcely be blamed! The intelligence that his eldest son had apparently formed a close connection with a member of a family which he holds in the greatest contempt came as a severe shock to him."

He nodded, grimacing. "Yes, I knew he would fly up into the boughs if he heard that I was having any dealings whatsoever with a Steane, which was why I hoped he never *would* hear of it. Do you wonder why I took her to Hetta, instead of bringing her here? It wasn't that I doubted *your* understanding of the case, I promise you! But his I did! Recollect, too, Mama, that I was already in his black books! He told me, on the occasion of my

175

last visit, that he didn't wish to see my face again, and, from what Simon told me, when I ran smash into him at Inglehurst on the day I took Cherry there, his temper had not improved!"

"Alas, no!" she sighed. "Poor Simon! I was so sorry for him, and he bore it all so patiently! But I was sorry for Papa too, because whenever he rakes any of you down, and says things he doesn't in the least mean, he is always thrown into gloom afterwards, and wishes he hadn't been so mifty. Not, of course, that he would admit it—though he did say after your last visit, dearest, that if you supposed he meant it when he told you he never wanted to see your face again you must be a bigger muttonhead than he had thought possible. He assured me that there was no occasion for me to worry about it, since he hadn't a doubt you'd come back very shortly—not that *he* cared a rush how long you stayed away! So you must never think that he doesn't hold you in affection!"

He burst out laughing. "Proof positive, Mama!"

"Well, of course it is! You know his way, Ashley! He would think it shocking weakness to betray to any of you how dearly he loves you! But I must say that nothing could have been more unfortunate than that you and Simon should have chanced to pay us visits at just that time. He was sadly out of frame, you know, not only because his gout was paining him so much, but because the new medicine which had been prescribed for him didn't suit his constitution at all. I'm bound to say that it did do his gout good, which was why he persevered with it, but it had a very lowering effect on him, so that I was glad when our good doctor substituted for it a diet-drink of dock-roots, which suits him much better." She smiled, and said: "But seeing you, and having made his peace with you, will have done him more good than all the medicines in the world."

He glanced quickly down at her. "Is that a hint to me that it's my duty to make Wolversham my headquarters, ma'am? I have a great regard for my father—indeed, I think few men have a better father!—but I couldn't live with him!"

"Well, I don't think he could live with you either," she replied composedly. "You would be certain to rub against each other, for you are both so dreadfully determined! You have only to go on in just the same way, giving us a look-in every now and then, and as long as you don't give him cause to suspect you of being on the brink of an imprudent marriage he will be very well pleased with you!"

"He need never fear, ma'am, that I could ever be so lost to all sense of what I owe not only to him, but to my name as well, as to do anything that would make him regard me as a—oh, as a broken feather in the Carrington wing!"

She smiled a little at that. "No, my dear: I am very sure he need not! And if you *had* wished to marry Miss Steane he would have tried to make the best of it, however disappointed he would have been, for he didn't dislike her, and he certainly didn't think her a *designing* girl. Indeed, he told me that he found it hard to believe she was Wilfred Steane's child! And, you know, dearest, even if he had taken her in the most violent dislike, and you had married her in the teeth of his opposition, he wouldn't have disowned you! No matter *what* any of you did, or *how* angry he was, that is something which he would never do, for it is wholly against his principles."

"Yes, I know it is," Desford agreed, a smile of affectionate amusement warming his eyes. "We all do—and it is what makes it quite impossible for any of us to do anything which we know would wound him to the heart! And it is also what makes him such an excellent parent! Horry nicked the nick when he told me, once, that, for his part, Papa (in one of his tantrums) was at liberty to lay anything he liked to his dish, because he could be depended on, in the last resort, to stand buff in defence of his sons!"

"Ah, you do know that, Ashley!" Lady Wroxton said, giving his arm an eloquent squeeze.

"Of course I do, Mama!" he said reassuringly. "But what a funny one he is! At one moment he can say that Wilfred Steane deserved to be disowned, and at the next give the cut direct to Nettlecombe for having done it!"

"For shame!" said Lady Wroxton, but with a quivering lip. "How dare you speak so improperly? You have quite misunderstood the matter! Naturally Papa said that, because it was perfectly true; but, in his opinion, Lord Nettlecombe behaved in a manner unworthy of a father, and that was true too! So there was nothing inconsistent in his having condemned both of them, and I will *not* permit you to call him a funny one!"

"Now that you have explained the matter to me, Mama, I perceive that I was quite beside the bridge to have done so," he replied.

She was not deceived by his air of grave remorse, but said, with an involuntary chuckle: "*Quite* beside it, wicked, odious, impertinent boy that you are!" She paused, and removed her hand from his arm to nip off a withered rose from one of the standards. "By the by, do you remember my telling you about Mr Cary Nethercott? Old Mr Bourne's nephew, I mean, who lately came into the property?"

"Yes. Why?"

"Oh, merely that I met him, when Papa and I drove over to Inglehurst! I never had, you know, so——"

"Met him at Inglehurst, did you? I suppose he called there to give Lady Silverdale some journal to read! Or had he another excuse?"

Startled by the sardonic note in his voice, she shot a quick glance at him, before answering with her usual calm: "My dear, how should I know? He was there when we arrived, sitting on the terrace with Hetta and Miss Steane, so what excuse he may have made for his visit I haven't a notion—if he made any! I formed the impression that he stands on such friendly terms with the Silverdales that he is free to drop in at Inglehurst whenever he chooses."

"Runs tame there, does he? How Hetta can tolerate such a prosy fellow I shall never know!"

"Oh, you've met him then?" she said.

"I should rather think I have! I trip over him every time I go to Inglehurst!"

"And you don't like him? I thought him a pleasant, well-conducted man."

"Well, I think him a dead bore!" said Desford.

She returned an indifferent answer, and almost immediately turned the subject, repressing, with a strong effort, a burning desire to pursue it.

The Viscount set out for London after partaking of a light luncheon, sped on his way by a recommendation from his father to post off to Bath first thing next day, and not to lie abed till all hours ("as you lazy young scamps like to do!"), because the sooner he finished with "this business" the better it would be for all concerned in it.

"For once, sir, I am in complete agreement with you!" returned the Viscount, a laugh in his eyes. "So much so that I shall sleep at Speenhamland tonight!"

"Oh, you will, will you? At the Pelican, no doubt!" said his lordship, with awful sarcasm.

"But of course, Papa! Where else should one put up on the Bath road?"

"I might have guessed you would choose the most expensive house in the country to honour with your patronage!" said the Earl. "When *I* was your age, Desford, I couldn't have stood the nonsense, let me tell you! But I had no bird-witted great-aunt to leave her fortune to me! Oh, well, it's no concern of mine how you waste the ready, but don't come to *me* when you find yourself in Dun Territory!"

"No, no, you'd disown me, wouldn't you, sir? I shouldn't dare!" said the Viscount, audaciously quizzing him.

"Be off with you, wastrel!" commanded his austere parent.

But when the Viscount's chaise had disappeared from sight he turned to nod at his wife, and to say: "This business has done him a deal of good, my lady! I own that I was a trifle put out when I first got wind of it, but there was never the least need for you to think he'd been caught by some designing hussy!"

"No, my dear," meekly agreed his life's companion.

"Of course it was no such thing! Not but what it was a lunk-headed thing to have done—However, I shall say no more on that head! The thing is that for the first time in his life he has a wolf by the ears, and he ain't running shy! He's ready to stand buff, and, damme, I'm proud of him! Sound as a roast, my lady!

Now, if only he would settle down—form an attachment to some eligible female—I'd hand Hartleigh over to him!"

"An excellent scheme!" said Lady Wroxton. "How delightful it will be, my love, to see Ashley where you and I lived until your father deceased!"

"Ay, but when?" responded his lordship gloomily. "That is the question, Maria!"

"Not so very long, I fancy!" said Lady Wroxton, with a smothered laugh.

CHAPTER XII

WHILE THE Viscount was impatiently awaiting the fashioning of a tyre to fit the wheel of his chaise, his youngest brother had been half-way back to London from Newmarket, with one of his chief cronies seated beside him in his curricle. Both gentlemen were in excellent spirits, having enjoyed a most profitable sojourn at Newmarket. Mr Carrington, in fact, was appreciably plumper in the pocket than his friend, for when, having boldly wagered his all on the Viscount's tip, and watched Mopsqueezer gallop home a length ahead of his closest rival, he had seen that a horse named Brother Benefactor was running in the last race he had instantly, ignoring the earnest pleas of his well-wishers not to be such a gudgeon, backed this animal to the tune of a hundred pounds. As it won by a head at the handsome price of ten-to-one, he left the course in high fettle, and with his pockets bulging with rolls of soft, one of which was considerably diminished at the end of the evening which he spent in entertaining several of his intimates to a sumptuous dinner at the White Hart.

Having a hard head and a resilient constitution, he arose on the following day feeling (as he himself expressed it) only a trifle off the hinges, and in unimpaired good spirits. The same could not have been said of his companion, whose appearance caused Simon to exclaim: "Lord, Philip, you look as blue as a razor!"

"I've got a devilish headache!" replied the sufferer, eyeing him with loathing.

"That's all right, old fellow!" said Simon encouragingly. "You'll be in a capital way as soon as you get out into the fresh air! Nothing like a drive on a fine, windy day to pluck a man up!"

Mr Harbledon vouchsafed no other response to this than a sound between a groan and a snarl. He climbed into the curricle, winced when it moved forward with a jerk, and for the next hour gave no other signs of life than moans when the curricle bounced over a bad stretch of ground, and one impassioned request to Simon to refrain from singing. Happily, his headache began to go off during the second hour, and by the time Simon pulled in his pair at the Green Man, in Harlow, he was so far restored as to be able to take more than an academic interest in the bill of fare, and even to discuss with the waiter the rival merits of a neck of venison and a dish of ox rumps, served with cabbage and a Spanish sauce.

Simon reached his lodging in Bury Street midway through the afternoon on the following day. Since neither he nor Mr Harbledon was pressed for time they had tacitly agreed to recruit nature by remaining in bed until an advanced hour. They had then eaten a leisurely and substantial breakfast, so that by the time they left the Green Man it was past noon. Still full of fraternal gratitude, Simon strolled round to Arlington Street, on the chance that he might find Desford at home. He was not much surprised when Aldham, who opened the door to him, said that his lordship was not in at the moment; but when he learned, in answer to a further enquiry, that his lordship had not yet returned from Harrowgate, he opened his eyes in astonishment, and ejaculated: *"Harrowgate?"*

"Yes, sir. So I believe," said Aldham.

Simon was not wanting in intelligence, and it did not take him more than a very few moments to realize what must have made his brother go off on such a long and tedious journey. He uttered an involuntary choke of laughter, but after eyeing Aldham speculatively decided that it would be useless to try to coax any further information out of him. Besides, for anything he knew, Aldham might not have been taken into Desford's confidence. So he contented himself with leaving a message for his brother, saying: "Oh, well, when he comes home tell him I shall be in London until the end of the week!"

"Certainly I will, Mr Simon!" said Aldham, much relieved to be rescued from the horns of a dilemma. He regarded Simon with indulgent fondness, having known him from the cradle, but he knew that Simon was inclined to be a rattlecap; and since he had learnt from Pedmore that one of the first duties incumbent upon a butler was to be unfailingly discreet, and never, on any account, to blab about his master's activities, he would have been hard put to it to answer any more searching questions without either betraying the Viscount, or offending Mr Simon.

Simon was engaged to join a party of friends at Brighton, and might well have gone there in advance of the rest of the party if he had not recollected that rooms at the Ship had been booked from the Saturday of that week. Only a greenhead would suppose that there was the smallest chance of obtaining any but the shabbiest of lodgings in Brighton, at the height of the season, if he had not booked accommodation there; so he was obliged to resign himself to several days spent in kicking his heels in London, which, in July, more nearly resembled a desert, to any member of the ton, than a fashionable metropolis. Not that London had nothing to offer for the entertainment of out of season visitors: it had several things, and Simon was considering, two days after his call in Arlington Street, whether the evening would be more amusingly spent at the Surrey Theatre, or at the Cockpit Royal, when the retired gentleman's gentleman who owned the house in Bury Street, and ministered to the three gentlemen at present lodging there, entered the room and presented him with a visiting-card, saying succinctly: "Gentleman to see you, sir."

The card bore, in florid script, an imposing legend: *Baron Monte Toscano*. Simon took one look at it, and handed it back. "Never heard of the fellow!" he said. "Tell him I'm not at home!"

A mellifluous voice spoke from the doorway. "I must beg a thousand pardons!" it said. "Too late did I realize that I had inadvertently presented this good man with the wrong card! Have I the honour of addressing Mr Simon Carrington? But I need not ask! You bear a marked resemblance to your father— who, I do trust, still enjoys good health?"

Considerably taken aback, Simon said: "Yes, I'm Simon Carrington, sir, but—but I fear you have the advantage of me!"

"Naturally!" said his visitor, smiling benignly at him. "I daresay you never saw me before in your life—in fact, I am quite sure of it, for until this moment you have been but a name to

183

me." He paused to wave a dismissive hand at the retired gentleman's gentleman, saying graciously: "Thank you, my good man! That will be all!"

"The name, sir, is Diddlebury—if you have no objection!" said his good man, in a voice which clearly showed his contempt for Mr Carrington's visitor.

"None at all, my man! A very good name, in its way!" said the visitor graciously.

Diddlebury, having looked in vain for a sign from Mr Carrington, reluctantly withdrew from the room.

"And now," said the visitor, "it behoves me to repair the foolish mistake I made, when I gave the wrong card to that fellow!" He drew out a fat card-case as he spoke, and searched in it, while Simon stared at him in amazement.

He was a middle-aged man, dressed in clothes as florid as his countenance. When the highest kick of fashion was a severity of style which banished from every Tulip's wardrobe all the frilled evening shirts which had been the rage only six months before, not to mention such enormities as flowered waistcoats, brightly coloured coats, or any other jewelry than a ring and a tie-pin, he was wearing a tightly fitting coat of rich purple; a shirt whose starched frill made him look like a pouter pigeon; and a richly embroidered waistcoat. A somewhat ornate quizzing-glass hung round his neck; a number of seals and fobs dangled from his waist; a flashing tie-pin was stuck into the folds of his cravat; and several rings embellished his fingers. He had probably been a handsome man in his youth, for his features were good, but the unmistakable signs of dissipation had impaired his complexion, set pouches beneath his eyes, and rendered the eyes themselves a trifle bloodshot.

"Ah, here we have it!" he said, selecting a card from his case. However, having taken the precaution of inspecting it through his quizzing-glass, he said: "No, that's not it! Can it be that I forgot —No! Here it is at last!"

Fascinated, Simon said: "Do you—do you carry different cards, sir?"

"Certainly! I find it convenient to use one card here, and

184

another there, for you must know that I am domiciled abroad, and spend much of my time in travel. But this card," he said, handing it to Simon with a flourish, "bears my true name, and will doubtless explain to you why I have sought you out!"

Simon took the card, and glanced at it with scant interest. But the name inscribed on it made him gasp: *"Wilfred Steane?* Then you *aren't* dead!"

"No, Mr Carrington, I am *not* dead," said Mr Steane, disposing himself in a chair, "I am very much alive. I may say that I am wholly at a loss to understand why anyone should have supposed me to have shuffled off this mortal coil. In the words of the poet. Shakespeare, I fancy."

"Yes, I know that," said Simon. "But I'm dashed if I know why you shouldn't understand why you was thought to have stuck your spoon in the wall! What else could anyone think when nothing was heard of you for years?"

"Was it to be supposed, young man, that if I had done any such thing I should have neglected to inform my only child of the circumstance? Not to mention the Creature in whose charge I left her!" demanded Mr Steane, in throbbing accents of reproach.

"You couldn't have," said Simon prosaically.

"I should have made arrangements," said Mr Steane vaguely. "In fact, I had made arrangements. But let that pass! I am not here to bandy idle words with you. I am here to discover where your brother is lying concealed, Mr Carrington!"

Simon's hackles began to rise. "I have two brothers, sir, and neither of them is lying concealed!"

"I refer to your brother Desford. My concern is not with your other brother, of whose existence I was unaware. I must own that until this morning I was unaware of your existence too." He heaved a deep sigh, and sadly shook his head. "One grows out of touch! *Eheu fugaces, Postume, Postume——!* No doubt you can supply the rest of that moving passage."

"Well, of course I can! Anyone could!"

"Labuntur anni," murmured Mr Steane. "How true! Alas, how true! Although you, standing as you do on the threshold of

185

life, cannot be expected to appreciate it. How well I remember the heedless, carefree days of my own youth, when——"

"Forgive me, sir!" said Simon, ruthlessly interrupting this rhetorical digression, "but you're wandering from the point! I collect that you wish me to tell you where my brother Desford is to be found. If I knew, I'd be happy to tell you, because he'd be devilish glad to see you, but I don't know! What I do know is that he is not *lying concealed* anywhere! And also," he added, with rising colour, and stammering a little, "Th-that there's no reason why he should be! And, what's more, I'll thank you not to make such—such false accusations against him!"

"All alike, you Carringtons!" said Mr Steane mournfully. "How vividly the past is recalled to my remembrance by your words! Your esteemed father, now——"

"We'll leave my father out of this discussion!" snapped Simon, by this time thoroughly incensed.

"Willingly, willingly, my dear boy! It is no pleasure to me to recollect how grievously he misjudged me. How little allowance he made for youth's indiscretions, how little he understood the straits to which a young man could be reduced by the harsh conduct of a parent who was—to put the matter in vulgar terms —a hog-grubber! I will go further: a flea-mint!"

"Well, you're out there!" retorted Simon. "I don't know much about what you did in your youth, sir, but I do know that my father gave yours the cut direct when he heard he'd disowned you!"

"Did he so?" said Mr Steane, much interested. "Then I have wronged him! I would I might have been present on the occasion! It would have supplied balm to my sorely wounded heart. But how, I ask myself, could I have guessed it? When I disclose to you that to me also he gave the cut direct you will realize that it was impossible for me to have done so."

"I daresay, but I shall be obliged to you, sir, if you will cut line, and tell me what your purpose is in coming to visit me! I've already told you that I don't know where Desford is, and I can only advise you to await his return to London! He has a house in

186

Arlington Street, and his servants are—are in hourly expectation of his return to it!"

"That he resides in Arlington Street I know," said Mr Steane. "Upon my arrival from Bath, I instantly made it my business to discover his direction—an easy task, his lordship being such a distinguished member of Society."

"Of course it was an easy task!" said Simon scornfully. "All you had to do was to consult a Street Directory!"

Mr Steane dismissed this with a lofty wave of his hand. "Be that as it may," he said, obscurely but with great dignity, "I did discover it, and instantly repaired to the inhospitable portals of his residence. These were opened to me by an individual whom I assumed to be his lordship's butler. He, like you, Mr Carrington, disclaimed all knowledge of his master's whereabouts. He was—not to put too fine a point upon it—strangely reticent. Very strangely reticent! I am neither a noddicock nor a souse-crown, young man—in fact, I am one who is up to every move on the board, ill though it becomes me to puff myself off! And I perceived, in the twinkling of a bedpost, that he was under orders to fob me off!"

"Well, if that's what you perceived it's time you bought a pair of spectacles!" replied Simon rudely. "How could Desford have given him any such orders when he thought you were dead? And, damn it, why the devil *should* he have done so? I daresay there's no one he would liefer meet than yourself! Yes, and if you care to leave me *your* direction I promise you I'll give it to my brother the instant I know where he is to be found! All I know at this present is that he went off to Harrowgate, early last week!"

Mr Steane appeared to subject this information to profound consideration. After an appreciable pause, he shook his head, and said with an indulgent smile: "It pains me to cast a doubt upon your veracity—and I would not wish you to think that I am insensible to the virtue of Loyalty! I assure you, young man, that I honour your noble determination to protect your brother, however much I may deplore his unworthiness. I will go further! If the interests of my beloved child were not so tragically involved, I should applaud it. But what, I ask myself, should take Lord Desford to Harrowgate? No doubt a salubrious resort, and one, as I recall, much patronized by persons afflicted with gout, scurvy, and paralytic debilities. But if you wish to persuade me that Desford, who cannot, by my reckoning, be above thirty years of age, suffers from any of these distressing diseases, you are—in vulgar parlance—doing it rather too brown."

"No, he don't suffer from those diseases! He don't suffer from any diseases, and he didn't go to Harrowgate for his health. Unless I'm much mistaken, he went there on what ought to be *your* business, Mr Steane! When I last saw him he was on the point of setting out to search for your father!"

"Tut, tut, my boy!" said Mr Steane reprovingly. "Too rare and thick altogether! I have never had any business in Harrowgate. Or, in point of fact, in any of the watering-places of its kind: they offer no scope at all to a man of my genius. As for my father, I have cut my connection with him. He has been as one dead to me for many years."

"Desford is searching for him to claim his protection for his granddaughter—your daughter, sir, whom you left destitute!" said Simon furiously. "Or is she too as one dead to you?"

"That I should have lived to hear such words addressed to me!" ejaculated Mr Steane, pressing a hand to his heart, and casting up his eyes. "My only child—my beloved child—the only relative I have in the world! And do not, I beg of you, speak to me of my erstwhile brother! I have not sunk so low as to claim relationship to that snivel-nose!" he added, descending abruptly from his histrionic heights. However, he rapidly recovered himself, and said: "I demand of you, young man, is not my presence in London proof of my devotion to the sole pledge left to me by my adored partner in the marital state?" Overcome by these reflections, he buried his face in his handkerchief, and became to all appearances bowed with grief.

"No, it ain't!" said Simon bluntly. "Anyone would think you'd plunged into a burning house, or some such thing!"

Affronted, Mr Steane raised his head, and said, with a good deal of feeling: "If you imagine that plunging into a burning

188

house is a riskier thing to do than to come boldly into this city, you are much mistaken! Why did I shake its dust from my feet do you suppose? Why did I choose to go into exile, leaving my beloved child—temporarily, of course—in the care of a female who had cozened me into believing her to be worthy of my trust?"

"I hardly like to say, sir!" promptly replied Simon. "But since you ask me I should think it was because the tipstaffs were after you!"

"Worse!" said Mr Steane tragically. "I do not propose to recount the circumstances which led to my ruin. Suffice it to say that from the hour of my birth misfortune has dogged my every step. My youth was blighted by a gripe-fisted parent, and a scaly scrub of a brother, who had not the common decency to cock up his toes when his life was despaired of! Not only did he rise up from what I confidently expected to be his death-bed, but less than a year later he fathered a son! That, young man, was the final straw!"

"Did—did you raise the recruits on a post obit bond?" asked Simon, awed.

"Naturally! Do not be misled into thinking that because I am not, I thank God, a muckworm, I am a lobcock! It was not in my father's power to cut me out of the Succession. If Jonas died, leaving a pack of daughters, I must, in due course, have inherited title, fortune, and all. Pardon me! The thought unmans me!" He disappeared once more into his handkerchief, emerging, after a few moments to say: "I shall not say that I was shattered. It was a blow that would indeed have crushed me had I been a pudding-heart, but I am not a pudding-heart: I have ever borne my reverses with becoming fortitude, and have seldom failed to make a recover. In this crisis, did I flinch? did I despair? No, Mr Carrington! I girded up my loins, as did—well, I forget who it was, but it's no matter!—and I did make a recover! You see in me, today, one who by his own exertions has raised himself from low tide to high water."

"Then why the deuce don't you settle your debts?" asked Simon sceptically.

Shocked by this suggestion, Mr Steane exclaimed: "Waste the ready on my creditors? I am not such a spill-good as *that,* I hope! Nor, let me tell you, as unmindful of my duty to my child! I had no other purpose in returning to the land of my birth than to succour her. Conceive what were my feelings when I arrived in Bath, yearning to clasp her in my arms, only to discover that the Creature to whom I had entrusted her had cast her off! Delivered her, in fact, into the hands of one of my bitterest enemies! And why? Because, if you please, in the midst of my struggles to bring myself about I had been obliged to defer the payment of her bills! Could she not have reposed as much confidence in my integrity as I had reposed in hers? Did she doubt that as soon as it became possible for me to do so I should have discharged my debt to her in full? Her only reply to these home-questions was a flood of tears." He paused, directing a challenging stare at Simon; but as Desford had divulged only the bare outlines of the circumstances which had led him to befriend Cherry, Simon had no comment to offer. So Mr Steane continued his narrative. "I repaired instantly to Amelia Bugle's country residence. It cost me a severe struggle to do so, but I mastered my repugnance: my parental feelings overcame all other considerations. And what was my reward? To be informed, Mr Carrington, that my innocent child had been ravished from the safety of her maternal relative's home by none other than my Lord Desford!"

"If that's what Lady Bugle told you, she was lying in her teeth!" Simon said. "He did no such thing! Lady Bugle treated Miss Steane so abominably that she ran away—meaning to seek refuge with her grandfather! All Desford did was to take her up in his curricle, when he overtook her trudging up to London!"

Mr Steane smiled pitifully at him. "Is that his story? My poor boy, it grieves me to be obliged to destroy your faith in your brother, but——"

"It needn't, for you won't do it!" interjected Simon, at white heat. "And I'll thank you not to call me your boy!"

"Young man," said Mr Steane sternly, "remember that you are speaking to one who is old enough to be your father!"

"And do you remember, sir, that you are speaking of one who is my brother!" Simon countered.

"Believe me," said Mr Steane earnestly, "I enter most sincerely into your feelings! I was never, I regret to say, blessed with a brother for whom I cherished the smallest partiality, but I can appreciate——"

"Partiality be damned!" interrupted Simon. "Ask anyone who knows him whether Desford is the sort of loose screw to *ravish* a chit of a girl away from her home! You'll get the same answer you've had from me!"

Mr Steane heaved another of his gusty sighs. "Alas, you force me to divulge to you, Mr Carrington, that I fear my unhappy child fell willingly into his arms! It rends me to the heart to be obliged to tell you this—and I need hardly describe to you how grievous a blow to me it was to learn that she had, in her innocence, succumbed to the lure of a libertine possessed of a handsome face, and engaging address. Not to mention the advantages of birth and fortune. I am led to believe that Lord Desford *is* possessed of these attributes?"

Revolted by this description of his eldest brother, Simon repudiated it, saying shortly: "No, he ain't! He's well-enough, I daresay—never thought about it, myself!—but as for *an engaging address*——! Lord, it makes him sound like a simpering, inching macaroni merchant! I'll have you know, sir, that Desford is a gentleman! What's more, your daughter didn't fall into his arms, because he never held them out to her! Not that I mean to say she would have done so if he had, for *I* am not one to cast aspersions on another man's close relations! And *also,* Mr Steane, if you *weren't* old enough to be my father I'd dashed well plant you a facer for having the infernal brass to call Desford a libertine!"

Mr Steane, listening to this heated speech with unimpaired equanimity, said compassionately, at the end of it: "I perceive that he has you in a string, and deeply do I pity you! You remind me so much of what I was in my youth! Hot-headed, perhaps, but replete with generous impulses, misplaced loyalties, and a touching faith in the virtue of those whom you have been taught

191

to revere! Sad, inexpressibly sad is it that it should have fallen to my lot to shatter that simple faith!"

"What the devil——?" demanded Simon explosively. "If you think that I was taught to revere Desford—or that I do revere him!—you're fair and far off, Mr Steane! Of course I don't! But—but—he's a damned good brother, and—and though I daresay he may have his faults he ain't a rabshackle—and that you may depend on!"

"Would that I could!" said Mr Steane regretfully. "Alas that I cannot! Are you ignorant, my poor young man, of the way of life your brother has pursued since he made his come-out, and—I am compelled to say—is still pursuing?"

Simon stared at him, wrath and incredulity in his eyes. The flush that had risen to his face when he had found himself compelled to violate every canon of decent reticence by upholding Desford's virtue darkened perceptibly. In a voice stiff with pride, he said: "My good sir, if, by those—those opprobrious words you mean to say that my brother has ever, at any time, or in any way, conducted himself in a manner unbefitting a man of honour, I take leave to tell you that you have either been grossly misinformed, or—or you are a damned liar!" He paused, his jaw dangerously outthrust, but as Mr Steane evinced no desire to pick up the gage so belligerently flung down, but continued to sit at his ease, blandly regarding him, he said haughtily: "I collect, sir, that when you speak of my brother's *way of life,* you refer to certain—certain connections he has had, from time to time, with members of the muslin company. But if you mean to tell me that you suspect him of seducing innocent females, or—or of littering the town with his butter-prints, you may spare your breath! As for the suggestion that he lured your daughter to elope with him—Good God, if it were not so damned insulting I could laugh myself into whoops at it! If he had fallen so desperately in love as to have done anything so kennel-raked, why the devil should he be doing his utmost to give her into her grandfather's keeping? Answer me that, if you can!"

Mr Steane shuddered eloquently, and replied in a manner worthy of a Kemble or a Kean: "If he has indeed done so, my dread is that he has wearied of her, and is seeking to fob her off!"

"What, in less than two days?" said Simon jeeringly. "A likely story!"

"My dear young greenhead," said Mr Steane, with a touch of asperity, "one can discover that a female is a dead bore in less than two *hours!* Not that I believe this Banbury story of his having gone off to Harrowgate in search of my father! It's a bag of moonshine! The more I think about it the greater becomes my conviction that he has abducted my innocent child, and bamboozled everyone into believing that he only did so because he thought she would be happier with her grandfather than with her aunt. Now, I don't doubt she may have been unhappy in that archwife's house, but if your precious brother thought she would be happier in my father's house he might be no better than a blubber-head, which I know very well he isn't! No, no, my boy! *You* may swallow that Canterbury tale, but don't expect me to! The plain truth is that he's bent on ruining my poor little Cherry, thinking that she has no one to protect her. He will discover his mistake! Her father will see her righted! Ay! even if he—her father, I mean, or, in a word, myself!—has to publish the story of his infamy to the world! If he has the smallest claim to be a man of honour he can do no less than marry her!"

"You've taken the wrong sow by the ear, sir!" said Simon, looking at him from between suddenly narrowed eyelids. "I'm happy to be able to inform you that your daughter's reputation is unblemished! So far from being bent on ruining her, my brother was bent on ensuring that no scandal should attach to her name! And I am even happier to inform you that she is residing, thanks to Desford's forethought, in an extremely respectable household!"

It would have been too much to have said that Mr Steane's countenance betrayed chagrin, but the bland smile certainly faded from his lips, and although his voice retained its smoothness its tone was somewhat flattened when he replied to what Simon, who had formed a pretty accurate idea of his character, believed to be an unwelcome piece of information. Simon began to feel a little uneasy, and to wish that he knew where Desford was to be found. Dash it all, it was Desford's business to deal with Mr Steane, not his! Desford would be well-served if he disclosed Cherry's exact whereabouts to this old countercoxcomb, and washed his hands of the whole affair.

"And where," enquired Mr Steane, "is this respectable household situated?"

"Oh, in Hertfordshire!" said Simon carelessly.

"In Hertfordshire!" said Mr Steane, sitting up with a jerk. "Can it be that I have wronged Lord Desford? Has he made her an offer? Do not be afraid to confide in me! To be sure, he should have obtained my permission to address himself to Cherry, but I am prepared to pardon that irregularity. Indeed, if he supposed me to be dead his informality must be thought excusable." He wagged a finger at Simon, and said archly: "No need to be discreet with me, my boy! I assure you I shall raise no objection to the match—provided, of course, that Lord Desford and I reach agreement over the Settlement, which I have no doubt we shall do. Ah, you are wondering how I have guessed that the respectable household to which you referred can be none other than Wolversham! I have never had the pleasure of visiting the house, but I have an excellent memory, and as soon as you spoke of Hertfordshire I recalled, in a flash, that Wolversham is in Hertfordshire. A fine old place, I believe: I shall look forward to seeing it."

Momentarily stunned, Simon pulled himself together, and lost no time in dispelling the illusion which was obviously working powerfully on Mr Steane's mind. "Good God, no!" he said. "Of course he hasn't taken her to Wolversham! He wouldn't dare! You must know as well as I do, sir, how my father regards you—well, you've told me yourself that he gave you the cut direct, so I needn't scruple to say that nothing would ever prevail upon him to give his consent to Desford's marriage to Miss Steane! Not that there's the least likelihood of his being asked to do so, because there ain't! Desford has *not* made her an offer, because, for one thing, he ain't in love with her; for another, there's no reason why he should; and for a third—well, never mind that!"

He had the satisfaction of seeing Mr Steane's radiant smile fade from his face, but it was short lived. A calculating look came into that gentleman's eyes, and his next words almost made the hair rise on Simon's scalp. "I fancy, young man," said Mr Steane, "that you will find you are mistaken. Yes. Very much mistaken! I can well believe that your honoured parent will not favour the match, but I venture to say that I believe he would favour still less an action of breach of promise brought against his heir."

"Breach of promise?" ejaculated Simon. "You'd catch cold at that, Mr Steane! Desford never made your daughter an offer of marriage!"

"How do you know that?" asked Mr Steane. "Were you present when he stole her out of her aunt's house?"

"No, I was not! But he told me how it came about that he was befriending Miss Steane——"

He stopped, for a slow smile had crept over Mr Steane's face, and he was shaking his head. "It is easy to see that you can have little knowledge of the law, young man. What your brother may have told you is not evidence. If it were admitted—which I can assure you it wouldn't be!—it could scarcely outweigh my unfortunate child's evidence!"

"Do you mean to say," gasped Simon, "that you think your daughter is the kind of girl who would stand up in a court of law, and commit perjury? Your memory isn't as good as you suppose, if that's what you think! Why, she's no more than a chit of a schoolgirl that hasn't cut her eye-teeth!"

"Ah!" said Mr Steane, putting Simon forcibly in mind of a cat confronted with a saucer of cream. "I collect, Mr Carrington, that you have met my little Cherry?"

"Yes, I've met her! And if she had accepted an offer from Desford, why, pray, didn't she tell me so?"

"So you have met her!" said Mr Steane thoughtfully. "No doubt in Lord Desford's company? Very significant! Ve-ry significant! One is led to suppose that he meant, at that time, to espouse her, for why, otherwise, should he have made her known to you?"

"He didn't! What I mean is," said Simon, becoming momently

195

more harassed, "I met her at—in the house to which he took her, and Desford didn't know I was there! I mean, he didn't expect me to be there, and she wasn't in his company when I met her! She was alone, in one of the saloons, waiting for Desford to explain the circumstances to Miss—to the lady in whose charge he placed her!"

"This," said Mr Steane, in a stricken voice, "is worse than I feared! Unhappy youth, has Lord Desford placed her in a *fancy-house?*"

"A fancy—No, of course he hasn't!" said Simon indignantly. "He took her to an old friend's house—a *very* respectable house, I'll have you know!"

"It doesn't sound like it to me," said Mr Steane simply.

"Oh, for God's sake, stop measuring twigs!" exclaimed Simon, quite exasperated. "You're talking the most idiotic hornswoggle I've been obliged to listen to in all my life! And I'll be damned if I'll listen to any more of it! Go back to my brother's house, and leave your card there—one that bears your true name!—and inform his butler where you are to be found! I promise you he will seek you out directly, for nothing could please him more than to know that Miss Steane's father is alive, and able to take charge of her. Though whether he will be pleased when he discovers what sort of a fellow you are is another matter!"

This savage rider failed to ruffle Mr Steane's serenity. "I venture to say that he would be very far from pleased—if he did seek me out—for he would recognize in me an avenging parent. A Nemesis, young man! It is inexpressibly painful to me to doubt your veracity, but I am forced against my will to say that I do not believe you. In fact, it has been borne in upon me that you lie as fast as a dog can trot, Mr Carrington. Or even faster! What a shocking thing that your revered parent—always such a high stickler—should have one son who is a profligate, and another—if you will pardon the expression!—a gull-catcher! And not even an expert in that delicate art!"

Simon strode across the room to the door, and wrenched it open. "Out!" he said.

Mr Steane continued to smile at him. "Certainly, certainly, if

196

you insist!" he said affably. "But consider! Is it quite wise of you to insist? You have not thought fit to disclose my unfortunate child's whereabouts to me, so there is no other course open to me than to repair to Wolversham, and to lay the facts of this distressing affair before your dear father. A course which I cannot feel that you would wish me to pursue, Mr Carrington."

He was right. Inwardly seething, Simon was obliged to choke down his rage, and to search wildly in his brain for a way of escape from what he recognized as a dilemma. Not having seen Desford since he had parted from him at Inglehurst, he was in ignorance of Desford's meeting with his father, and on one point his determination was fixed: not through his agency was Lord Wroxton going to hear of the scrape Desford had got himself into. Lord Wroxton could be depended on to stand buff, but he would be furious with Desford for having, in the first place, befriended Cherry Steane, and in the second place for having made it necessary for him to treat with her father, or even to receive such a sneaking rascal in his house. If ever a flashy clever-shins meant mischief, Simon thought, this one did! And who knew what mischief he might be able to work, except Desford himself? Simon did not for a moment believe that Des had made Cherry an offer of marriage, but if Cherry, prompted by her father, asserted that he had done so a rare case of pickles it would be! Considering the Honourable Wilfred Steane with narrowed eyes, Simon thought that while his object might be to achieve a brilliant match for his daughter it was far more probable that his real aim was pecuniary gain. Would my Lord Wroxton tip over the hush-money to keep his proud name free from the sort of shabby scandal with which it might well be smirched? Yes, Simon thought, he would! *Damn* Des for going off the lord knew where at just such a moment! If this cunning fox were to be kept away from Wolversham, there was nothing for it but to disclose to him that so far from having been dumped in a fancy-house Cherry had been placed in the care of a lady of unim-peachable respectability. He was extremely reluctant to furnish Mr Steane with her precise direction, for not only had he an extremely vivid notion of what Lady Silverdale's feelings would

197

be if that genteel hedge-bird presented himself at Inglehurst, but for anything he knew Desford might by this time have removed Cherry to some other asylum. The obvious way out of the dilemma was to persuade Mr Steane to await Desford's return to London: dash it all, it was he who had taken the wretched girl under his protection, and it was for him to decide whether or not to hand her over to her disreputable parent! But, whatever he did it was all Lombard Street to an eggshell that he would not, once he had set eyes on Mr Steane, present him to the Silverdale ladies.

The problem seemed to be insoluble, but just as Mr Steane said, in a voice of unctuous triumph: "Well, young man?" a brilliant idea shot into Simon's head. He said, shrugging his shoulders: "Oh, very well! If you won't take my word for it that your daughter is in safe hands, I shall be compelled to give you her direction, I suppose! Mind, I'm strongly tempted to urge you to visit my father—lord, what a settler he'd tip you!—but he ain't in very plump currant at the moment, and it wouldn't do him any good to fly into one of his pelters. It wouldn't do you any good either, because he wouldn't believe a word of your story. More likely to have you kicked out of the house! If you ever succeeded in entering it, which I'll go bail you wouldn't! He ain't receiving anyone but his family, and his closest friends, until he's in better cue, and you had as well go rabbit-hunting with a dead ferret as try to get past his butler! However, my mother wouldn't like it above half if there was to be a brawl, so I will inform you that when Desford found that your father was gone out of town he escorted Miss Steane to Inglehurst—which is Lady Silverdale's country house! She, let me further inform you, moves in the first circles, and is as starched-up as my father! So rid your mind of anxiety, Mr Steane!"

He ended on a confident note, for he had not failed to perceive a change in Mr Steane's expression, and was happy to know that he had succeeded in piercing his armour of self-satisfaction. He still smiled, but with tightened lips; and his pouched eyes had lost their look of tolerant amusement. But when he spoke it was as silkily as ever. He said: "I wonder what I can have said to make you take me for a looby? I assure you, my guileless young friend, you are making a sad mistake! I am, in common parlance, up to all the rigs! Do, pray, explain to me how it came about that a starched-up lady of the first consideration—I am not acquainted with her, but I take your word for that!—welcomed to her house a girl who was brought to her by your brother— unattended by an abigail, too!"

"If your memory is as good as you would have me believe it is, you must surely recall that I told you Desford had taken your daughter to the house of an *old friend!*"

"My memory, Mr Carrington, is excellent, for I also recall that when, not so many minutes past, you hovered on the brink of uttering the name of the female into those hands your brother had delivered my innocent child you uttered a single, betraying word! Not *Lady,* young man, but *Miss!*"

"Very likely I did," replied Simon coolly. "Miss Silverdale, in fact. My brother's thoughts naturally flew to her when he was at his wits' end to know what to do with Miss Steane, rather than to her mother. You see, he is betrothed to her!"

"What?" gasped Mr Steane, for the first time shaken off his balance. "I don't believe it!"

Simon raised his brows. "Don't believe it?" he repeated, in a puzzled voice. "Why don't you believe it?"

Mr Steane made a gallant attempt to recover his poise, but the announcement had been so unexpected that all he could think of to say was: "Profligate though he may be, I cannot believe that Lord Desford is so lost to all sense of propriety—of common decency!—as to take a girl he had seduced from her home to the lady to whom he had become affianced, and to claim her protection for that girl!"

"I should think not indeed!" responded Simon readily. "Of course he did no such thing! What's more, Miss Silverdale is far too well acquainted with him to suspect him of it! What you mean, sir, is that you don't wish to believe it, because no one but a barndoor savage could suppose that even the biggest rogue unhung would do such a thing!"

But Mr Steane's agile brain had been working. He stabbed a

199

forefinger at Simon, and demanded: "And why, young man, did you not inform me at the outset of this circumstance?"

"Because," replied Simon, "owing to my father's being in a tender state still, and to Lady Silverdale's wish to give a dress-party in honour of the betrothal at which he could not be present without knocking himself up, it has been agreed that no announcement of the engagement should be made until he is quite stout again. *We,* of course, know of it, and so, I daresay, do Desford's cronies, but as far as the scaff and raff of society are concerned it is a secret. So I beg you won't spread it about, Mr Steane! A fine trimming my brother would give me if he knew I'd betrayed his confidence!"

Mr Steane rose to his feet, saying: "I shall not conceal from you, young man, that I am by no means satisfied. It has already been made plain to me that you are—not to wrap the matter up in clean linen!—an accomplished fibster. Reluctant though I may be—indeed I *am!*—to bring a blush of embarrassment to any delicately nurtured female's cheeks—I perceive that it is my duty, as a parent, to discover from Miss Silverdale the truth of this shocking affair. Not to mention, of course, my ardent desire to clasp my child to my bosom again! If you will be so good, Mr Carrington, as to inform me as to the precise locality of Miss Silverdale's abode, I will relieve you of my presence!"

"Oh, it's in Hertfordshire!" said Simon carelessly. "Ask anyone in Ware the way to Inglehurst: they'll tell you!" He added, as Mr Steane picked up his hat: "But you'd be better advised to await my brother's return! I daresay Lady Silverdale may consent to receive you if you go to Inglehurst under his wing, but she's devilish high in the instep, I warn you, and the chances are that if you go alone you won't get over the doorstep!"

"You are insolent, my good boy," replied Mr Steane loftily. "You are also foolish beyond permission. How, pray, does it come about that this model of propriety has—according to your story—received my daughter into her distinguished household?"

"Why, because she was sorry for her, of course!" said Simon. "Just as anyone would be for a girl who had been deserted by her sole surviving parent, and cast destitute upon the world!"

Mr Steane, casting upon him a look of ineffable disdain, stalked wordlessly out of the room.

Young Mr Carrington, wasting no more than two minutes over a self-congratulatory review of his encounter with as sly a rogue as had ever, as yet, tried to tap him on the shoulder, realized that if his masterly (if far from truthful) handling of the situation were not to be overset it behoved him to make all possible speed to Inglehurst, to warn Hetta of the ordeal in store for her, and to inform her that he had recklessly betrothed her to Desford.

He was shrewd enough to feel pretty confident that Mr Steane, in spite of his air of opulence and his boast that he had raised himself from low tide to high water, was not quite so flush in the pocket as he pretended to be. It was unlikely that he would go to the expense of hiring a post-chaise and four to carry him to Inglehurst. If he hired a chaise at all, it would be a chaise and pair, but it was more probable, Simon thought, that he would travel to Ware on the Mail, or even a stage-coach, and hire a carriage there to carry him to Inglehurst. At the same time, it would not do to make too sure of this. Young Mr Carrington, that promising spring of fashion, saw that Adventure was beckoning to him, and responded to the invitation with the alacrity of a schoolboy. In less than half-an-hour he had shed his elegant pantaloons for a pair of riding-breeches; dragged off his natty Hessians; thrust his feet into his riding-boots, and hauled them up over his calves; exchanged his town-coat, with its long tails and buckram-wadded shoulders, for one more suitable for a gentleman about to take part in equestrian exercise; snatched a low-crowned beaver from his wardrobe, and a pair of gloves from a drawer in his dressing-table; a whip from the what-not littered with a heterogeneous assortment of his possessions; and was bounding down the stairs. His arrival on the doorstep co-incided with the appearance, round the corner of the street, of his groom, leading the goodlooking hack on which young Mr Carrington frequently lionized in the park, and accompanied by the page-boy who had been sent to summon him.

A word to his groom, a shilling tossed to the page, and he was off almost before his feet had found the stirrups. But in spite of his delightful sense of urgency, and of being (as he himself would have phrased it) prime for a lark, young Mr Carrington had so far outgrown the heedless impulses of his schooldays as to defer his dash into Hertfordshire until he should have called, for the second time, at his brother's house in Arlington Street.

Aldham, hurrying up from the basement to answer an imperative summons conveyed by a tug at the bell which set it jangling so noisily and insistently that Mrs Aldham very nearly suffered a spasm, was pardonably incensed when he discovered that it was only Mr Simon, trying to bring the house down over their heads. "Well, for goodness' sake, sir!" he said indignantly. "Anyone would think you was that Bonaparty, escaped off St Helena! And don't you try to bring that horse into the house, Mr Simon, for that I will not permit you to do!"

Simon, who, in default of finding any loafer in the street, had been obliged to lead his hack on to the flagway, to the foot of the few shallow steps which led up to the door of the house, retorted: "I don't want to bring him into the house! All I want is to know where his lordship is! *Do you know?*"

"No, Mr Simon, I do not know!"

"Oh, don't be so damned discreet!" said Simon explosively. "This is important, man!"

"Mr Simon, I promise and swear that I'm telling you the truth! All his lordship said, when he went off, was that he didn't expect to be gone above a day or two, but he didn't tell me where he was going to, and it wasn't my place to ask him!"

"But—he has returned from Harrowgate, has he?" Simon said, frowning. "Did you give him my message?"

"Yes, sir, I gave it to him in your very words," Aldham assured him. " 'Tell him I shall be in London till the end of the week,' you said. And so I did, but his lordship only said to tell you, if you should come enquiring for him again, that he would give you a look-in when he came back. Which, Mr Simon, we are expecting him to do at any moment, Mrs Adlham being poised, as you might say, over the kitchen-stove, with a pigeon pie ready to be popped into the oven, and a couple of collops——"

"The devil fly away with the collops!" interrupted Simon wrathfully. "Where's his lordship's man? Where's Stebbing?"

"His lordship gave Tain leave of absence, sir, him having taken a chill on the way back from Harrowgate; and Stebbing's gone with him—with my lord, I mean—being that my lord has gone off in his curricle this time, and not travelling post."

"In his curricle? Then he can't have gone far from London! If he should return today, tell him—No. Here, hold my horse, Aldham! I'll scribble a note for his lordship!"

With these words he thrust his bridle into Aldham's hands, and strode into the house, leaving that devoted but long suffering retainer to cast his eyes up in a mute appeal to heaven to grant him patience. It was wholly beneath his dignity to hold even his master's horse, but he accepted the charge without demur, and upon Simon's emergence from the house a bare three minutes later he went so far as to offer him a leg-up, and to chuckle when Simon vaingloriously refused this assistance.

"Pooh!" said Simon. "Do you take me for a cripple? Here, take this note, and see you give it to my brother the instant he arrives!"

"I will, Mr Simon," promised Aldham. "Now hold a minute while I tighten the girths! If I'm not taking a liberty, where might you be bound for, sir?"

"Oh, only to Inglehurst!" answered Simon airily. "Thank you: that's the dandy!" He then favoured Aldham with a smile, and a wave of his hand, and rode off at a brisk trot towards Piccadilly.

"And in which sort the wind is," Aldham said, when recounting this episode to his wife, "I know no more than you do, my dearie! Though that's not to say I haven't got my suspicions! And one thing I *will* say for Mr Simon! For all his carryings-on he's not one to cut his stick when my lord's in trouble, which I'm much afraid he may be!"

CHAPTER XIII

SIMON, KNOWING the country in the midst of which his birthplace was situated like the back of his hand, reached Inglehurst shortly after three o'clock that afternoon, and turned in at the lodge-gates hard on the heels of a landaulette, displaying on its panels the lozenge-shield proclaiming the widowhood of its owner, and drawn, at a sedate trot, by a pair of well-matched but sluggish bays. Uncertain of the identity of its solitary occupant (for she was holding up a parasol to protect her complexion from the strong sunlight), he kept at a discreet distance in the rear, until it drew up below the terrace of the house, and he saw, as she shut her parasol, and alighted from the carriage, that the unknown lady was not, as he had feared, Lady Silverdale, but her daughter. He then urged his tired mount forward, and called out, as Henrietta was on the point of walking up the broad, shallow steps to the house: "Hetta, Hetta! Stay a minute! I want to speak to you!"

She paused, quickly turning her head, and exclaimed: "Simon! Good God, what in the world are you doing here? I had supposed you to be in Brighton! Have you ridden over from Wolversham?"

"No, I've come from London," he replied, dismounting, and handing his bridle to one of the footmen who had jumped down from his perch at the back of the landaulette. With a brief request to the man to give the horse into the head groom's charge, he turned, and grasped the hand Hetta was holding out to him, saying in an urgent undervoice: "Something very important to say to you! Must see you in private!"

She looked a little startled. "Oh, what is it, Simon? If it's bad news, pray don't try to break it gently to me! Your parents? Desford? Some accident has befallen one of them?"

"No, no, it ain't that!" he assured her. "I've come to warn

205

you, because it is bad news—devilish bad news! Wilfred Steane is on his way here!"

"*Wilfred Steane?*" she exclaimed. "But I thought he was dead!"

"Well, he ain't," said Simon. "He's very much alive! Came to visit me this morning."

"Oh, what a horrid creature you are! Trying to frighten me out of my skin, with your talk of bad news! I don't call *that* bad news!"

"You will when you've seen him," said Simon. "He's a shocking fellow!"

"Oh, dear, how unfortunate!" she said, quite dismayed.

"You may well say so! I'll tell you what passed between us, but not here! Won't do for any of the servants to overhear us."

"No, indeed! Come into the house! You can wait for me in the Green saloon. I won't be above a couple of minutes, but I must show myself to Mama! I've been sitting with poor Mrs Mitcham all the morning, and you know what Mama is! If I venture to go more than five miles from home she is convinced that some dreadful fate will overtake me! Either I shall be robbed by highwaymen, or that there will be some accident to the carriage in which I shall be hideously hurt! It is too absurd, but it's useless to argue with her. I expect I shall find her in high fidgets, for I've been absent for nearly five hours!"

She hurried up the steps, the folds of the delicate primrose muslin dress she was wearing gathered in one hand; and when she reached the terrace she saw that Grimshaw was waiting to receive her in the open doorway, an expression on his face of portentous gloom. "Thank God you have come home, Miss Hetta!" he said earnestly.

"Well, of course I've come home!" she replied, with a touch of impatience. "I haven't been to the North Pole! I have been, as you very well know, a distance of no more than twelve miles, and since I had my mother's coachman to drive me there, and both her footmen to protect me from any eccentric highwaymen who *might* have chanced to fall upon the carriage, and to rescue me if those showy slugs had bolted, and overturned us, you

206

cannot have been under the smallest apprehension that any disaster had befallen me!"

"No, miss, I was under no such apprehension. It is her ladyship's state which makes me thankful to see you back. She has suffered a terrible shock, and, I regret to say, is in great affliction."

"Good heavens, is my mother ill? Has there been some accident?" she cried.

"Not, so to say, an *accident,* Miss Hetta," replied Grimshaw, heaving a deep sigh, and casting a reproachful look at her. "But when the terrible news was conveyed to her ladyship she felt a very severe spasm and went into strong hysterics."

"But *what* news?" demanded Henrietta, in considerable alarm.

"I regret to be obliged to inform you, miss," said Grimshaw, in a tone of ghoulish satisfaction, "that we have every reason to fear that Sir Charles has eloped with Miss Steane."

"Oh, my God!" muttered Simon, at Henrietta's elbow. "Now we *are* in the basket!"

"Fiddle!" she snapped. "How dare you talk such moonshine, Grimshaw? Who had the spiteful impudence to tell such a ridiculous story to her ladyship? Was it you, or was it Cardle? I can believe it of either of you, for you have both tried, from the moment Miss Steane set foot inside this house, to make her ladyship believe that she was an odious schemer! But it is you and Cardle who are the odious schemers! I don't wish to hear another word from you—though I promise you *you* will hear a great many words from Sir Charles when I tell him of this piece of wicked mischief-making! I am going to my mother now, but I am expecting a visit from Miss Steane's father, Mr Wilfred Steane. When he arrives, you will show him into the library, and advise me of it."

Before this blaze of wrath, as alarming as it was unprecedented, Grimshaw quailed. "Yes, Miss Hetta!" he said hastily. "Her ladyship is laid down on the sofa in the drawing-room, miss! Being a little restored by some drops of laudanum. It wasn't me that broke it to her that Sir Charles was gone off with Miss Steane, and I'm sure *I* wouldn't have said anything about it until you was come home——"

207

"That will do!" said Henrietta superbly.

"Yes, miss!" said Grimshaw, almost cringing. "I will show Mr Steane into the library, exactly as you say, miss!"

"Or the Baron Monte Toscano!" interpolated Simon.

Henrietta had started in the direction of the drawing-room, but she checked at this, and looked over her shoulder, saying quickly: "No, no, Simon! I can't receive strangers at such a moment!"

"Same man!" he explained, in an undervoice. "Explain it to you later! But for the lord's sake, Hetta, don't see him until you've first seen me! Something dashed important to warn you about!"

She looked bewildered, but promised she would join him in the Green saloon as soon as might be possible.

The scene that met her eyes when she entered the drawing-room bore eloquent testimony to Lady Silverdale's attack of the vapours. Her ladyship lay moaning softly on the sofa; Cardle was waving smelling-salts under her nose with one hand, and with the other dabbing her brow with a handkerchief drenched in vinegar; and on the table beside the sofa was a collection of bottles, ranging from laudanum and tincture of Valerian-root, to Hungary Water and Godfrey's Cordial.

"Thank God you are come home at last, Miss Hetta!" cried Cardle dramatically. "See what that wicked creature has done to her ladyship!"

"Oh, Hetta!" quavered Lady Silverdale, opening her eyes, and holding out a limp hand.

"Yes, Mama, I'm here," said Henrietta soothingly. She took the limp hand, and patted it, and said coldly: "You may go, Cardle."

"Nothing," announced Cardle, bridling, "shall induce me to leave my beloved mistress!"

"Your mistress doesn't need you while she has me to look after her," said Henrietta. "This show of devotion would be more affecting if you had not quite deliberately thrown her into such agitation! I'll speak to you later: for the present, you will please leave me to be private with her ladyship."

"That I should have lived to hear such words addressed to

me!" uttered Cardle, clasping her hands to her spare bosom, and casting up her eyes to the ceiling. "I that have served her blessed ladyship faithfully all these years!"

"Yes, yes, but go away now!" said her blessed ladyship, reviving sufficiently to push away the vinegar-soaked handkerchief. "I don't want this nasty-smelling stuff! You know I don't like it! Oh, Hetta, thank you, dearest!" she added, receiving from her thoughtful daughter a fresh handkerchief, sprinkled with lavender-water, and sniffing it. "So refreshing! You see, Cardle, that Miss Hetta knows just what to do to make me better, so you needn't scruple to leave me in her care! And take away the vinegar, and the laudanum, and *all* those bottles, except the asafoetida drops, in case I should feel another spasm coming upon me! And give me my smelling-salts, please! And perhaps you should leave the cinnamon water, but *not* Godfrey's Cordial, which I am persuaded doesn't suit my constitution. And don't, I beg of you, Cardle, start sobbing, for my nerves are shattered, and I find myself in a very agitated state, and nothing upsets me more than to have people crying over me!"

At the end of this speech, which had increased in vigour surprising in a lady who had, at the start of it, presented the appearance of one who was almost beyond human aid, Cardle saw nothing for it but to withdraw, which she did, with the utmost reluctance, and with many shuddering sighs indicative of her wounded sensibilities. When she had gathered up the rejected remedies, she went with bowed shoulders to the door, turning as she reached it to bestow a last pitiful look at her mistress, and one of venomous dislike at Henrietta.

"Well, now," said Henrietta cheerfully, "we can be comfortable together, Mama!"

"I shall never again know a moment's comfort!" said Lady Silverdale, relapsing slightly. "Oh, Hetta, you don't know what has happened!"

"No, I don't," agreed Henrietta, sitting down beside her mother, and casting her very becoming hat of satin-straw on to a near-by chair. "Grimshaw told me a ridiculous Banbury story, not one word of which am I such a goose as to believe, so do, pray, Mama, tell me what really happened here today!"

"Alas, it is no Banbury story! Charlie has run off with that wretched girl Desford persuaded me to house for him! I shall never forgive him, never! Heaven knows it was much against my will that I consented to take her, for I didn't like her. There was always something about her that seemed to me to show a want of conduct. Those inching manners, you know, were beyond the line of being pleasing. You must recall my saying so to you, several times!"

"No, I don't recall that," said Henrietta dryly. "It doesn't signify, however. What does signify is this nonsensical notion that Charlie has run off with Cherry Steane. It is too absurd, Mama! Cherry doesn't like him any better than she likes any young man!"

"That was just her artfulness! Exactly what one might have expected of Wilfred Steane's daughter! I see *now* that she was all the time determined to get a husband. There can be no doubt that she first set her cap at Desford, only he, being up to snuff (more shame to him!), no sooner saw what her game was than he got rid of her—at *my* expense! Hetta, when you refused to marry Desford you had a fortunate escape! I own, I was disappointed at the time, however little you may have guessed it, but I have lived to be thankful that you are not today the wife of such an unprincipled rake! You would have been miserable, dearest! And if ever I reproached you for refusing his offer I tell you now that nothing would prevail upon me to consent to your union with him!"

"As the question doesn't arise," said Henrietta calmly, "must we waste time in discussing Desford's morals?"

"Certainly not!" said Lady Silverdale. "*I* have no wish to discuss them! I don't wish ever to see him again, or even to waste a thought on him! In fact, if he has the effrontery to show his face here, Grimshaw will have instructions to refuse him admittance! Foisting that wretched girl on to me—*throwing* her in poor Charlie's way—coaxing you into believing his glib tale——!"

Knowing that no purpose would be served by entering into

argument with her fuming parent, Henrietta sat in unresponsive silence until Lady Silverdale had talked herself out of breath. She then said: "What makes you suppose, ma'am, that Charlie has eloped with Cherry?"

"He did it in a tantrum, of course!"

Henrietta looked amused. "I shouldn't have thought that even such a skip-brain as Charlie would elope because he was in a tantrum—and with a girl for whom he has never shown a sign of partiality, too!"

"He's not a skip-brain!" said Lady Silverdale, firing up. "And as for not showing partiality, with my own eyes I saw him, not an hour after you had left the house, Hetta, *hugging and kissing her!*"

"Hugging her? Pray, how did he contrive to do that, with one arm in a sling, and two broken ribs?" asked Henrietta sceptically.

"He had his left arm round her, of course, and he *did* kiss her, for I came into the room just as he was doing it! And, what is more, Hetta, she made no effort to push him away from her!"

"You should be grateful to her for that, ma'am! Considering it was only yesterday that Dr Foston was shaking his head, and warning us that Charlie must take the greatest care, because though one of the broken ribs is mending the other is causing him to feel anxious, I think Cherry showed remarkable restraint not to struggle with him! I don't doubt that she was terrified of what might be the result of pushing him away."

"How can you be so blind, Henrietta, as to let yourself be taken-in in this foolish way?" demanded Lady Silverdale. "*I* noticed many days ago that she was a flirt—indeed, I felt obliged to warn her not to encourage gentlemen to make up to her!—and Cardle tells me——"

"I wish to hear nothing of what Cardle tells you, ma'am!" Henrietta said, rather hotly. "It is of no consequence whatsoever! She resented Cherry from the start, and hasn't ceased to try to set you against the poor child!"

"Cardle is devoted to me," said Lady Silverdale. "*She* at least has my interests at heart!"

Henrietta started to speak, checked herself, and, after a

momentary pause, said: "What happened when you surprised Charlie kissing Cherry?"

"He released her immediately, and if ever guilt was plain to be seen in anyone's face it was in Cherry's! She was in too much confusion to be able to speak. She stammered something, turning as red as fire, and ran out of the room. And you are not to suppose, Hetta, that I didn't give Charlie a scold! I scolded him extremely severely, for whatever you may say, I do *not* ignore his faults. Not that I think it *was* his fault, but he should not have allowed himself to be led into impropriety."

"So then he flew into one of his stupid rages, and was probably very rude to you," nodded Henrietta.

"Yes, he was!" said Lady Silverdale, with feeling. "He actually told me—*shouted* at me!—to 'stubble it!' And when I asked him if he wanted to break my heart, he walked out of the room, and slammed the door in a way he must *know* is excessively bad for my nerves!"

"Well, I think that was more improper than to have kissed Cherry," said Henrietta, her mouth suitably grave, but an irrepressible twinkle in her eyes. "I expect he will be sorry now, and be ready to beg your pardon, so don't be distressed about it, Mama!"

"He has *gone!*" said Lady Silverdale tragically.

"Nonsense! I daresay he flung himself out of the house in a miff, but he will be back as soon as he has recovered his temper, depend upon it!"

"Alas, you do not know all! Cherry has gone too!" disclosed Lady Silverdale, recruiting her forces with the vinaigrette. "And if you imagine, Hetta, that I said anything to drive her out of the house in that highty-tighty fashion, you are much mistaken! Naturally I was obliged to read her a lecture, exactly as I should to you, if you ever conducted yourself with such a want of delicacy, which, thank God, you never would do!"

"And what did she say, ma'am, in answer to this gentle scold?"

"Oh, she said it hadn't been her fault, and that Charlie had taken her by surprise, and a great deal more to that wheedling tune! So I told her—perfectly kindly—that no gentleman kisses

212

a girl unless he has received encouragement to do so; and I warned her of what might well befall her if she didn't learn to behave with more propriety. Then I said (because she began to cry) that I wasn't angry with her, and should do my best to forget the incident, and I told her to go up to her bedchamber until she was more composed."

"Unfortunate girl!" ejaculated Henrietta. "How *could* you, Mama? When she has been so grateful to you, and so good to you! Telling her such a—such a *plumper,* too! And she's such a goose that I expect she believed no gentleman kisses a girl unless she encourages him, and has run off to cry her eyes out! Now I shall have to go in search of her!"

Lady Silverdale was so much incensed that she bounced up from her moribund position, and sat bolt upright. "You are as unnatural as your brother!" she declared, in a trembling voice. "Is it nothing to you that your mother should have spent the day in an agony of anxiety? Oh, no! All you care for is that miserable little wretch you've made into a bosom-piece! As for going in search of her, she has already been searched for, and neither she nor Charlie is on the premises! And, what is more, Cardle saw her running down the backstairs not twenty minutes after I sent her to her room, and she was wearing her bonnet and shawl, *and* the nankeen boots I procured for her! And you call *that* gratitude!"

Henrietta was frowning slightly. "She must have gone for a walk beyond our grounds, then. Foolish of her, but if she was as upset as I collect she was, she was probably bent on finding a retreat where she wouldn't be looked for. Or perhaps of seeking relief from her feelings in exercise: it's what I should do in like circumstances!"

"Wait!" commanded Lady Silverdale. "A little later, a closed vehicle was seen to be drawn up a few yards beyond the farmgate, and one of the undergardeners saw Charlie come out into the lane, *with his hat pulled down over his eyes,* so that he shouldn't be recognized, of course, but James did recognize him, because he was wearing that olive-green coat, which I *cannot* like, and it is perfectly true, Hetta: he *was* wearing it today!

And he looked round to be sure no one was following him, and then climbed up into the carriage. So James was in a puzzle to know what to do, because *all* the servants know that Dr Foston has expressly forbidden Charlie to ride, *or* to drive, for at least another week, and he was afraid Charlie would do himself an injury. So he made up his mind to come up to the house, and try whether he could get a word in Pyworthy's ear—not that that would have been of any use, because Charlie has Pyworthy in a string! I'm sure I am glad to think Charlie's valet is so devoted to him, but there's reason in all things, and when it comes to pretending to *me* that he doesn't know where Charlie is, or what he's doing, as he does, over and over again—well, I think it the outside of enough!"

"Mama," said Henrietta, with determined patience, "Simon Carrington is waiting for me, with an urgent message, in the Green saloon, so do, pray, tell me——"

"I am telling you, but if you keep interrupting me I may as well hold my peace," replied Lady Silverdale, in an offended voice. "And as for Simon Carrington, I forbid you to invite him to dine here, Hetta! I don't accuse him of aiding and abetting Desford, though it wouldn't surprise me if he is, but I don't wish to set eyes on *any* Carrington!"

"Very well, ma'am. Did James tell Pyworthy that Cherry was in that carriage?"

"He didn't see Pyworthy," said Lady Silverdale stiffly. "He saw Grimshaw!"

"And told him that?"

"No, but he knew there was *someone* in the carriage, for the door was opened from inside it, and he saw Charlie laughing, and saying something, and who else could it have been than——"

"And on this you, and Cardle, and Grimshaw have fabricated the most fantastic Canterbury tale I ever heard! The romances you are so fond of reading, ma'am, are nothing to it!"

"But, Hetta, it is not a Canterbury tale! Where could Charlie have been going to, in that secret way, except to——"

"For heaven's sake, Mama, don't say Gretna Green!" begged Henrietta, torn between exasperation and amusement. "Without as much as one cloak-bag between the pair of them! My guess is that Charlie has gone off on some expedition he knows you'd disapprove of; and if he does himself an injury he will be well-served! What is more important is to discover what has become of Cherry! For how long has she been missing?"

"Hours! Both of them!" asserted her ladyship. "And how you can be so heartless as to say that Cherry is more important than your only brother——"

"I don't believe he'll come to any harm," said Henrietta impatiently. "Dr Foston only said that because he knows him too well to think that he would be prudent unless he were frightened into it! But I do fear that Cherry may have met with some accident, and I am going to send out a search-party, to look for her!"

She rose quickly, but was startled by a little scream from her mother. *"Charlie!"* uttered Lady Silverdale, and sank back against the sofa cushions with one plump hand pressed to her heart.

Sir Charles came impetuously into the room. It was evident from his expression, and from his stammering utterance, that so far from having recovered his temper he was in a towering rage. "I sh-should like to know, m-ma'am, what the dev—*deuce*—you mean by s-setting the servants to spy on me? By God, I think it beats the Dutch! Don't you frown at me, Hetta! I'll say what I dashed well choose! It's coming to something when a man can't move two steps out of his house without being followed, and spied on by his own servants, and being scolded by his butler for daring to go out without informing the whole household why he was going out, and where he was going, and when he would come back! There's no bearing it, and so I warn you, ma'am!"

"Unhappy boy!" said his mother dramatically. *"Where is Cherry?"*

"How the deuce should I know? And if you mean to give me any more jobations, I'm off! All that grand fussation just because I snatched a kiss! Anyone would think I'd tried to rape the girl!"

"Charles! If you have no respect for *my* sensibility, have you none for your sister's?"

215

"Well, I'm sorry," he said sulkily. "But it's enough to make a man go off on the ear when such a riot is kicked up over a mere trifle!"

"I know well that you were not to blame," said Lady Silverdale, dabbing at her eyes. "You shouldn't have done it, for you are old enough to know better, but I've no doubt you never would have done it had she not invited you to! So we shall say no more about it!"

He flushed darkly. "Oh, yes, we shall say more about it!" he said furiously. "She did not invite me to kiss her! As a matter of fact, she threatened to box my ears if I didn't let her go, silly little wet-goose! So don't you ring a peal over her, ma'am, because I won't have her blamed for what she couldn't help!"

"Charlie," interposed Henrietta quietly, "between them, Cardle and Grimshaw put it into my mother's head that you had eloped with Cherry, so you cannot be surprised to find her in a great deal of agitation! So do try to moderate your language!"

"Eloped with her?" he gasped. "Next you'll say you thought I was on my way to the Border! In a hired hack, and with a girl I don't even like above half! If you mean to tell me *you* thought anything so addle-brained, you must have rats in the garret, Hetta, and that's all there is to it!"

"Oh, no, I didn't!" she assured him. "But if you don't know where she may be I must send the grooms and the gardeners out to search for her immediately."

"If she was not in that carriage, who was?" suddenly demanded Lady Silverdale. "Do not ask me to believe that it was one of your friends, for I should hope none of them would visit you in that sly fashion! There is some mystery about this, and I am feeling very uneasy. I can feel my palpitations coming on already. Charlie, do not be afraid to confide in me! Have you got into a scrape?"

He drew an audible breath, and said, as one goaded beyond endurance: "Much chance I've had of getting into a scrape since I've been tied by the heels here! If you must know, it was Pyworthy in the hack, and I went off with him to watch a mill! And if you want me to tell you why I sent him to hire a hack,

216

and bring it round to the farm-gate, it was because I knew dashed well what kind of a bobbery there would be if you got wind of it, ma'am!"

Henrietta gave a low chuckle. "I guessed as much!" she said, picking up her hat, and going to the door. "I'll leave you to make your peace with Mama."

"Yes, but if you mean to set the men scouring the countryside, I wish you won't!" he said uneasily. "Dash it, she can't have come to any harm, and we don't want to set people talking!"

"Unfortunately, finding Cherry is a matter of considerable urgency," she replied sweetly. "I have good reason to believe that her father is coming here to claim her, and is likely to arrive at any moment. Perhaps you would like to relieve me of the task of telling him that she can't be found?"

"No, I dashed well shouldn't!" he said fervently. "Hetta, are you bamming me? How do you know he's coming here? Good God, I thought he was dead!"

"Well, he isn't. And I know he is coming here, because Simon Carrington rode out from London to warn me of it!"

Lady Silverdale, recovering from the stupefaction which had caused her jaw to drop and her eyes to start alarmingly, shrieked after her daughter's retreating form: "Don't dare to bring him in here, Hetta! I can't and I won't meet him. Cherry is your responsibility, not mine!"

"Don't fall into a twitter, Mama!" Henrietta said. "I haven't the smallest intention of bringing him in here!"

CHAPTER XIV

HENRIETTA FOUND that Grimshaw was hovering in the wide corridor which led from the hall to the drawing-room, and at once gave him the necessary directions for an organized search for Miss Steane. He received these in a manner which showed her that the cumulative effects of having received a rating from herself and of being rattled off, probably in a most intemperate language, by his raging young master, had been so salutary as to render him, temporarily at least, all eagerness to oblige. He tried to detain her by excusing his own share in the day's evil happenings, but as he very meanly cast all the blame on to Cardle she had little compunction in cutting short his protestations. She then went quickly to the Green saloon, where she found Simon pacing round the room in a fret of impatience.

"Good God, Hetta, I thought you was never coming!" he exclaimed. "I've been feeling like a cat on a hot bakestone!"

"You look like one!" she told him. "I came as soon as I could, but my mother was in such a taking——"

"What, has Charlie indeed eloped with Miss Steane?" he demanded incredulously. "What a hare-brained thing to do!"

"No, of course he hasn't! He came in a few minutes ago. He went off to watch a prize-fight, and stole out of the house so that my mother should know nothing about it. That's no matter! But what is more serious is that Cherry has been missing for several hours, and since my mother, egged on by her woman, and by Grimshaw, had it firmly fixed in her head that she had run off with Charlie no one has made the least push to find her. I've told Grimshaw to send the men out immediately to search for her, and can only trust that they do find her before her father arrives."

He blinked at her. "Yes, but—Did she steal out of the house too? What I mean is, queer sort of thing to do, isn't it? Not telling anyone she was going out. Come to think of it, it ain't the thing for a girl of her age to jaunter off without leave! I know Griselda never did so—in fact, I'm pretty sure my mother never allowed her to go out walking beyond the grounds without someone to bear her company, even if it was only her abigail."

"Oh, no, nor did mine! But the case is a little different, Simon! You won't repeat this, but it seems that there was a—a slight rumpus this morning, owing to my mother's having found Charlie trying to flirt with Cherry, and—and refining a great deal too much upon it! And I am afraid that what she said to Cherry upset the child so much that she ran out of the house, to—to walk off her agitation, and may have lost her way, or—or met with some accident!"

"Dash it, Hetta, this ain't the wilds of Yorkshire!" objected Simon. "If she lost her way, anyone could have set her right! And I can't for the life of me see what sort of an accident she could have met with! Sounds to me as though she's run away. Seems to make a habit of it!"

"Oh, Simon, surely she could not be so idiotish?" Henrietta said.

"Well, I don't know," he said dubiously. "Of course, I wasn't talking to her above twenty minutes, but she didn't seem to me a needle-witted girl by any means."

"No," she sighed. "She is a dear little creature, but sadly gooseish."

"Good thing if you were rid of her," he said. "Good thing for Des too! If it weren't for this curst father of hers, I'd say let her go! But we shall find ourselves in the briars if he sails in expecting to clasp her to his fat bosom—yes, that's the way he talks! At least, he didn't say 'fat': that's a what-do-you-call it by me!—and you are obliged to tell him she's run away, and can't be found!"

"*I* shall certainly be in the briars, but why *you* should be I can't conceive!" she replied, with some asperity. "And it would not be a good thing if she ran away from us under any circumstances whatever! Des entrusted her to my care, and if you think it would be a good thing if I betrayed his confidence so dismally you must be all about in your head!"

"No, no!" he said hastily. "What I meant to say was, not quite such a *bad* thing! The fact of the matter is, Hetta, that this ramshackle fellow is a pretty ugly customer, and it's as plain as a pack-saddle that what he means to do is to force Des to marry the girl—or, if that fails, to bleed him for the damage done to her reputation!"

"Des didn't damage her reputation!" she cried.

"No, I know he didn't, and so I told the old shagbag! But the thing is I can't prove he didn't, because all I know is what Des told me. And that ain't evidence, as Mr Lickpenny Steane took care to inform me! Confound Des, going off the lord only knows where, and leaving me to cope with this case of pickles! Ten to one I shall make a rare mess of it! The devil of it is, Hetta, that no one knows where he is, so I can't——"

"He is in Bath," she interrupted. "He came here on his way back from Harrowgate, and had formed the intention of visiting the lady who owns a school in Bath, where Cherry was educated, you know, to beg her help in finding a genteel situation for Cherry—Nettlecombe not having come up to scratch."

"In Bath? But that's where Steane went to! And then came up to London—no, I rather think he said he went first to the Bugles' place! He must have missed running into Des, for he certainly hadn't seen him when he came to call on me. In fact, he came to discover from me where Des was. Yes, and that puts me in mind of something that went clean out of my head in the hurry I was in! Dashed if I didn't forget to ask Aldham what the dickens he meant by sending Steane round to me! Because it must have been Aldham, when Steane was badgering him to say where Des was! Fobbing the fellow off on to me! Jupiter, if I don't give him a tongue-banger when I get back to London!" He paused, and then said, in a milder tone: "Oh, well! I daresay it was all for the best! At least I was able to head him! Now, you listen to me, Hetta! I wouldn't have sent him here if I could have avoided it!"

"But, Simon, surely you must have done so?" she protested.

"He may be a disreputable person, but he is Cherry's father, and none of us has any right to hide her from him!"

"Well, I wouldn't do it," he said frankly. "But, then, she don't hit my fancy. But I've a strong notion Des will do everything in his power to keep her out of Steane's hands—once he's taken the fellow's measure, which he will do, in a pig's whisper! Trouble with Des is that he's too chivalrous by half! Not but what I daresay if I'd been such a sapskull as to have picked the girl up and promised to take care of her I might feel a trifle queasy at handing her over to Steane."

"You know, Simon," she said, "for some reason or other, the suspicion that you don't like Mr Steane has taken strong possession of my mind! But apart from his ambitious scheme to win a rich and titled husband for her—which, I own, gives one no very good idea of his character, but which might, after all, spring from a wish to do his utmost to ensure for her the sort of life any father must wish for his daughter, and which, from anything I have heard of him, he is not himself in the position to provide for her—apart from this, is there any reason why he shouldn't be allowed to take her into his own care? I can't but feel that in coming to find her he does show that he holds her in considerable affection." She stopped, wrinkling her brow. "Though it does seem odd of him to have left her for such a long time without a word, or a sign. However, there may be some reason for that!"

"He was probably in gaol," said Simon. "For anything I know, he may practise all kinds of roguery, but I fancy his chief business is fuzzing, cogging, and sleeving. And I should think," he added, "that he'd be pretty good at drinking young 'uns into a proper state for plucking! A Captain Sharp, Hetta!" he said, seeing that she was looking bewildered. "Sort of fellow who carries a bale of flat-size aces in his pocket, and knows how to fuzz the cards!"

"Good God! Do you mean he is a cheating gamester?" she gasped. "You cannot possibly know that, Simon!"

"Oh, can't I just?" he retorted. "You *must* think I'm a slow-top! What else could I think of a fellow that carries half-a-dozen visiting-cards in his pocket-book, all of 'em with different names, and says that places like Bath and Harrowgate offer no scope for a man of his genius? Of course they don't! There's no deep play in the watering-places where people go for their health! And if you think Des will be ready to give her up to a rascal that will drag her all over Europe with him, rubbing shoulders with all the rags and tags of society, you can't know Des as well as I thought you did!"

"No, no, indeed he wouldn't be!" she said, very much shocked. "But, surely, if that is the kind of life Mr Steane leads, he cannot wish to be saddled with Cherry? Why should he?"

"I don't know, and I don't mean to waste my time trying to hit upon the reason. What I want you to understand, Hetta, is that he means mischief, and dangerous mischief, what's more! When I saw what his game was, and realized what a deuced unpleasant scandal he could start, if he accused Des of seducing that tiresome girl, promising to marry her, and then tipping her the double, I told him that so far from doing any of those things Des had placed her in the care of some old friends of ours, and had himself posted off to find her grandfather. He pretended that he didn't believe it. He even had the curst insolence to say—Well, never mind that! So I was forced to tell him that the girl was residing with Lady Silverdale, who was a widow, moving in the first circles, and as starched-up as my father! I meant it for the best, Hetta, but it gave him the chance to land me a heavy facer. He asked me how it came about that such a lady had consented to receive into her house a girl brought to her by a man of Desford's reputation—oh, yes! I was forgetting that piece of lying insolence! Des, you'll be interested to learn, is a rake and a libertine!—without her maid, or any other attendant!" He broke off suddenly, and jerked up his head, listening to the sound of an approaching carriage. "Oh, my God, here he is!" he said. Two strides took him to the window, and while Henrietta waited in some anxiety, he stood watching the chaise-and-pair until it drew up below the terrace. He then uttered a groan, and said: "Ay, it's Steane all right and tight!"

"I was never nearer in my life to playing least-in-sight!"

confessed Henrietta. "What am I to say to him, Simon? I promise you I am in a perfect quake!"

"No need for you to be in a quake!" answered Simon, in a heartening tone. "But there's just one thing I must mention!"

"Yes, there is need! I've *lost* Cherry! And if she isn't found— Oh, I do wish Desford were here!"

"For the lord's sake, Hetta, don't *you* get in a stew!" begged Simon, alarmed. "And as for Des—You know, I've been thinking about him, and it's my belief he will be here! If he went to Bath, we know he reached the place *behind* Steane, don't we?"

"Do we?" she said distractedly.

"Of course we do! Steane didn't meet him there, and the schooldame, whatever her name may be, didn't tell him she had seen him. All she told him was that Lady Bugle had fetched Cherry away, and had taken her to live with her. I wish you will take a damper, Hetta! If you mean to fly into the twitters we *shall* be bowled out!"

This severity had its effect. She said: "No, no, I promise you I won't! But I find my mind is less strong than I believed it to be —in fact, it is all chaos! Oh, heavens, that is Grimshaw's step! In another moment Mr Steane will be upon us!"

"No, he won't. Grimshaw will show him into the library, and it won't hurt him to kick his heels there for a while. Never mind him, just mind me! If Des visited Miss Thingummy *after* she'd seen Steane, what would he do? Drive back to London as fast as he could, of course!"

"Unless he followed Steane to Maplewood," she said doubtfully.

"No," said Simon, shaking his head. "I own I did think of that myself, but the more I consider the matter the more I feel he wouldn't have done any such thing. Well, do but put yourself in his shoes, Hetta! He knew that Cherry wasn't living with her aunt, and he must have known that the Bugles wouldn't have encouraged that old court-card to linger in their house! I daresay he didn't know that Lady Bugle had told Steane that *he* had 'ravished' her away, but he must have thought the chances were that Steane would have left that place before he could reach it."

She had been regarding him intently, trying to get her thoughts into order, but at this she said quickly: "He did know that! Lady Emborough wrote to your mama, telling her that she had received a visit from Lady Bugle, demanding to know what Des had done with her niece, and I informed Des of it!"

"That settles it, then!" said Simon. "Des would have returned to London immediately! And when he reached Arlington Street Aldham gave him the letter I scribbled—there can be no doubt about that!—and as soon as he had read it it's Carlton House to a Charley's shelter that he set out instantly to join me here. I shouldn't wonder at it if he were to arrive at any minute!"

He was interrupted by Grimshaw, who came in to announce Mr Steane's arrival, but when Grimshaw had withdrawn, he said: "There's just one more thing I must warn you about, Hetta! Well, as a matter of fact, it's why I rode out here as fast as I could! Steane thinks you're betrothed to Des."

Henrietta had been tidying her ruffled hair in front of the mirror, but at this she turned, showing Simon a startled face. "Thinks I'm betrothed to Des? Why should he think anything of the sort?"

"Well," said Simon, a trifle conscience-stricken, "I told him you were!"

"Simon!" she uttered wrathfully. "How could you have told him so when you must know there isn't a word of truth in it?"

"It was the only thing I could hit upon to account for Lady Silverdale's having received Cherry, under such dashed havey-cavey circumstances," he explained. "And also it seemed to me the surest way of sending him to grass, if it came to an action for breach of promise. Well, it stands to reason that if Des was betrothed to you he wouldn't have offered another female marriage, or brought her to visit you!"

"I think it was an infamous thing to have done!" she said, those expressive eyes of hers flaming with anger.

"No, no!" he assured her. "Only thing I could do! I promise you Desford won't care a straw!"

"Desford!" she said chokingly. "And what about me, pray?"

225

"Hang it all!" he protested. "Why should you care either? Ten to one it won't leak out, because unless I'm much mistaken Steane don't mean to stay in England a day longer than he need. Besides, I told him the engagement hadn't been announced yet—I said that was on account of my father's health, by the by: not stout enough yet for dress-parties—so if he does blab it abroad you have only to deny it, or cry off, if you prefer."

"Oh, how abominable you are! I'll never forgive you for this!" she told him, an indignant flush reddening her cheeks.

"Well, never mind that!" he said, in a consolatory tone. "If I'd guessed you might object to it, I wouldn't have done it, but I did do it, and there's nothing for it but to stick to it. You must see that, Hetta!"

"I don't!" she snapped.

"Do you mean to say that you're going to tell Steane you ain't engaged to Des?" he gasped. "Of all the shabby things to do! I wouldn't have believed it of you! I thought you was too much of a right one to run away just when poor old Des most needs your help! Turning missish at such a moment! Dashed well stabbing him in the back!"

"Oh, be quiet!" she said crossly. "If this horrible creature is rag-mannered enough to ask me, I shan't deny it. But what I *shall* do, Mr Simon Carrington, is to give you your own again!"

"That's the hammer!" he said encouragingly. "I knew I could depend on you! Always said you were as sound as a trout! Now, you go and hold up your nose at that oily old rascal —and take care you don't let him guess I'm here, for it won't do if he realizes I came to warn you!"

With these kindly words, he patted her on the shoulder, and held open the door for her, meeting the scathing glance she threw at him with eyes brimming with laughter.

He then shut the door again, and retired to the broad window-seat to await the arrival of his brother. He had no doubt that Desford would arrive; the only doubt it was possible for one of his sanguine temperament to entertain was whether Desford would reach Inglehurst in time to deal with Mr Wilfred Steane before poor Hetta had been driven into the last ditch. But the longer he pondered over the question the more convinced did he become that Desford would arrive in time to take the management of what (damn it all!) were his affairs, not his brother's, or Hetta's, into his own hands. It wouldn't be like Des not to make all haste to their rescue, he decided.

And his confidence was justified. Twenty minutes after Henrietta had joined Mr Steane in the library a postchaise-and-four swept round the bend in the avenue, and brought young Mr Carrington to his feet. So sure was he that its passenger was Desford that he did not wait to watch the steps being let down, but went hastily out into the hall, and intercepted Grimshaw, who was treading majestically across it towards the door. "No need for you to trouble yourself!" he said. "It's only my brother! I'll let him in!"

Grimshaw looked at once surprised and disapproving, but he bowed, and went back to his own quarters, reflecting that Mr Simon always was a regrettably harum-scarum young man, much too prone to brush aside the ordinary conventions of Polite Society.

Simon went bounding down the steps just as Desford alighted from the chaise, and called out: "Lord, am I glad to see you, Des! You old slip-gibbet!"

"I'll be bound you are," said the Viscount, receiving this unflattering appellation, and the playful punch to his ribs which accompanied it, as marks of affection, which, indeed, they were. "I'm much obliged to you, bantling: no reason why you should be called upon to enter into this imbroglio!"

"Oh, gammon!" said Simon. "A pretty fellow I should be to have given you the bag! And a rare hank you'd be in if I had, let me tell you!" He lowered his voice, and said seriously: "It's worse than you know, Des."

"Good God, is it?" He nodded to his head postilion, saying briefly: "I don't know how long I shall be: probably an hour or two. We shall spend the night at Wolversham." He turned back to Simon, as the chaise moved on towards the stables, and asked: "Has Steane arrived yet?"

"Yes, about half-an-hour ago. He's with Hetta, in the library."

"Then I had best lose no time in joining them."

"Oh, yes, you had, dear boy!" said Simon, acquiring a firm grip on his arm. "What you had best do is to listen to what I have to tell you, if you don't wish to make mice feet of the business! We'll take a little stroll along the terrace, as far as that damned uncomfortable stone seat, where we shan't be overheard."

"If you're going to tell me that Steane is a fat rascal, I know it already. I visited Miss Fletching the day after Steane had been there, bullocking her until the poor lady succumbed to an attack of the vapours. I don't know what upset her most: the thundering scold she got from him, or the discovery that he had grown very fat. From what she said to me, I'd no difficulty in gathering that he hasn't altered since the days when he was obliged to fly the country. What's his lay? Card-sharping?"

"Undoubtedly, I should think, though I daresay he ain't particular. Any form of flat-catching, from the looks of him! His present lay, my boy, is to compel you to marry his precious daughter!"

The Viscount burst out laughing. "Well, he'll be queered on that suit!"

"If I were you, Des, I wouldn't be too sure of that," said Simon.

"My dear lad, I am quite certain of it! I met her for the first time at a ball the Bugles gave, and had a conversation with her; on the following day I encountered her on my way to London, took her up into my curricle, and conveyed her first to London, and then brought her here, since when I haven't laid eyes on her. So if Steane has any notion of accusing me of having seduced her the sooner he rids himself of it the better it will be for him." He saw that Simon was looking unusually grave, and said, in a little amusement: "I'm not shamming it, you know!"

"Well, of course I know it! But this fellow could make nasty mischief. What if he set it about that you stole Cherry away from her aunt's house, under a promise to marry her?"

"Good God, is he as bad as that?"

Simon nodded. "I daresay you could disprove a charge of having made off with her, and kept her until you was tired of her——"

"What, in one day? Doing it too brown, Simon!"

"The point is can you prove it was only one day? I shouldn't think that Bugle woman would support you: she's already told Steane you ravished Cherry out of the house. Seems one of her daughters overheard what you and Cherry were saying, on the night of that ball."

"Well, she didn't overhear me trying to persuade Cherry to run off with me. And considering upwards of half-a-dozen people saw me leave Hazelfield some time after breakfast on the following morning, and the Silverdales took charge of Cherry that same evening, I don't think that cock will fight!"

"No, very likely not, but you wouldn't want such an on-dit to be running round the town, would you? You know what all the tattlemongers would say: No smoke without fire! and the lord knows there are enough of them on the town!" He grinned, watching the kindling of the Viscount's eyes, and the hardening of the lines about his mouth. "Never mind looking like bull-beef, Des! *Would* you want that?"

The Viscount did not answer for a moment, but sat frowning down at his own finger-nails. He had turned his closed hand over, and seemed to find the row of well-kept nails interesting. But presently he straightened his fingers, and looked up, meeting Simon's eyes. "No, I wouldn't," he replied. He smiled faintly. "But I hardly think he will attempt anything of that sort. For one thing, it would be to lay himself open to reprisal; and for another, he must surely know that he is in extremely ill-odour here. No one for whose opinion I care a button would believe a word he said."

"What about your enemies?"

"I haven't any!"

229

"Why, you old windy-wallets!" exclaimed Simon indignantly. "Talk of ringing one's own bell——!"

The Viscount laughed. "No, no, how can you say so?"

"Let me tell you, Des, that this is no laughing matter!" said Simon severely. "I don't say you couldn't beat him all to sticks if he accuses you of having seduced Cherry, for very likely you could—though I don't think you'd enjoy it. But you wouldn't find it as easy to fight an action for breach of promise!"

"Why not? For that to succeed Cherry's testimony would be needed, and he won't get that."

"Anyone would take you for a mooncalf!" said Simon, quite exasperated. "Next you'll say he's welcome to try it! Well, if you've no objection to setting yourself up as a subject for steward's room gossip, what do you imagine the parents would feel about it?"

"But, Simon, how could he possibly bring such an action without support from Cherry?"

"He could start one, couldn't he? What do they call it? File a suit? Because he knows you'd pay through the nose to stop him!"

"I'm damned if I would!"

"And what about my father? Ay, that's another pair of sleeves, ain't it? *He* would! I sent that old hedge-bird here because he threatened to go to Wolversham, and hoax my father with his lying story! And the next thing was that he had the infernal brass to ask me how it came about that Lady Silverdale had been persuaded to receive Cherry at the hands of such a libertine as you are, brother! So I said that you were betrothed to Hetta!"

"You said *what?*" Desford demanded, taken aback.

"Well, I thought there was nothing for it but to go the whole pile," explained Simon. "It seemed to me to be the best thing I could say, because if he believed it he was bound to see that it turned his scheme to accuse you of having promised to marry Cherry into a case of crabs. Which he did see! Never saw a man look so blue in my life! But if you don't like it I'm sorry, but considering you and Hetta have been as thick as inkleweavers for the lord knows how many years, I didn't think you'd care a straw for it!"

"I don't," said Desford, a queer little smile hovering round his mouth. "But my father already knows the true story! I told it him myself, on my way back from Harrowgate."

"Told him—Des, you didn't!" uttered Simon, turning pale with dismay. "How *could* you have done anything so blubber-headed?"

There was a good deal of amusement in the Viscount's eyes, but he answered meekly: "Well, as he had already got wind of the business, and had driven over here with Mama to discover what sort of a girl I had apparently become entangled with, it seemed to be the only thing I could do."

"Lord!" said Simon, with an eloquent shiver. "You've got more bottom than I have, Des! Did he come the ugly?"

"Not at all! You should know him better than to think he would, when any of us three were in the suds! Oh, he read me one of his scolds, but he told me to come to him if I found myself at the end of my rope! Mind you, he'd met Cherry by that time, and knew at a glance that she wasn't a designing harpy!"

"So I might have spared myself the trouble of heading him away from Wolversham!" said Simon wrathfully. "Upon my word, Des——"

"Oh, no! I'm grateful to you for having done so! He wouldn't have believed Steane's story, but it's more than likely that he would have paid him handsomely to keep his mouth shut, and I'm damned if I'll allow Steane to put the screw on him! He told me himself that when he came here it was with the intention of buying Cherry off, if he found that she was a designing harpy. Never mind that! Did you come here to warn Hetta that she is engaged to me?"

"Yes, of course! I had to!"

"And how did she take it?"

"I'm bound to own that she flew up into the boughs, which surprised me. What I mean is, not like her to turn missish all at once! However, I pointed out to her that if the story were to leak out she could either deny it, or cry off, so she mended her

231

temper, and promised she'd stand buff. No need to fear she may run shy! I'll say this for Hetta: she may be a trifle freakish now and then, but she's a right one at heart!"

"Yes, the pick of the basket!" Desford said, getting up. "And the sooner I go to her rescue——"

"Stay a moment, Des! They are all in an uproar, because that troublesome girl seems to have loped off!"

"Cherry? Good God, why?"

"Oh, Hetta thinks it was because Lady Silverdale found Charlie kissing her, and gave her a scold! She also thinks Cherry may have met with an accident, and she's sent off most of the men to search for her. The devil of it is, of course, that if they don't find her Steane will be sure to cut up rough. Very likely he'll accuse the Silverdales of having ill-used her!"

"Oh, my God, as though we weren't in bad enough loaf already!" groaned the Viscount, striding away towards the door into the house.

"Hi, wait!" Simon called, suddenly bethinking himself of something, and jumping up from the seat. He thrust a hand into his pocket, pulled out a package, and hurried after his brother. "Here you are, old chap!" he said, holding it out, with a shy smile. "Very much obliged to you!"

"But what is it?"

"A roll of soft, you gudgeon! The monkey you lent me!"

"Chuff it!" recommended the Viscount. "I told you at the time that I wasn't going to let you break *my* shins! Did Mopsqueezer win?"

"I should rather think he did! What's more, there was a horse entered for the last race, called Brother Benefactor, so I put all my winnings on him, and he came home at ten-to-one! Bound to, of course!"

The Viscount gave a shout of laughter. "Lord, what a cockleheaded thing to do! No, stop pushing that roll at me! I don't want it! You may be said to have earned it, what's more!" He laid a hand on Simon's shoulder, and gave him a little shake. "You must have been having the devil of a time in the bumblebroth I brewed! Thank you, bantling!"

232

"Oh, fudge!" Simon said, deeply flushing. "I wish you would take it! I'm fairly swimming in lard, you know!"

"You won't be, by the time you return from Brighton!" retorted the Viscount.

CHAPTER XV

WHEN HENRIETTA entered the library, nothing in her face or in her bearing betrayed her inward misgivings. She came in with her graceful, unhurried step, and looked across the room at her visitor, her brows faintly raised; and said, not uncivilly, but with a suggestion of high-bred reserve in her manner: "Mr Steane?" She watched him execute a flourishing bow, and moved forward to a straight chair by the table in the middle of the room, saying, as she sat down on it: "Pray, will you not be seated? Am I right in supposing you to be poor Cherry's father?"

"Yes, ma'am, you are indeed right!" he answered. "Her sole surviving parent, separated from her by a cruel fate for too long, alas, and tortured by anxiety!"

She raised her brows rather higher, and said, in a polite, discouraging voice: "Indeed?" She had the satisfaction of seeing that she had slightly discomfited him, and continued, with strengthened assurance: "I regret, sir, that my mother—er—finds herself unable to receive you. She is a trifle indisposed today."

"I shall not dream of intruding upon her," he said graciously. "My sole desire—I may say, my burning desire!—is to clasp my beloved child to my heart again. For this did I steel myself to revisit the land of my birth, with its poignant memories of my late, adored helpmate: inexpressibly painful to a man of sensibility, I assure you, Miss Silverdale! I presume I do have the honour of addressing Miss Silverdale?"

"Yes, I am Miss Silverdale," she replied. "It is unfortunate that you did not warn us of your intention to visit us today, for it so happens that Cherry is not, at the moment, here. She went out walking some time ago, and is not yet returned. However, I daresay you will not have long to wait before being—reunited with her."

"Every moment that withholds her from me is an hour! You must pardon the natural impatience of a father, ma'am! I can scarcely bear to wait five minutes to see with my own eyes that she is safe and well."

"She was perfectly safe and well when I last saw her," said Henrietta calmly, "but as she went out some hours ago I own I am a little uneasy, and have sent some of our servants to search for her, in case she may have met with an accident, or lost her way."

He instantly assumed an expression of horror, and demanded in a shocked tone: "Do you tell me, ma'am, that she was actually permitted to go out unattended? I had not thought such a thing to have been possible!"

"It was certainly imprudent," she said, maintaining her air of calm. "Had I been at home at the time I should have told her that she must take one of the footmen, or one of the maids, but I drove out myself quite early this morning, to visit an invalid, and so knew nothing about it, until I returned, an hour ago."

"Had I known to what dangers, to what neglect, my tender, innocent child was being exposed——!" he groaned. "But how could I have known? How could I have guessed that the woman to whose care I committed her would prove herself to be utterly unworthy of my trust, and would cast her on the world, careless into what hands she might fall?"

"Well, she didn't. She gave her into her aunt's hands. And I can't but feel, sir, that if you had kept her informed of your whereabouts she would have written to you, to tell you that Lady Bugle had taken Cherry to live with her."

"I shall not weary you, ma'am, with an account of the circumstances which obliged me to withhold my direction from Miss Fletching," he said loftily. "I am a man of many affairs, and they take me all over Europe. In fact, I rarely know from one day to the next *where* they will take me, or for how long. I believed my child to be safe and happy in Miss Fletching's charge. Never for an instant did I entertain the thought that she would hand her over to one who has ever been—after my

236

father and my brother—my worst enemy! She has much to answer for, and she shall answer for it! As I have told her!"

"Forgive me!" said Henrietta, "but have not you more to answer for than Miss Fletching, sir? It seems strangely unnatural for a father—particularly such an affectionate father as yourself!—to leave his daughter for so long without a word that she was forced to mourn him as dead!"

Mr Steane dismissed this with a wave of his hand. "If I had been dead she would have been informed of it," he said. "It was quite unnecessary for me to write to her. I will go further: it would have been folly to have done so, for who knows but what she might have wished to leave school, and join me abroad? I was not, at that time, in a position to provide her with a settled home."

"Oh!" said Henrietta. "Are you now in that position, sir?"

"Certainly!" he replied. "That is to say, as settled as one can ever hope to be. But of what use is it to dwell upon what might have been? I must resolutely banish the temptation to take the poor child away. I must deny myself the solace of her company. I must resign myself to loneliness. My duty is inescapable: I must see her righted in the eyes of the world!"

"Good gracious, has she ever been wronged?" Henrietta said, opening her eyes at him. "If you are talking of her having run away from her aunt, you must let me tell you that you are making a mountain out of a molehill, Mr Steane! To be sure, it was rather a hurly-burly thing to do, and might have led her into dangerous trouble; but since, as good luck would have it, Lord Desford overtook her on the road, and brought her here, no harm has come of it."

He heaved a deep sigh, that verged on a moan, and covered his eyes with one fat hand. "Alas that it should fall to my lot to destroy your belief in Lord Desford's integrity!"

"Oh, you won't do that!" she said brightly. "So pray don't fall into the dismals!"

He let his hand drop, and said, with a touch of asperity: "That may be the story Lord Desford told you, ma'am, but——"

237

"It is. And it is also the story Cherry told me," interpolated Henrietta.

"Instructed, I have no doubt at all, by his lordship! It is not the story I heard from Amelia Bugle! Far from it indeed! Very far from it! She told me that although she had been unable to discover when it was that Desford first met Cherry, it was certainly before the night of the ball at her house, when one of her daughters was a witness of his secret assignation with her, and in the course of which the elopement must have been planned."

"What nonsense!" said Henrietta contemptuously. "Elopement, indeed! I wonder you should have let yourself be bamboozled by such a ridiculous tale, sir! It's easy enough to see why she told it, of course: she was scared that you might discover that it was her abominable treatment that drove Cherry to run away! But that is the plain truth! As for Lord Desford's part in the business, you may think yourself very much obliged to him, for if he had not taken her up in his curricle, heaven knows what might have happened to her! I may add that as soon as he had established her in my mother's care he left immediately to find Lord Nettlecombe! He ran him to earth at Harrowgate—and any other man would have abandoned the search when he discovered that he would be obliged to travel more than two hundred miles to reach his lordship!"

Mr Steane shook his head at her, a sad, pitying smile curling his lips. "That," he sighed, "is the tale Desford's young brother tried to hoax me with. I do not for a moment mean to suggest that *you* are trying to hoax me, Miss Silverdale, for it is plain to me that you too have been hoaxed. For how is it possible that Lord Desford—a man who has been on the town I know not how many years—should have supposed that my father would have contemplated for as much as a moment such a journey? *You* may not be aware that he is as scaly a snudge as was ever born, but Lord Desford must surely know it! Why, he has scarcely stirred out of Albemarle Street for years past! If he did find that his health demanded a change of air, the farthest he would have gone from London would have been Tunbridge

Wells. Though I rather fancy," he added, considering the matter, "that he would have retired to Nettlecombe Manor. Lodgings in watering-places, you know, are never to be had dog-cheap. As for the cost of travelling to Harrowgate—no, no, ma'am! That is doing it much too brown, believe me!"

"Nevertheless, he did go to Harrowgate, and is there at this moment. Perhaps his bride persuaded him to undertake the expense of the journey," said Henrietta, with a wonderful air of innocence.

"His what?" ejaculated Mr Steane, starting upright in his chair, and staring at her very hard.

"Oh, didn't you know that he was lately married?" she said. "Desford didn't know either, until he was introduced to the lady. I understand she was used to be his housekeeper. Not, I fear, the pink of gentility, but I feel, don't you, that it was very sensible of him to marry someone whom he can trust to look after him, and to manage his household exactly as he likes!"

She had introduced this new topic in the hope of diverting Mr Steane from the real object of his visit, and the gambit succeeded to admiration, though not in the way she had expected. Instead of going into a passion, he burst into a guffaw, slapping his thigh, and gasping: "By God, that's the best joke I've heard in years! Caught in parson's mousetrap, is he? Damme if I don't write to felicitate him! That'll sting him on the raw! Why, he cast me off for eloping with Jane Wisset, and though I don't say she was of the first rank she wasn't a housekeeper!" He went off into another guffaw, which ended in a wheezing cough; and as soon as he was able to fetch his breath again, invited Henrietta to describe his stepmother to him. She was unable to do this, but she did regale him with some of the things Desford had told her. He was particularly delighted by the quarrel between the newly married couple which had sprung up over the silk shawl, and again slapped his thigh, declaring that it served the old hunks right. He then said, wistfully, that he wished he could have seen his brother's face when the news had been broken to him. He began to chuckle, but another thought occurred to him, and brought a cloud to his brow. "The

239

worst of it is he can't cut Jonas out of the inheritance," he said gloomily. "Still," he added after brooding over this reflection for a few moments, and speaking in a more hopeful tone: "I shouldn't wonder at it if this housekeeper makes the old muckworm bleed freely, so the chances are Jonas won't come into as big a fortune as he expected to." He favoured Henrietta with a bland smile, and said: "One should always try to look on the bright side. It has ever been my rule. You would be astonished, I daresay, how often the worst disasters do have a brighter aspect."

She was as much diverted as she was shocked by this simple revelation of Mr Steane's character, and felt herself unable to do more than murmur an affirmative. Any hope that she might have entertained of Mr Steane's forgetting his daughter's predicament in the contemplation of his brother's rage and chagrin were dispelled by his next words. "Well, well!" he said. "Little did I think that I should enjoy such an excellent joke today! But it will not do, Miss Silverdale! Jokes are out of place at such a time, when my breast is racked with anxiety. I accept that Lord Desford did go to Harrowgate; and I can only say that if he was such a dummy as to think he could fob my unfortunate child off on to her grandfather he has been like a woodcock, justly slain by its own treachery. Or words to that effect. My memory fails me, but I know a woodcock comes into it."

What she might have been goaded to retort remained unspoken, for at this moment the Viscount came into the room. The thought that flashed into her mind was that he might have been designed to form a contrast to Wilfred Steane. There were fewer than twenty years between them, and it was easy to see that Steane had been a handsome man in his youth. But his good looks had been ruined by dissipation; and his figure spoke just as surely as his face of a life of indolence and over-indulgence. Nor were these faults remedied by his manner, or his dress. In both he favoured a florid style, which made him appear, in Henrietta's critical eyes, disastrously like a demi-beau playing off the airs of an exquisite. Desford, on the other hand, was complete to a shade, she thought. He had a handsome countenance; a lithe, athletic figure; and if the plain coat of blue superfine which he wore had had a label stitched to it bearing the name of Weston it could not have proclaimed the name of its maker more surely than did its superb cut. His air was distinguished; his manners very easy, and unaffected; and while there was no suggestion of the Pink, or the Bond Street Spark, about his trim person it was generally agreed in tonnish circles that his quiet elegance was the Real thing.

He shut the door, and advanced towards Henrietta, who had exclaimed thankfully: "Desford!"

"Hetta, my love!" he responded, smiling at her, and kissing her hand. He stood holding it in a warm clasp for a minute, as he said: "Had you despaired of me? I think you must have, and I do beg your pardon! I had hoped to have been with you before this."

She returned the pressure of his fingers, and then drew her hand away, saying playfully: "Well, at all events, you've arrived in time to make the acquaintance of Cherry's father, who isn't dead, after all! You must allow me to make you known to each other: Mr Wilfred Steane, Lord Desford!"

The Viscount turned, and raised his quizzing-glass, and through it surveyed Mr Steane, not for very long, but with daunting effect. Henrietta was forced to bite her lip quite savagely to suppress the laughter that bubbled up in her. It was so very unlike Des to do anything so odiously top-lofty! "Oh," he said. He bowed slightly. "I am happy to make your acquaintance, sir."

"I would I might say the same!" returned Mr Steane. "Alas that we should meet, sir, under such unhappy circumstances!"

The Viscount looked surprised. "I beg your pardon?"

"Lord Desford, I have much to say to you, but it would be better that I should speak privately to you!"

"Oh, I have no secrets from Miss Silverdale!" said Desford.

"My respect for a lady's delicate sensibilities has hitherto sealed my lips," said Steane reprovingly. "Far be it from me to

241

ask a question that might bring a blush to female cheeks! But I have such a question to put to you, my lord!"

"Then by all means do put it to me!" invited Desford. "Never mind Miss Silverdale's sensibilities! I daresay they aren't by half as delicate as you suppose—in fact, I'm quite sure they are not! You don't wish to retire, do you, Hetta?"

"Certainly not! I have not the remotest intention of doing so, either. I cut my eye-teeth many years ago, Mr Steane, and if what you have already said to me failed to bring a blush to my cheeks it is not very likely that whatever you are about to say will succeed in doing so! Pray ask Lord Desford any question you choose!"

Mr Steane appeared to be grieved by this response, for he sighed, and shook his head, and murmured: "Modern manners! It was not so in my young days! But so be it! Lord Desford, are you betrothed to Miss Silverdale?"

"Well, I certainly hope I am!" replied the Viscount, turning his laughing eyes towards Henrietta. "But what in the world has that to say to anything? I might add—do forgive me!—what in the world has it to do with you, sir?"

Mr Steane was not really surprised. He had known from the moment Desford had entered the room, and had exchanged smiles with Henrietta, that a strong attachment existed between them. But he was much incensed, and said, far from urbanely: "Then I wonder at your shamelessness, sir, in luring my child away from the protection of her aunt's home with false promises of marriage! As for your effrontery in bringing her to your affianced wife——"

"Don't you think," suggested the Viscount, "that foolhardiness would be a better word? Or shall we come down from these impassioned heights? I don't know what you hope to achieve by mouthing such fustian rubbish, for I am persuaded you cannot possibly be so bacon-brained as to suppose that I am guilty of any of these crimes. The mere circumstance of my having placed Cherry in Miss Silverdale's care must absolve me from the two other charges you have laid at my door, but if you wish me to deny them categorically I'll willingly do so!

So far from luring Cherry from Maplewood, when I found her trudging up to London I did my possible to persuade her to return to her aunt. I did not offer her marriage, or, perhaps I should add, a carte blanche! Finally, I brought her to Miss Silverdale because, for reasons which must be even better known to you than they are to me, my father would have taken strong exception to her presence under his roof!"

"Be that as it may," said Mr Steane, struggling against the odds, "you cannot—if there is any truth in you, which I am much inclined to doubt!—deny that you have placed her in a very equivocal situation!"

"I can and do deny it!" replied the Viscount.

"A man of honour," persisted Mr Steane, with the doggedness of despair, "would have restored her to her aunt!"

"That may be your notion of honour, but it isn't mine," said the Viscount. "To have forced her into my curricle, and then to have driven her back to a house where she had been so wretchedly unhappy that she fled from it, preferring to seek some means, however menial, of earning her bread to enduring any more unkindness from her aunt and her cousins, would have been an act of wicked cruelty! Moreover, I hadn't a shadow of right to do it! She begged me to carry her to her grandfather's house in London, hoping that he might allow her to remain there, and convinced that if he refused to do that he would at least house her until she had established herself in some suitable situation."

"Well, if you thought he'd do any such thing, either you don't know the old snudge, or you're a gudgeon!" said Mr Steane. "And from what I can see of you it's my belief you're the slyest thing in nature! Up to every move on the board!"

"Oh, not quite that!" said Desford. "Only to your moves, Steane!"

"You remind me very much of your father," said Mr Steane, eyeing him with considerable dislike.

"Thank you!" said Desford, bowing.

"Also that young cub of a brother of yours! Both of a hair! No respect for your seniors! A pair of stiff-rumped, bumptious

243

bouncers! Don't think you can put the change on me, Desford, trying to hoax me with your Banbury stories, because you can't!"

"Oh, I shouldn't dream of doing so!" instantly replied his lordship. "I never compete against experts!"

Henrietta said apologetically: "Pray forgive me, but are you not straying a little away from the point at issue? Whether Desford was a gudgeon to think that Lord Nettlecombe would receive Cherry, or whether he thought what any man must have thought, doesn't seem to me to have any bearing on the case. He did drive her to London, only to find Lord Nettlecombe's house shut up. He then brought her to me. What, Mr Steane, do you suggest he should rather have done?"

"Thrown in the close!" murmured the Viscount irrepressibly.

"I must decline to enter into argument with you, ma'am," said Steane, with immense dignity. "I never argue with females. I will merely say that in accosting my daughter on the highway, coaxing her to climb into his curricle, and driving off with her his lordship behaved with great impropriety—if no worse! And since he abandoned her here—if she *is* here, which I gravely doubt!—what has he done to redress the injury her reputation has suffered at his hands? He would have me think that he sought my father out in the belief that he would take the child to his bosom——"

"Not a bit of it!" interrupted Desford. "I hoped I could shame him into making her an allowance, that's all!"

"Well, if that's what you hoped you *must* be a gudgeon!" said Mr Steane frankly. "Not that you did, of course! What you hoped was to be able to fob her off on to the old man, and you wouldn't have cared if he'd offered to engage her as a cook-maid as long as you were rid of her!"

"Some such offer was made," said Desford. "Not, indeed, by your father, but by your stepmother. I refused it."

"Yes, it's all very well to say that, but how should I know if you're speaking the truth? All I know is that I return to England to find that my poor little girl has been tossed about amongst a set of unscrupulous persons, cast adrift in a harsh world——"

"Take a damper!" said the Viscount. "None of that is true, as

244

well you know! The unscrupulous person who cast her adrift is yourself, so let us have less of this theatrical bombast! You wish to know what I have done to redress the injury to her reputation she has suffered at my hands, and my answer is, Nothing—because her reputation has suffered no injury either at my hands, or at anyone else's! But when I found that your father had gone out of town, the lord only knew where, and that Cherry had nowhere to go, not one acquaintance in London, and only a shilling or two in her purse, I realized that little though I might like it I must hold myself responsible for her. With your arrival, my responsibility has come to an end. But before I knew that you were not dead, but actually in this country, I drove down to Bath, to take counsel of Miss Fletching. I was a day behind you, Mr Steane. Miss Fletching most sincerely pities Cherry, and is, I think, very fond of her. She offers her a home, until she can hear of a situation which Cherry might like. She has one in her eye already, with an invalid lady whom she describes as very charming and gentle, but all depends upon her present companion, who is torn between her duty to her lately widowed parent, and her wish to remain with her kind mistress."

"Oh, Des, it would be the very thing for Cherry!" Henrietta cried.

"What!" ejaculated Mr Steane, powerfully affected. "The very thing for my beloved child to become a paid dependant? Over my dead body!" He buried his face in his handkerchief, but emerged from it for a moment to direct a look of wounded reproach at Desford, and to say in a broken voice: "That I should have lived to hear my heart's last treasure so insulted!" He disappeared again into the handkerchief, but re-emerged to say bitterly: "Shabby, my Lord Desford, that's what I call it!"

Desford's lips quivered, and his eyes met Henrietta's, which were brimful of the same appreciative amusement that had put to flight his growing exasperation. The look held, and in each pair of eyes was a warmth behind the laughter.

Mr Steane's voice intruded upon this interlude. "And where," he demanded, "*is* my little Charity? Answer that, one of you, before you make plans to degrade her!"

"Well, I am afraid we can't answer it just at this moment!" said Henrietta guiltily. "Desford, you will think me dreadfully careless, but while I was visiting an old friend this morning, Cherry went out for a walk, and—and hasn't yet come back!"

"Mislaid her, have you? I learned from—Grimshaw—that she's missing, but I don't doubt she has done nothing more dangerous than lose her way, and will soon be back."

"If she has not been spirited away," said Mr Steane darkly. "My mind is full of foreboding. I wonder if I shall ever see her again?"

"Yes, and immediately!" said Henrietta, hurrying across the room to the door. "That's her voice! Heavens, what a relief!"

She opened the door as she spoke. "Oh, Cherry, you *naughty* child! Where in the world——" She broke off abruptly, for a surprising sight met her eyes. Cherry was being carried towards the staircase by Mr Cary Nethercott, her bonnet hanging by its ribbon over one arm, a mutilated boot clutched in one hand, and the other gripping the collar of Mr Nethercott's rough shooting-jacket.

"Dear, dear Miss Silverdale, don't be vexed with me!" she begged. "I know it was stupid of me to run out, but indeed I didn't mean to make you anxious! Only I lost my way, and couldn't find it, and at last I was so dreadfully tired that I made up my mind to ask the first person I met to show me how to get back to Inglehurst. But it was ages before I saw a single soul, and then it was a horrid man in a gig, who—who looked at me in *such* a way that—that I said it was of no consequence, and walked on as fast as I could. And then he called after me, and started to get down from the gig, and I ran for my life, into the woods, and, oh, Miss Silverdale, I tore my dress on the brambles, besides catching my foot in a horrid, trailing root, or branch, or something, and falling into a bed of nettles! And when I tried to get up I couldn't, because it hurt me so much that I thought I was going to faint."

"Well, what a chapter of accidents!" said Henrietta. She saw that one of Cherry's ankles was heavily bandaged, and exclaimed: "Oh, dear, dear, I collect you sprained your ankle!

Poor Cherry!" She smiled at Cary Nethercott. "Was she in your woods? Was that how you found her? How kind of you to have brought her home! I am very much obliged to you!"

"Yes, that was how it was," he answered. "I took my gun out, hoping to get a wood-pigeon or two, but instead I got a far prettier bird, as you see, Miss Hetta! Unfortunately I had no knife on me, so I thought it best to carry Cherry to my own house immediately, so that I could cut the boot off, and tell my housekeeper to apply cold poultices, to take down the swelling. I sent my man off to fetch Foston, fearing, you know, that there might be a broken bone, but he assured me that it was only a very bad sprain. You will say that I should have brought her back to you as soon as Foston had bound up her foot and ankle, but she was so much exhausted by the pain of having it inspected by Foston that I thought it best that she should rest until the pain had gone off."

"You can't think how much it hurt, dear Miss Silverdale! But Mr Nethercott held my hand tightly all the time, and so I was able to bear it."

"What a perfectly horrid day you've had!" said Henrietta. "I'm so sorry, my dear: none of it would have happened if I hadn't been absent!"

"Oh, no, no, no!" Cherry said, her eyes and cheeks glowing, and a seraphic smile trembling on her mouth. "It has been the happiest day of my whole life! Oh, Miss Silverdale, Mr Nethercott has asked me to marry him! Please, please say I may!"

"Good God!—I mean, you have no need to ask my permission, you goose! I have nothing to do but to wish you both very happy, which you may be sure I do, with all my heart! But there is someone here who has come especially to see you, and whom I am persuaded you will be very glad to meet again. Bring her into the library, Mr Nethercott, and put her on the sofa, so that she can keep her foot up."

"Who," demanded Mr Steane of the Viscount, "is this fellow who presumes to offer for my daughter without so much as a by your leave?"

"Cary Nethercott. An excellent fellow!" replied the Viscount enthusiastically.

He moved over to the sofa, and arranged the cushions on it, just as Cary Nethercott bore Cherry tenderly into the room. She exclaimed: "Lord Desford! Indeed I'm glad to meet him again, Miss Silverdale, for I owe everything to him! How do you do, sir? I have wanted so much to thank you for having brought me here, and I never did, you know!"

He smiled, but said: "Miss Silverdale didn't mean that you would be glad to meet *me* again, Cherry. Look, do you recognize that gentleman?"

She turned her head, and for the first time caught sight of Mr Steane. She stared at him blankly for an instant, and then gave a tiny gasp, and said: *"Papa?"*

"My child!" uttered Mr Steane. "At last I may clasp you to my bosom again!" This, however, he was unable to do, since she had been set down on the sofa, and the corset he wore made it impossible for him to stoop so low. He compromised by putting an arm round her shoulders, and kissing her brow. "My little Charity!" he said fondly.

"I thought you were dead, Papa!" she said wonderingly. "I'm so happy to know you aren't! But why did you never write to me, or to poor Miss Fletching?"

"Do not speak to me of that woman!" he commanded, sidestepping this home-question. "Never would I have left you in her charge had I known how shamefully she would betray my trust, my poor child!"

"Oh, *no,* Papa!" she cried distressfully. "How can you say so, when she was so kind to me, and kept me at the school for nothing?"

"She delivered you up to Amelia Bugle, and that I can never forgive!" declared Mr Steane.

"But, Papa, you make it sound as if I wasn't willing to go with my aunt, but I promise you I was! I wanted to have a *home* so much. You don't know how much!" She found that Mr Nethercott, standing behind the head of the sofa, had dropped a hand on her shoulder, and she nursed it gratefully to her cheek, tears

248

on the ends of her eyelashes. She winked them away, and continued to address her father, with a good deal of urgency: "So, pray, Papa, don't go away again without paying her what she is owed!"

"Had I found you as I left you, happy in her care, I would have paid and overpaid her, but I did not so find you! I found you, after an unceasing search which was attended by such pangs of anxiety as only a father can know, being buffeted about the world, and not one penny will I pay her!" said Mr Steane resolutely.

"In other words," said Desford, "you mean to tip her the double!"

"Papa, you *cannot* behave so shabbily! You *must* not!" Cherry cried, in considerable agitation.

"I think, my love," said Mr Nethercott, "that you had best leave me to deal with this matter."

"But it isn't right that you should deal with it!" she said indignantly. "It isn't your debt! It's Papa's!"

"I do not acknowledge it," stated Mr Steane majestically. "She may consider herself fortunate that I have decided not to bring an action against her for gross neglect of her duty. That is my last word!"

"In that case," said Mr Nethercott matter-of-factly, "I will carry Cherry upstairs. You must realize, I am persuaded, sir, that she has had a very exhausting day, and has been quite knocked-up by it. Miss Hetta, will you conduct me to her bedchamber, if you please?"

"Indeed, I will!" Henrietta replied. "No, no, don't argue, Cherry! Mr Nethercott is perfectly right, and I am going to put you to bed directly. You shall have your dinner sent up to you, —and your Papa may visit you tomorrow!"

"How kind you are! How *very* kind you are, Miss Silverdale!" Cherry sighed. "I own I *am* feeling rather fagged, so—so if you won't think it very uncivil of me, Papa, I believe I will go to bed! Oh, Lord Desford, in case I don't see you again, goodbye, and thank you a thousand, thousand times for all you've done for me!"

He took the hand she stretched out to him, and kissed it, saying in a rallying voice: "But you will be constantly seeing me, you little pea-goose! We are to be neighbours!"

"As to that," said Mr Steane haughtily, "I have by no means decided to give my consent to this marriage. I shall require Mr Nethercott to satisfy me as to his ability to support my daughter in a manner befitting her breeding."

Mr Nethercott, already in the doorway with his fair burden, paused to say with unruffled composure that he would do himself the honour of laying before his prospective father-in-law all the relevant facts concerning his birth, fortune, and situation in life as soon as he had carried Cherry up to her room. He then continued on his purposeful way, preceded by Henrietta, and telling his betrothed, very kindly, to hush, when she attempted to argue that her marriage had nothing whatsoever to do with her father.

The Viscount shut the door, and strolled back to his chair, regarding Mr Steane with a pronounced twinkle in his eyes. "You are to be congratulated, Mr Steane," he said. "Your daughter is making a very creditable marriage, and you need never suffer pangs of anxiety about her again."

"There is that, of course," acknowledged Mr Steane heavily. "But when I think of the plans I have been making for years—I should have known better! All my life, Desford, I have been quite the dregs of my family as to luck. It disheartens a man! There's no denying that!" He turned his jaundiced gaze upon the Viscount, and added: "Not that you know anything about it! You seem to me to have the devil's own luck! Well, consider what has happened this day! You wouldn't have braced it through if this fellow, Nethercott, hadn't dropped out of the sky like a honey-fall for you!"

"Oh, yes, I should!" said the Viscount. "Not to use words with the bark on them, your intention was to bludgeon me into marrying Cherry, but you chose the wrong man, Steane: there was never the least hope of buttoning that scheme up!"

"I abandoned all thought of your marrying Cherry when I learned of your betrothal," Mr Steane replied. "Never shall it be said of me that I wrecked the happiness of an innocent female—however deluded she may be! But I fancy, my lord, you'd have come down handsomely to keep this scandalous business quiet! Or, at any hand, that stiff-necked father of yours would!"

"From what I know of my stiff-necked father, Mr Steane, I think he would have been far more likely to have driven you out of the country."

"Well, it's a waste of time to discuss the matter!" said Mr Steane irritably.

"Of course it is! Consider instead how much cause you have to be thankful that your only daughter has had the good fortune to become attached to a man who will certainly make her an admirable husband!"

"My only daughter! She's another disappointment! There's no end to them. I had hopes of her when she was a child: seemed to be a bright, coming little thing. She could have been very useful to me."

"In what way?" asked Desford curiously.

"Oh, many ways!" said Mr Steane. "I hoped she might act as hostess in the establishment I have set up in Paris, but I saw at a glance that she's too like her mother. Pretty enough, but not up to snuff. Wouldn't know how to go on at all. A pity! Sheer waste of my time and blunt to have come to England."

Since he seemed to be slipping rapidly into a maudlin frame of mind, the Viscount was relieved to see Mr Nethercott come back into the room. He was accompanied by Henrietta, and it was immediately plain to the Viscount that it was she who had prompted him to suggest to Mr Steane that it would be more convenient to discuss such matters as Settlements at Marley House.

"I think that an excellent notion!" she said warmly. "You will wish to inspect Cherry's future home, I expect, Mr Steane. And if you care to visit her tomorrow, Mr Nethercott has been kind enough to say that he will be happy to put you up for the night!"

"I am obliged to you, sir," said Mr Steane, reverting to his grand manner. "I shall be happy to avail myself of your hospi-

251

tality—but without prejudice, understand!" He then took a punctilious leave of Henrietta, bowed stiffly to the Viscount, and allowed himself to be ushered out of the room by the impassive Mr Nethercott.

"You unprincipled woman!" said the Viscount, when the door was fairly shut behind the departing visitors. "You should be ashamed of yourself! Saddling the unfortunate man with that old rumstick!"

"Oh, did you guess it was my doing?" she said, breaking into pent-up laughter.

"Guess!" he said scornfully. "I knew it the instant you came in looking as demure as a nun's hen!"

"Oh, no, did I? But I had to get rid of him, Des, or Mama would have taken to her bed! What with thinking Charlie had eloped with Cherry, and then hearing that Wilfred Steane was on his way to visit us, she's been having spasms, and vapours, and every sort of ache and ill, and is now in the worst of ill-humours! I shall have to go to her, or she will fall utterly into the hips. But before I do go, tell me what you feel about this astonishing betrothal! Will it do, or is he too old for her? I've noticed that she seems to prefer old men, but——"

"Never mind what I think! What do you think, Hetta?"

"How can I say? I think she is so amiable, and sweet-tempered, that she will be happy, as long as he is kind to her. As for him, he seems to be extremely fond of her, so perhaps he won't find her a trifle boring."

"Fond of her! He must be nutty on her to be willing to marry her now that he's seen her father!"

She laughed. "You know, Des, I didn't think he could be as bad as people say, but he's worse! If he weren't such a funny one I couldn't have borne to sit there listening to him! But when I was discussing her prospects with Mr Nethercott one day, he said that her parentage ought not to weigh against her in the mind of a man who fell in love with her. So I daresay he won't think her father worth a moment's consideration!"

"Hetta, tell me the truth! Has it hurt you?" he asked bluntly.

"Good God, no! Though it has sadly lowered my crest, I

own! I was vain enough to think that he came here to visit me, not Cherry!"

"When I first met him, dangling after you, none of us had ever heard of Cherry," he reminded her.

"I might have known you'd roast me for having been cut out by Cherry! What an odious creature you are, Des!" she said affably. "By the by, do you and Simon mean to spend the night at Wolversham? I wish I might invite you both to dine with us, but I daren't! Mama has taken you in the most violent dislike, for having foisted Cherry on to us, and she never wants to see the face of a Carrington again! So for the present I must say goodbye to you!"

"Just a moment before you do that!" he said. "You and I, my pippin, have still something to discuss!"

He spoke lightly, but the smile had vanished from his eyes, which were fixed on her face with a look in them that made her feel, for the first time in all their dealings, as shy as a schoolgirl. She said hurriedly: "Oh, you refer, I collect, to that nonsensical story Simon made up about us! I must say I was excessively vexed with him, but I don't think any harm will come of it! Simon says that if it does leak out that we are secretly engaged we have only to deny it, or for one or other of us to cry off."

He returned no answer, and when she ventured to steal a look at him she found that he was still watching her intently. In an attempt to relieve what, for some inscrutable reason, she felt to be an embarrassing situation, she said, with a very creditable assumption of her usual liveliness: "If it comes to that, I collect the task of crying off will be mine! I can never understand why it is thought very improper for a gentleman to cry off an engagement, but no such thing if the lady does it!"

"No," he agreed, but not as if he had been attending to her. "I give you fair warning, Hetta, that if it does come to that the task *will* be yours, for I have not the most remote intention—or desire—to cry off." He paused for an instant, trying to read her face, but when she lifted her eyes, as though compelled, to his, his mouth twisted, and he said in a voice she had never heard before: "But you shan't! I won't let you! Oh, Hetta, my dear

253

pippin, I've been such a fool! I've loved you all my life, and never knew how much until I thought I was going to lose you! Don't say it's too late!"

A tiny smile wavered on her lips. She said simply: "No, Des. N-not if you really mean it!"

"I never meant anything more in my life!" he said, and went to her, holding out his arms. She walked straight into them, and they closed tightly round her. "My best of friends!" he said huskily, and kissed her.

This idyll was interrupted by Lady Silverdale, who came into the room, saying in the voice of one who had passed the limits of her endurance: "I do think, Hetta, that you might have come to tell me——" She broke off, and exclaimed in scandalized accents: "Hen-ri-etta!" Then, as Desford looked quickly round, and she perceived who it was who was embracing her daughter, her note changed. "Desford!" she cried joyfully. "Oh, my dear, dear boy! Oh, how happy this makes me! Hetta, my darling child! Now I don't care *what* happens!"

"But, Mama!" objected Hetta, wickedly quizzing her. "You told me that nothing would prevail upon you to give your consent to my marrying Des! Why, you even congratulated me on my fortunate escape from such a fate!"

"Nonsense, Hetta!" said Lady Silverdale, very properly dismissing this untimely reminiscence. "It has been the one wish of my life! I have always been excessively fond of him, and, what's more, I have never wavered from my conviction that he is just the man for you!"

"Thank you, ma'am!" said Desford, raising her hand to his lips. "I *hope* I may be just the man for Hetta, but all I *know* is that she is just the woman for me!"

"Dear Ashley! Very prettily said!" she approved. "It is what one so particularly likes in you! To be sure, I was not quite pleased with you when you brought Wilfred Steane's child here, but that's not of the smallest consequence *now!* But I must say, Hetta, it was as much as I could do to say what was proper when she told me, just now, that she had accepted an offer from Mr Nethercott. It seemed to me that there was to be no end to the gentlemen she steals from you! First it was Desford; then it was Charlie—not, of course, that he is one of your suitors, but the *principle* is the same—and now it's Mr Nethercott! Well, she's welcome to him, for I never thought him worthy of you, never! Desford, you will stay to dine with us, of course. Hetta, run and warn Ufford—No, I'll see him myself, and Charlie must talk to Grimshaw about champagne. Bless you, my dear ones!" With these words she went away to confer with the cook, her gait at startling variance from the tottering steps which had brought her into the room a few minutes earlier.

The lovers then resumed their previous occupation, only to be almost immediately interrupted by Simon, who strolled in, checked on the threshold in surprise at the sight which met his eyes, and burst into a shout of laughter. Reproved in no uncertain terms by his elder brother, he was quite unrepentant. "Oh, isn't there anything to laugh at!" he said, kissing Hetta's cheek, and painfully wringing the Viscount's hand. "Here's the pair of you, smelling of April and May ever since I can remember, and it ain't until *I* put it into your heads that it occurs to either of you to stop huffling and get spliced! Well, I told you you didn't how how nacky my best was, Des, but you know now!"

He then took his leave of them, declining an invitation to join the dinner-party on the score of its being imperative that he should be in London before it became too dark to see his way. "I'm off to Brighton in the morning," he explained. "But if you should get into any more scrapes, Des, just send me word, and I'll post straight back to rescue you!"